THE LUMEN CALIGO

~FALLEN~

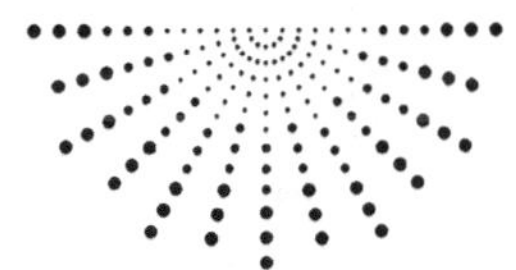

LAWRENCE C. COBB

ISBN: 978-1-964605-00-5 (SC)

ISBN: 978-1-964605-01-2 (HC)

ISBN: 978-1-964605-02-9 (E)

Cover design: Tony Midi

End Chapter Art: Tony Midi

Copyright Page Art: Plotnikkova

CONTENTS

For my friends and family. Thank you for teaching me that too much exposure to the light will leave you blind and not enough exposure to darkness will leave you ignorant. Balance is key. Actions speak louder than words. Thank you.

Lawrence C. Cobb

PROLOGUE

There are three types of people in the world. Those with white wings. Those with black wings. And those with none. Every 350 years a fourth is born called the *Lumen Caligo*. One side of his wings there is white. On the other side, there is black.

Throughout time, the Lumen Caligo acted as a peacekeeper for all the nations, leading them to times of peace, prosperity, and power ...

Then, the Lumen Caligo of the 1600s mysteriously vanished at the brink of war between the nations. His last letter was something called "The Isolation Order".

It requested that the nations return to their lands of origin. Fearing the destruction that could unfold and respecting the title of The Lumen Caligo, the nations returned to their lands and vowed to remain isolated from the rest of the world until the Lumen Caligo returned ...

On a sunset beach in California, a man sits in solitude ... Not knowing the role he will play for the changing and shaping of the world ... *This* is where our story begins.

Animated trailer for your viewing pleasure.

1

ISOLATIONS VISITOR

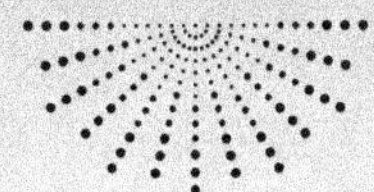

THE SUN WAS SETTING ... everything was calm. Amber and gold reflected off the ocean's blue face. The reflection danced like a pair of ballerinas until it reached the banks of the shore. Sitting on the sand looking out towards the sunset was a man deep in thought.

He watched the sun go down as if he expected it to say something.

He was only vaguely aware of the sound of drums coming from the apartment complex behind him and the man flying a drone to get the "perfect shot" of the sunset. Neither mattered. His thoughts and emotions were as rampant as the colors dancing off the ocean's surface.

The man's name was Martin Weatherford. Even sitting down, you could tell the man was tall—6'4", at the very least. He had prominent cheek bones and three freckles on his left cheek that formed a perfect triangle. A reddish hue from a recovering sun burn adorned the exposed parts of his skin. Then there were his eyes ... A vibrant blue that were as intimidating to look at as they were beautiful. His eyes were filled with remorse and fierce sadness. Like a leech, gloom sapped his hope away.

The sun began its reunion with the water, its final moments on the horizon before its farewell. Martin's thoughts changed with the sun.

Why sun-set? Set has so many different definitions. Not to mention over twenty expressions starting from the word set. Set in motion ... set forth ... set one's heart upon ...

Martin closed his eyes tightly. He had set his heart upon many things and had failed repeatedly. The creation of a family, fulfilling his father's expectations, impressing his nation ... Yet it all felt small in comparison to the betrayal he felt. He tried to be understanding of the situation and everything he had been told ... but that was not how he was raised.

"Actions speak louder than words," he echoed. "What I set in motion is my doing and no one else's. I am to act on situations ... not be acted upon."

The drone crashed into the waves. Its constant buzzing was engulfed by the low roar of the ocean. A muffled whimper put a smirk on Martin's face as the man set out to salvage the drone. In the distance, yells from the drummer's parents silenced the beat. The calm made a welcome return. The sound of crashing waves set in all around him.

Set ... Having a specified direction in motion. I envy you, Mr. Sun ...

Martin stood up and brushed the sand off of his hands.

"Time to head back home," he said to the ocean.

Martin made his way southward alongside the breaking waves. He lived almost as close to the Mexican border as possible. The town of Imperial Beach, California, had become his new home. 1112 Seaside Avenue was his safe haven. Although it had only been six months since he had isolated himself, he felt subtle changes freeing him from past attachments. His new haircut was an example of this change. Past societal pressures had pushed him to nearly commit some unspeakable things. He shuddered at the thought.

Martin gazed back towards the horizon as he reached where the sand met the cement. The sky was in splendid display, its colors splashing across the ocean and the clouds. All that was missing was the hallelujah chorus.

Something reached into the deepest corners of Martin's mourning heart that he hadn't experienced in a very long time ... Optimism. For the first time since he'd left home over a year ago, he felt optimism's blissful reassurance. Things may not have been ideal, but somehow, he knew they would get better. With the last sliver of light, the sun made its escape behind the horizon, leaving remnants of red and amber speckled across the water and clouds.

"May I also leave an imprint on humankind as beautiful as you when I am gone, Mr. Sun," whispered Martin.

With that, Martin gestured toward the sun like a monk praying with his ring fingers bent. An odd gesture to the outside world, but one of the highest respects to those familiar with its meaning.

Martin walked around the corner to the front entrance of his apartment. He rented from a large woman who owned the place by the name of Arlene Palermo. An orthopedic surgeon by trade, she was of Portuguese descent and *loved* theatrics. She was a big fan of Martin because he had read every Shakespeare play she had and could quote lines and discuss the underlying meanings.

From Trinculo's lines from *The Tempest* to *Hamlet's* "To be or not to be" speech, Martin had them down. (Although most things he read he never forgot.) Safe to say, Martin was Arlene Palermo's favorite tenant and made no effort to hide it. Every time their paths crossed, she would greet Martin in the most formal of speech from which Martin would match. It was common courtesy for Martin, but just like common sense, common courtesy "wasn't so common" as Arlene would say.

Ms. Palermo stood on the sidewalk looking completely preoccupied by something. She whipped around, frantically looking in all directions before quickly resting her eyes on Martin. Panic was in her eyes and no sign of theatrics were on display. Genuine surprise filled her expressive face.

"Good evening Ms. Palermo, is everything alright?" asked Martin.

"Martin! Oh, thank goodness you've arrived! I was cleaning the windows when I looked down and saw someone come to your front door covered head to toe in a tattered robe. I thought it strange because it's been rather warm lately but then as I was walking to the door there was this flash of light and it startled me so much that I hesitated and then—"

"Ms. Palermo! Please calm down, madam. I'm sure it was just some local kids attempting some sort of prank."

"No, but that's just it, Martin dear! When I worked up the courage to shoo him away, he was nowhere to be found. What's more ...

As soon as I made it down the stairs, what did I see? A child on your front step!"

Silence fell between them as confusion overtook Martin.

"Come with me, my dear. I should have gone to the child first instead of looking for the deserter. Come, come, come ..."

Ms. Palermo walked to the front of the apartment with Martin faster than he had ever seen her move. She was surprisingly spry despite her age and size. Reaching the front of Martin's apartment, their demeanor quickly changed to a quieter one. There was, in fact, a baby sound asleep in what appeared to be singed blankets. The faint smell of smoke hung in the air.

"Ms. Palermo, may I?" whispered Martin, gesturing to the child.

"By all means, Martin dear."

Inspecting the child carefully, Martin started looking for any other contents the child may have arrived with. The child had golden-brown skin and brown hair with amber sprinkled throughout. It lit up with the light making it look like coals on the baby's head. Martin's eyes settled on a piece of paper tucked underneath the child's head. As carefully as he could, he lifted the baby's head and beckoned Ms. Palermo over.

"Please grab the letter, Ms. Palermo."

She glided over quietly, leaned in, and gently slid the paper out from under the infant's head. Cautiously, Martin lowered the child's head back to its original position. Right before he could retrieve his hand, the baby gently grabbed his ring finger. Reassurance filled the baby's face, coupled with an adorable yawn. Martin smiled.

Gently, Martin picked up the child and cradled him in his arms.In response, the child immediately turned over to make itself more comfortable.

What have you been through, young one? Who are you?

Returning his gaze to Ms. Palermo, her face changed expressions almost as fast as it changed colors. Glancing at the piece of paper, her eyes widened and then looked back at Martin.

"It's addressed to you!" Ms. Palermo hissed, causing the child to flinch. The child squeezed Martin's ring finger a little bit tighter.

"What?!" Martin mouthed, his eyes widening with surprise.

Did they find me? No, that's impossible. I was too thorough and far too random. Even I didn't know where I would end up when I set off...

Martin rolled his eyes.

There is that word again.

"Come into my apartment where it's more comfortable, Ms. Palermo. When you're ready, go ahead and read the letter."

With the ripped letter in hand, she whipped out an ungodly amount of keys from her pocket. The keys jangled while she located the one that opened Martin's apartment. With a swift turn, she opened the door. Martin turned on the living room lights with his hip and then turned to Ms. Palermo. With a nod, she began to read.

Martin... He is everything you have grown up knowing and everything I hoped he would be Words cannot fully express how much he means to me and I would do anything to see he doesn't get hurt again by the circumstances surrounding me. Before he takes his rightful place leading the nation, he will need you. Grant him some of the light that has so abundantly been placed inside of you. The hate between us is a long and complicated one, nevertheless, there is no one I trust more. I will tell you everything that has transpired between us in person the next time we meet ... but before I sign off I will say this much ... I love him for all he is, but hate myself for all the pain I have caused him. Bring him back to me when

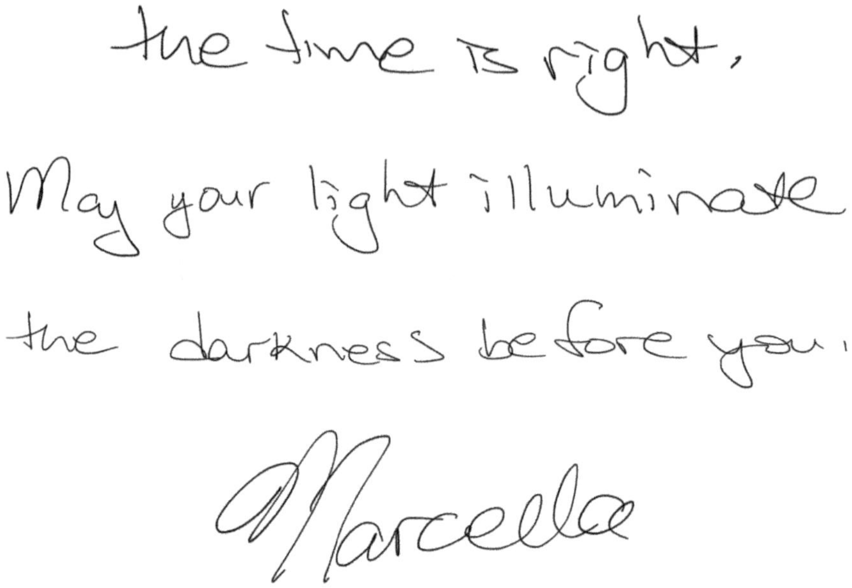

The hand writing was absolutely horrid. There could be no mistake ... the writing was hers. The parchment was smaller than normal, covered in soot and ripped cleanly at the top and a little bit by the signature. The rip must have been recent because that was the cleanest part of the paper. Confusion and questions filled Martin's mind as he re-read the letter in Ms. Palermo's hand. The envelope had the baby's name on it. Cyrus Ganymede ... Martin shook his head.

How did they find me? Is this really her child? What should I do?

Looking back to Ms. Palermo, Martin asked, "Did you see anything else Ms. Palermo?"

"You arrived only moments after I descended. I have told you everything, Martin dear," she replied with both the fear and the strength of someone desperately trying to clear their name.

"I will unwrap him from this blanket to see if anything else came with him."

"Careful he doesn't get a chill ...

Just as soon as Martin began, he stopped.

He might be ...

"Ms. Palermo, could you be a doll and warm up some milk for the child? He might be hungry when he wakes," asked Martin with a thick layer of charisma and a breathtaking smile he knew would surely convince her.

"Oh! Of course, Martin dear. So considerate of you really, why didn't I think of that? It will be ready in a flash!"

Raising her finger up as if it were a sword, she pointed herself towards the kitchen and marched over like a member of a marching band. Never a dull moment with Ms. Palermo.

As she rummaged through the cabinets, Martin turned his back to the kitchen. He glanced behind his shoulder to make sure Ms. Palermo was preoccupied with the task he had given her.

As carefully as a collector unwrapping a relic, Martin began unraveling the child from his blue blanket. Besides some light burns and smudges from the ash, the child's face was spotless. Martin switched from cradling the baby in his arms to an upright position against his chest.

"So, do you know this Marcella?" Ms. Palermo asked as a pan clanged to the ground.

The clanging from the kitchen woke the child. A pained and tired cry escaped his lips.

"Yes ... I know this Marcella. At least, I thought I knew her ..." Martin slowly uncovered the child's neck. The blanket was the most burned on the backside and Martin could see that some of the flames had scorched Cyrus' neck. No wonder he'd started to cry. The skin was red and slightly blistered.

"What will you do with the child? We could make some calls to the boy's extended family after the milk is ready."

Martin unwrapped the rest of the blanket, revealing the child's torso. Martin's eyes widened, and he let out an audible gasp. Utter disbelief filled his chest as he almost dropped the child. Startled by the sudden movement, the child began to cry loudly.

"Oh dear," said Ms. Palermo, peeking her head from the kitchen.

"It must have been all the ruckus I made when I dropped that pan.

The milk should be simmering in a minute or two. Would you like me to hold the little guy for a bit?"

Quickly covering the child's torso, Martin whirled around.

"Ms. Palermo!" Martin said louder than he should have.

"What is it?!" Distress returned to her face. Martin collected himself and then continued.

"The child is burned on his neck. Look!" Martin said, revealing just enough evidence.

Ms. Palermo began changing colors again. Great big tears welled up in her green eyes as she beheld the child's blistered red skin.

"Let's take Cyrus in right now and get him treated," said Martin.

"I don't think his burns are too bad, but I would ask you to look over him when we get to the hospital."

"Of course, dear! This little angel deserves nothing but the best." Martin gave a slight smirk at the comment."After we finish at the hospital, I'll need to make a stop at the supermarket. It's a little bare in here for a child. Perhaps you can help me?" Martin said, raising an optimistic eyebrow.

Like a soldier who had come to terms with the battle before her, courage and determination returned to Ms. Palermo. She gulped and then nodded fiercely.

"Absolutely. Be quick now."

Ms. Palermo turned off the stove, poured the lukewarm milk into the drain, and then went and collected her things from her apartment upstairs. She returned panting after a couple of seconds with her purse and an overcoat.

"One more thing, Ms. Palermo, before we embark," Martin said with stout conviction. "There will be no calls after we are done. I will be raising the child. I am now Cyrus' caretaker."

The look of determination on Martin's face was quickly matched by Ms. Palermo's. With the same conviction, she placed one hand on the back of the child's head and the other on Martin's shoulder.

Looking directly into Martin's eyes she said, "Of course you are."

2
GRADUATION

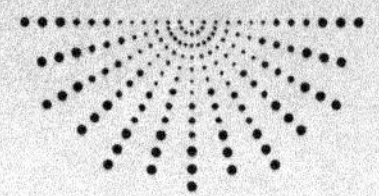

11 Years Later

CYRUS YAWNED. GRADUATION WAS taking *forever*. Graduating middle school was something of an accomplish-ment and meant a lot... to the parents. This graduation ceremony had a speaker, which Cyrus believed was a bit excessive. Him.

"Your scholastic excellence in spite of your challenges inspire your fellow classmates. Being the top of your class at such a young age is an impressive accomplishment, Cyrus. Your classmates will be happy to hear from you at the graduation," his principal had said the week prior.

Cyrus chuckled to himself. His classmates were in the same boat he was ... trying to make the ceremony go as fast as possible so summer could *finally* begin. The only thing "inspiring" about this cere-mony would be the end.

Being the top of a middle school class was hardly something Cyrus considered as an accomplishment. School had always been easy for him. Skipping two grades and graduating middle school at age eleven was no big deal to Cyrus, but his classmates didn't like him any better for it either. No one likes being reminded someone three years younger can outscore them on every test. The way they treated him was like he was an alien from outer space.

Speaking of aliens, where is Martian sitting again?

Cyrus scanned the audience and quickly found him. Front and center, as usual. Cyrus hadn't been able to pronounce his "T's" as a child so "Martin" came out as "Martian." Even long after Cyrus had started pronouncing his words correctly, *Martian* stuck around. He might as well have been a Martian with how he acted. Martin was the smartest person in the room everywhere he went. He spoke with unparalleled eloquence no matter the situation and had the memory of an elephant.

Everyone has a formal and non-formal mode they switch on and off depending on the situation and circumstance. Martin had formal and super formal.

Cyrus had grown used to the flabbergasted looks on the faces of teachers, parents, and principals every time Martin opened his mouth. He used to find it entertaining but it quickly got old. He lived with it, after all, so he was exposed to it day in and day out.

Sitting next to Martin was Ms. Palermo. Giddy and smiling, she was enthusiastic about watching Cyrus speak. She was treating this like it was opening night of a Broadway Musical, and Cyrus was the lead.

She really needs to get out more ...

Cyrus allowed a small smile. He was grateful for their support. Even if this ceremony for graduating middle school was a complete waste of time, he had two people in the crowd who cared for him.

"Our next speaker is one of your fellow classmates and has overcome some tremendous obstacles in his life. May I present your valedictorian, Cyrus Weatherford!"

A weak applause from his fellow students was overshadowed by some very enthusiastic cheers from Ms. Palermo.

"YEAH CYRUS!!! WOOT WOOT!"

A feigned smile to hide his embarrassment crept across Cyrus' face. He then pushed the controls on his wheelchair and made his way to the lowered pulpit.

The ceremony was finally over. Parents gushed and smiles returned to all of the kids' faces. Cyrus was also smiling.

Summer is here!

To Cyrus, this meant series binging, comic books, and some extra free time. There was a catch in Cyrus' house though. Martin put education and well-being as a top priority ... therefore, Cyrus had to spend as much time reading as he did watching series, movies or animes. Cyrus thought he found a loophole for his reading requirements by choosing comic books and animated stories, but Martin quickly caught on.

The rule became he had to alternate between the two. Every other book had to be an actual book. He could not read two comic books in a row. (A rule Cyrus found very annoying while Martin found it motivating.) As Martin would say, "You'll find that most books in this world don't have pictures to go along with them. Best start getting used to it."

Martin made his way up to the stage with Ms. Palermo, smiling as they went.

"Cyrus that was wonderful!!! Absolutely splendid oral presentation. The delivery along with the message you conveyed... These kids truly do not know how lucky they were to have you as their speaker!" swooned Ms. Palermo.

Martin smiled at the enthusiasm Ms. Palermo displayed then turned to Cyrus and said with a slight smirk, "Yes, your oral presentation was wonderful. What would you compare his speech to, Ms. Palermo?"

Here we go ...

Cyrus hated when Martin did this. He would egg Ms. Palermo on and ask her to compare something Cyrus said or did to a favorite play she had seen or a show she was watching. It always left Cyrus red in the cheeks. She always went overboard.

"I want to compare it to the speech King Théoden gave his

Rohirrim right before breaching the Orcs ranks," she started thoughtfully.

"The one where they all yell 'Death!' before they begin their charge?!" Martin said with less than believable enthusiasm.

Cyrus shot Martin a dirty look.

"Yes! That one! Thank you, Martin dear. The feeling right before the charge, the motivation I felt along with the emotion that was evoked. The feeling was similar as you delivered your message. Excellent oral presentation, just excellent ..." said Ms. Palermo, trailing off.

"Can we not use the words oral presentation' around these middle schoolers, please? They already have enough ammunition against me from my speech," asked Cyrus desperately. He could hear soft chuckles around him and felt his cheeks start to blush.

Martin smiled a devilish smile, the type he gave when he was about to say something he thought was clever. Cyrus braced for impact.

Turning to Ms. Palermo he said, "Very well... We will make our rounds and then return home. Cyrus, say thank you to Ms. Palermo for attending your graduation and listening to your speech ... Oral leave you here."

Ms. Palermo snorted.

~

Cyrus didn't want to hang around, but Martin insisted he thank his teachers. It took another hour before they reached the car. Martin shook every single teachers' hand, looked them in the eye, and acknowledged their hard work. Cyrus echoed everything Martin said and graciously thanked each one.

Despite being impatient to get home as quickly as possible, Cyrus knew how important manners were. Martin had drilled into him again and again that courtesy and gratitude were true signs of intelligence.

"Common courtesy is not so common, Cyrus. Don't be a commoner," he would say.

The looks on the teachers' faces mirrored the energy Martin displayed. Appreciation filled their faces and Cyrus couldn't help but feel glad every time one of his teachers faces lit up. At the end of the day, Cyrus saw with his own eyes how saying thank you with true sincerity filled peoples hearts. Always a learning experience with Martin.

The drive back was exciting. No more school! The amount of binge watching and video games he had planned was unreal. He had three video games he wanted to play all the way through —two of them he had already finished but was starting over for the joy of it. The third one was Martin's gift to Cyrus for finishing at the top of his class.

The main character was the last fighter added to his favorite fighting game. It was a big deal. Cyrus could hardly wait.

He beamed as he looked at his reflection in the window of the car. Cyrus had a very unique look. He had light brown skin with a ton of dark freckles canvased across his face. Curly brown hair with auburn strands speckled his head like burning sparks. Yet, that wasn't his most interesting feature. Cyrus had Heterochromia iridium-two different colored eyes. Cyrus' left eye was a hazel brown, almost yellow, while his right eye was bluer than the sky on a clear day.

Cyrus had always liked his appearance because it was unique from everyone elses. His peers in school tended to avoid him, though. The look' mixed with his intelligence was a little too much for people his age to handle. Parents and teachers lapped it up, though.

The bump right before their house jolted Cyrus from his trance. They had finally arrived, 1112 Seacoast Drive. A pretty easy address to remember. Martin got out first, as usual, and looped around to the passenger side to help Cyrus. They had an ADA van equipped with a ramp that would slide out so Cyrus could wheel in and out of the car. Luckily, Martin had always lived on the first floor. Ms. Palermo used to live on the second floor but moved to the first floor about seven years ago. Her mobility had been deteriorating and stairs had become more difficult for her. She was Martin and Cyrus' next door neighbor.

For better or worse.

Cyrus had been diagnosed when he was 5 years old with a condition called *Duchenne Muscular Dystrophy*, *DMD* for short. His reflexes became slower and slower as he grew and he'd become almost completely paralyzed from the neck down. He had been wheelchair bound since his first memories. The upside was the acronym *DMD* sounded like Dungeons and Dragons, which Cyrus thought was kind of cool.

Cyrus still had control of his arms below the elbows and could rotate his head slightly. Everything else was paralyzed. Being able to move even a little bit lifted Cyrus' spirits because he hated feeling helpless, primarily when it came to eating. He was always thankful to Martin for being able and willing to help him ... but Cyrus still felt a twinge of embarrassment. He couldn't help it.

Part of the reason he believed Martin always gave him things to do was because he didn't want him to feel sorry for himself. It was annoying most of the time, but Cyrus understood this ploy early on and kept doing them regardless. Although he would never admit it to Martin, being busy did keep Cyrus' mind off the fact that he was wheelchair bound.

"Being busy is the best remedy for feeling sorry for oneself," Martin would say.

As they made their way into the house, Cyrus set his wheelchair to full speed and zoomed quickly to—as Martin liked to call-"the spot". Right in front of the TV, right in the cross breeze of the house with viewing access to the kitchen. Ideal in all aspects.

"Martian, please hand me the controller? I can hardly wait," asked Cyrus, trying to contain his excitement. The game had been downloading since 8 A.M.

"Steady now, Cyrus. Allow me to place your personal items in your room before that," replied Martin with a smile.

"OK ..." Cyrus said a little deflated.

"But ... I will do it quickly."

With that, Martin briskly glided to Cyrus' room. Five seconds later, he reappeared and handed Cyrus the controller. Martin was the greatest guy sometimes. With palpable excitement, Cyrus switched the console on and anxiously awaited for the game as Martin made his way to the kitchen.

"Couple things to remember for these next couple days, Cyrus. First, tomorrow, Ms. Palermo will be preparing dinner as a way of saying congratulations. Best behavior please and compliment the food regardless of what is served. I don't want another eggplant parmesan incident."

Cyrus smiled. It was funny in hind sight. Ms. Palermo had under-cooked the eggplant so it had retained its squishy texture. It was Cyrus' first time having eggplant, and he didn't know what to expect.

Right as they'd started eating, Cyrus asked Martin-right in front of Ms. Palermo—if the eggplant was still supposed to be raw ... Good times.

"Second, after dinner, I want to play one game of chess with you.

Don't tank it this time, or I'll make you play another."

Last time they'd played, Cyrus had intentionally lost as fast as he could so he could get back to the show he was watching. The entire time, Martin kept eying him and asking, "Are you sure?"

Martin caught on and also decided to play terribly. This annoyed Cyrus because it made the game go longer. The game deteriorated to such a point where Cyrus began thinking he could beat Martin. Once Martin saw the effort return, he stopped tanking and handily defeated Cyrus. Cyrus had never beaten Martin.

"Lastly, I was speaking with some of your teachers and all of them recommended you as a tutor. I then went to the high school looking for something that aligned with these recommendations and found something."

Dread filled Cyrus' heart. Every time Martin went on one of his little missions to find something for Cyrus, he did.

"In order for you to graduate, you need community service and after talking with Principal Hemrick, I discovered that Mar Vista High School has a transfer student tutor program. You start Monday, 10-12, every day of the week."

Cyrus jaw dropped.

10-12?! Everyday?!

Cyrus already had those two hours planned out.

Next week is super hero week!

"Martian please..." pleaded Cyrus. "Let me have one summer without a random class, coding seminar, painting lesson or anything else along those lines."

"It's already decided, Cyrus. You have a brilliant mind, and you must share that with others. That is the best way to grow. It will also give you an opportunity to be the first point of contact for incoming students. Befriend them. Moving to a new place can be an uncomfortable experience. Make it a positive one for them."

Cyrus shook his head in disbelief. He had been looking forward to letting his brain rot completely with the amount of video games, movies and books he had lined up.

"I need to give you your injections before you dive into your story. The faster I do that, the faster you can start."

Cyrus grimaced a little bit. With the condition that he had, Martin had signed him up for an experimental treatment that called for injections all along his vertebrae. Being that he was paralyzed for the most part, he didn't feel too much pain, but after the injections were finished, it left his body achy and sore. It was not comfortable, but it was hopefully going to make him better.

Cyrus knew his time was limited. Most kids with his condition never saw twenty. It always felt like there was a giant axe over his head, and as much as Martin kept him busy, he always held that image in the back of his mind. Time seemed to be against him from a very young age. Death was something he had come to terms with. Cyrus' natural optimism along with Martin's missions' were what held back the lurking tides of despair.

"OK .. Could we do that now so I can at least enjoy my first weekend of freedom uninterrupted?" asked Cyrus.

Martin nodded, retrieved the needles and medicine and then began. Despite the treatment being experimental, Cyrus had been undergoing it as long as he could remember. He did not have too many memories using his legs. The sickness got him from a young age.

Cyrus winced as he felt the needles pierce his flesh by his neck. As the shots continued descending, he felt them less and less. It was never pleasant. Cyrus usually had a reoccurring dream after his injections where he could not only run but was able to fly. The sense of freedom he felt was so liberating, emotion would swell in his chest and he would wake up with tears of happiness.

What he would give to feel that in real life.

3

TERRIFIC TUTOR

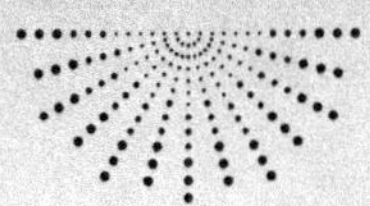

CYRUS WOKE UP AT 8 AM. This was late for him considering he usually woke up at 6:30 every morning during the school year. In Cyrus' mind, however, it might as well have been three in the morn-ing. It was summer vacation. There should have been a requirement of nothing earlier than 10 AM.

It usually took an hour for Martin to help Cyrus get ready, have breakfast and leave. Martin was obsessed with routine. Cyrus could hear rustling in the kitchen and the smell of bacon accompanied with its usual sizzle.

Cyrus was still upset at Martin. He had spent the weekend using every known method of persuasion to try to get out of tutoring. From "I don't know the material well enough" to telling Martin it was his summer and he was being forced into helping people against his will.

Amused, Martin responded the same way every time.

"You're going, Cyrus. You need to learn how to help people with what you know. Especially when you don't want to."

It was pointless. The man was impenetrable. Convincing Martin to let him off the hook was harder than breaking into Fort Knox. The truth was, Cyrus was anxious. Friends weren't a strong suit of his. He knew how to socialize when the time came, but he was shy. Being

23

confined to a wheelchair made it so he couldn't do most activities with the other kids in his grade. Not to mention puberty was running rampant with his classmates while it hadn't hit him ... yet. Cyrus shuddered at the thought of having the puberty talk with Martin.

Cyrus found comfort in books and reading. Martin told Cyrus that, like himself, he was a social introvert. He had his thoughts and knew how to share them but he also knew how to hide them.

Cyrus rolled his head, stretching as he woke. He stayed quiet and closed his eyes.

Maybe Martian forgot? I could pretend to be asleep and at least make us late?

Cyrus opened his eyes.

Yeah right... forget or be late. Not Martian.

The elephant memory combined with the punctuality of a product geek on release day ... That was Martin. There was no way around it. Cyrus sighed in defeat.

"Cyrus, you up? Carpe diem. Time to seize the day. Breakfast is about ready."

"T'll be up in a minute."

No tones of amnesia there ...

The sound of plates being set on the table along with the intoxicating smell of bacon signaled it was time to get up. Footsteps came down the hall and then Cyrus' door opened.

"Good morning, sunshine," said Martin with a smile. "Breakfast is served."

Martin lifted Cyrus out of the bed and placed him in his wheelchair. Cyrus felt like a rag doll. Embarrassment still tugged at Cyrus but whenever Martin detected it, he usually defused it by calling Cyrus "my little rag doll" or dancing moronically in circles until Cyrus smiled. Martin always told Cyrus he relied on him for his arm workout. The man had dad jokes for days, but they made Cyrus smile.

Martin wheeled him to the table and helped him with his breakfast. The bacon, per usual, tasted as good as it smelled. After breakfast, began the usual routine. Shower, dress, prepare for the day, injection.

Martin worked at the hospital with Ms. Palermo, and together they researched treatments for DMD.

It seemed like the heavens had smiled upon Cyrus when he was diagnosed. Despite the intensity of his diagnosis, his doctor lived next door and his guardian was trained to attend to his needs. Martin had become a registered nurse and assisted Ms. Palermo in her practice.

Ms. Palermo was an Orthopedic Surgeon, one of the best around She always said she would retire, but she had been saying that for as long as Cyrus could remember.

Martin opened the front door and then looked back towards Cyrus. The moment their eyes met, Cyrus slumped his neck and closed his eyes in dramatic fashion. Martin was deliberately taking away his summer.

"Chin up, rag doll. It's a beautiful day to help someone."

They made their way to the car and loaded up. This wasn't how Cyrus had envisioned his summer vacation. Ms. Palermo peeked her head out her front door and shouted a loud farewell. During the drive, he counted the things he would rather do than tutor incoming students.

Eat broccoli. Have a staring contest with the sun. Talk to Ms. Palermo about her favorite musicals. This. Is. The. Pits.

"Welcome to Mar Vista High School, my young Mariner," said Martin.

"Thanks."

He was now a Mariner ... yay. School was school and thus far, the social aspect had greatly disappointed Cyrus. Mostly because, as Martin had told him, he was a 35-year-old stuck in an 11-year-old body. To this, Cyrus would respond that Martin was a 75-year-old grandpa stuck in a 30-year-old body. Martin always graciously thanked him for the 'compliment'.

Cyrus IQ along with the maturity for his age, made most conversations boring for him. He was of the opinion that most of what the teenagers talked about was inconsequential and petty. The hormones talked 75% of the time and gossip the other 25%. *First world problems*, tended to be his thought whenever people in his grade spoke.

A bright green roof and a painted Poseidon welcomed Cyrus to his summer of purgatory. They made their way to the first classroom after the main gym. A dull grey color oozed across the walls.

Not the most appealing color to encourage education.

The building was labeled with a large J' before you entered.

What does the 'J" stand for? Jail, probably.

They entered the classroom, and Cyrus noticed four other souls in the room. There were two male students, one female student and a female teacher.

Martin quickly took charge. He introduced himself and Cyrus to the teacher—a woman as bland as the building. She was thin with pursed lips and a straight nose. Dark blue eyes hid behind spherical glasses and greying brunette hair. Her name was Ms. Dougle, and as Martin began to speak, his contagious eloquence shot an involuntary smile to her pursed lips.

There it is ... The Martian charm.

Cyrus rolled his eyes.

After coming to her senses, Ms. Dougle turned around and began introducing everyone.

"The two young men are Luis and Todd. Luis is from Texas, and Todd is from Michigan."

The two boys turned, waved unenthusiastically and returned back to their phones.

Luis was a short-set Latino, most likely Mexican. He had the pubescent mustache hairs that most of the other boys in Cyrus' grade had.

Some of the girls too. Cyrus suppressed a smile.

Todd, on the other hand, looked like he hadn't seen a lot of sun. He had a few freckles much lighter than Cyrus. Messy brown hair sprouted from his head. His teeth protruded from his face reminding Cyrus of a foal. Todd's expression was that of shock when he saw Cyrus.

"The young lady is ... Oh, I have such a hard time with this name..." Ms. Dougle trailed off. "How do you pronounce your name again? Is it ... Ow Lolo?"

Thick curly brown hair whipped around in the corner and revealed a golden-skinned girl with a fierce expression.

"It's Auli'i," she said as if she were correcting a child.

"Ow ... lee ... me ..." said Ms. Dougle hopefully.

The girl sighed and shook her head. "I'll help you. 'Ow' like someone stepped on your toe. 'Lee' like the name and then 'e' like the letter. Ow-Lee-e. Auli'i."

Martin seemed intrigued.

"Where are you from, Ms. Auli'i?" asked Martin executing the name flawlessly.

Auli'i smiled at his success. "I am from Hawaii, Mr. ... What was your name?"

"My name is Martin Weatherford, and this is Cyrus. Hawaii, the big island? Or are you from one of the other seven inhabited islands?"

Auli'i's smile changed to raised eyebrows.

"Well. Mr. Weatherford. It seems you know something about geography. I was born on Oahu, the main island where most of the population and military bases reside."

"You have lived in a beautiful place, Ms. Auli'i. I myself have never been, but I do hope I can visit one day. Pleasure meeting you." Auli'i smiled and nodded her head. Martin turned to Cyrus, gave a nod in her direction and then flashed a smile. Cyrus looked the other way.

"Thank you so much, Ms. Dougle. Use him as you see fit. Cyrus, I will see you at noon. Farewell, everyone."

Use him as you see fit?! What am I, a slave?

Cyrus felt abandoned.

This is so unfair.

Ms. Dougle turned to the class. "We will be covering basics in Algebra. Let's start with a quick lesson then I will have Cyrus help Luis, and I will help you two." After the lesson, Ms. Dougle handed out worksheets that were due at the end of class.

Cyrus' summer sentence had begun. Algebra was a subject Cyrus found extremely easy. Luis was in a bad mood and pretended he knew the material. Every question they began, Cyrus asked if he knew where to start, to which Luis would say he knew and didn't need to prove anything. Then, he would proceed to do it wrong, and Cyrus would step in and help him finish the problem. Pretty soon, Luis started making Cyrus do the worksheet. He would ask Cyrus to start, saying he would check his work. Cyrus tried to be helpful and understanding, but he quickly caught on to Luis' scheme.

This kid is just using me ... I'm not doing another problem for him.

The kid was very snide about having done nothing thus far. Cyrus, on the other hand, was very annoyed. Arriving to question 13, Luis tried the same routine.

"OK, go for it. I'll take notes on this one, too." Cyrus stared at the kid, feeling his rage build up.

"Actually, this one, I'm going to let you do."

"No, it's fine! Keep going, you're really on a roll."

"No..." said Cyrus with a shrug. "The rest I will merely supervise. *You've* got this."

Disgust filled Luis' face as he stared down Cyrus.

Perking up what little chest he had, he looked at Cyrus and whispered menacingly, "Why not? You have something better to do?!"

"Yes, I do. Help *YOU* learn how to do it," replied Cyrus in a normal voice.

"Well, then I'm going to get some help from someone who actually knows what they're doing. Ms. Dougle! I need some help. Cyrus doesn't know what he's doing."

Ms. Dougle was busy helping Todd and Auli'i but she bought it.

"Very well. Auli'i, could you switch places with Luis, please?" Todd's eyes widened. He also seemed uncomfortable with Luis' presence.

"Of course, Ms. Dougle," said Auli'i graciously.

Scooping her things, she made it over to the table before Luis had even begun to stand.

Luis quickly grabbed his things. As he left, he looked over to Cyrus and mouthed the words 'stupid'. Auli'i i furrowed her brow. Luis' eyes met hers, and she made no attempt to hide how unimpressed she was. Luis sneered at her too, then scampered over to Ms. Dougle.

Cyrus found himself getting more and more angry with Martin for forcing him into this.

Auli'i took her seat in front of Cyrus, and then gave him a warm smile. Cyrus felt his cheeks turn red

"Sorry about that jerk," whispered Auli'i. "I know I introduced myself to your father but I'm Auli'i. Auli'i Fualautoalasi."

Auli'i extended her hand. Cyrus blinked a couple of times, trying to comprehend what the heck she had just said.

"Cyrus. Cyrus Weatherford," he replied, wiggling his fingers.

Auli'i reached over and shook his hand with a smile. Luis coughed loudly and shot them both a look.

"Was he trying to make you do everything?" asked Auli'i.

Cyrus jaw dropped. "Yeah... he did ... uh .. How'd you know?"

"Same thing with that Todd kid. Not the brightest one of the bunch. I could visibly see Ms. Dougle getting annoyed at his lack of effort," she said shaking her head.

Cyrus smiled. Maybe it wasn't going to be that bad of a day after all.

Returning to a normal voice, Auli'i asked, "I have a couple questions on some of these. I was able to get through about half. Could you help me?"

"Yeah! Yeah just fine. What can I ... uh ... help you with on the assignment?"

This Auli'i is exotic looking, thought Cyrus.

Cyrus began helping Auli'i solve some equations with fractions in them. Auli'i was smart and only asked for help when she wanted clarification and when she'd finished a problem. She was motivated and that made Cyrus job infinitely easier.

An hour flew by, and when the clock reached 11, Ms. Dougle excused herself for a moment to go to the restroom.

Noticing the lack of adult supervision, Luis looked up and then, in what Cyrus guessed was an attempt to impress Auli'i, said to Cyrus,

"That's a nice ride you got. Must have been what got you the girl." He imitated rolling the wheels of a wheelchair.

Todd contorted his face and began uttering horse sounds. Cyrus believed Todd was laughing but wasn't sure.

Luis fed off of Todd's horse laugh, but as he turned back around, Auli'i was pointing a finger in his face. Cyrus hadn't even seen her move.

"You apologize to Cyrus this moment."

Luis flinched from surprise. Todd's horse laugh squealed to a halt.

"I was just kidding," Luis said with a nervous laugh.

"I'm not. Apologize."

The A/C was the only sound in the room.

Luis sat up straight. "I'm not apologizing to that cripple-" Auli i grabbed Luis by the ear, and in the blink of an eye, stood him up, marched him to the classroom entrance and threw him out.

Not missing a beat, Auli'i pirouetted and returned to her seat with the grace of a ballerina. Todd's bucktooth jaw had dropped. Cyrus sat in stunned silence.

"So, problem 13 has these integers. Can you make sure I did this one correctly?"

Cyrus stared at her, bewilderment quite apparent on his face. Auli i stared back.

"I don't like bullies."

Cyrus returned to the page with a nervous smile.

Ms. Dougle returned five minutes later, quickly scanned the room, then asked where Luis was.

"He was being an a—" began Auli'i.

"Being called by his parents, Ms. Dougle. Apparently, there was a family function today. He got a call and off he went. I couldn't tell exactly what it was because it was in Spanish," said Cyrus, borrowing some 'Martian charm.

Auli'i gave him a smirk and a raised eyebrow of approval. Auli'i then shot Todd a serious look that seemed to say, *Right?!* Todd flinched and shook his horsey noggin.

Ms. Dougle shrugged her shoulders and went back to helping Todd.

"Thanks for the save," said Auli'i with a smile. "I was just going to come clean and tell her what I did."

Her smile was breathtaking. The white of her teeth contrasted her golden-brown skin.

"My pleasure. I figured this Luis kid wouldn't be in a hurry to tell anyone he was ushered out the door by a girl."

"What do you mean, 'by a girl'?" Her expression turned serious.

Cyrus got a little nervous. It had not been his intent to offend her.

In situations like this, Cyrus had a sarcastic defense mechanism that usually kicked in. This time, he was coming up blank.

"I only meant his pride was hurt. No bully wants to admit they were beaten by a girl, someone younger or, in my case, a 'cripple.'" Auli'i's expression softened with a hint of pain. Cyrus felt a twinge of guilt. He usually didn't play the cripple card, but after what he saw, he definitely wanted to be on Auli'i's good side.

"You're probably right. Bully or not, he had it coming. My mother and I just got away from a bully."

Cyrus became very cautious. He hadn't really talked with anybody seriously about their life. He was used to being, well ... ignored.

"Was it uhhh... was it ... someone from ... your school?"

"No ... It was my father."

"I'm ... uhhh. I'm so sorry."

"Sorry? Sorry for what?"

"Your pain."

They sat in silence for a minute.

"You want to know something, Cyrus?" asked Auli'i with a half smile.

"S-s-sure."

"You seem to have a personality that is as interesting as your appearance. Do you want to be my first friend here in San Diego?"

Friend?

The word seemed foreign but Cyrus couldn't shake the warm feeling from head to toe. Cyrus became aware of the baboon-ish smile that had crept across his face.

After he regained his composure, he replied with, "Sure. Just don't beat me up, OK? Otherwise, you'll only have Todd left."

"Don't give me a reason to."

They both smiled horsey smiles.

4

THE CHIEF

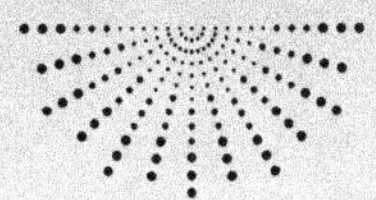

JUNE TUTORING HAD FLOWN by and Cyrus was the better for it. Auli'i and Cyrus had really bonded during Cyrus' indentured servitude.

Martin gave him the eye every time he picked him up. Cyrus forced himself not to smile to avoid the looks from Martin. The look of *credit belongs to me* that Cyrus hated. He knew Martin did it jokingly to irritate him, but Cyrus hated the thought of Martin using this experience to justify future activities. The proof was in the pudding though ... Cyrus had perhaps made the coolest friend possible.

Auli'i was cultured in every sense of the word. She was well read, feisty as a firecracker and could keep up with Cyrus' semantics. She was better at roasting Cyrus than he was of her, and she reminded him of that fact constantly. She said it was to, "establish dominance." To which Cyrus would shake his head and try to hide his smile. Cyrus' sarcastic comments *never* went unnoticed by Auli'i, and she always had one in response. They were two peas in a pod.

Auli'i was not very familiar with tablets or phones which *really* surprised Cyrus since everyone his age or older had a phone and was always on it. Cyrus showed Auli'i how to use them and just like everything else, she picked it up quick.

A woman by the name of Kamalani was Auli'i's mother. She had made quite the impression on Cyrus by smothering him in the most back breaking hug and wettest kiss he had ever received. Martin had also been taken by surprise but was absolutely charmed by the woman.

Kamalani had started a new job so she couldn't always pick up Auli'i.

The moment Cyrus found this out, he insisted Auli'i catch a ride with them back home. It didn't take a lot of convincing, and Kamalani was over the moon. They lived in the opposite direction in-between an old donut shop and the drive-in theater where the flea market took place.

It was a considerable distance to walk.

"Fine, I'll let you hang around me a little bit more, geez" Auli'i had said.

"You flatter yourself. I'm just doing my good deed for the month." Cyrus got a flick to the ear for that comment. She was incredibly fast.

Auli'i had extended an invitation for Cyrus and Martin to come over for lunch after their last day of tutoring. Auli'i's mother was cooking up a fish called 'Mahi-mahi' Cyrus had never eaten it, but Martin was particularly interested when she told him about the fish.

When Cyrus asked him if he'd had it before, he said cryptically,

"Yes, but it's been a while."

"You clean up nice," said Auli'i with a flirtatious look as Cyrus rolled into the classroom.

"Wish I could say the same," replied Cyrus.

Auli'i chuckled. They'd finished tutoring, and although it would be a month until school started back up, they'd promised to still see each other outside of school.

"So, what we gonna do?" asked Auli'i.

"I don't know, whatcha want to do?"

"I don't know, whatcha want to do?" replied Auli'i with an eye roll. "But seriously, what are we going to do?"

"First, we will watch phase one of those superhero movies I've been talking about. You really must live under a rock. How have you not seen them?"

Auli'i rolled her eyes.

"Then, we'll walk the beach at sunset looking for shells and sand dollars."

"You mean I'll go for the sunset walk while you roll beside me."

"I could sue you for making fun of a cripple."

"Do it. I'm smarter than you so I would get the lawsuit thrown out on baseless charges."

"Baseless?! You got a lot of nerve young lady."

"Young lady? I am fourteen and you are eleven. That is no way to talk to your superior, young man."

"Hmph ... Well, look who's tutoring who. Age doesn't account for everything. I can't help that I am a child prodigy."

"With California's public education system right now, I don't think skipping a grade or two counts for much," laughed Auli'i.

"Hey, it's not my fault the material is so easy, or the fact that Martian drills me at home. My big brain, being confined to a chair and Martian's regimented schedule all contributed to me skipping those grades."

"Yes, yes ... but of course, darling."

Cyrus chuckled softly.

"Can I ask you a question?" asked Auli'i, flipping back to normal.

"Fire away."

"Why do you call him Martian?"

"Have you not seen the way he acts?"

Auli'i shrugged and nodded in agreement.

"No, that's not it. As a kid I had difficulty pronouncing my T's. He thought it was cute ... I think it's funny. We both win. Plus, he is very different from anyone else I've ever met. So, it just kinda fits, you know?"

"Why don't you call him dad?"

"I ... well... there was this time when I was in kindergarten and we had to make finger paintings for our parents. Everyone was busy painting and as the teacher was making her rounds and she asked me who I was making mine for. You can imagine her confusion when I said Martian."

They both took a minute to laugh.

"When I went home that day and gave him the painting, he loved it, of course. Because, you know, I'm a genius." Cyrus did an upper-crust impression.

Auli'i rolled her eyes while laughing.

"I asked him what you just asked me." Attempting his best Martin impression, "I adopted you, Cyrus. I am not your father, but I am indeed your guardian. Dare I say, guardian angel. One day you will meet your parents, and when you do, I would still like to be your Martian, if you'll let me."

"Awwwwww. That is sooo cute."

Cyrus shook his head, embarrassed. "Mehhhh... Depends."

"So, when are you going to meet them?"

"He said sixteen or when I start walking."

Auli'i raised her eyebrows in shock. "When you start walking?! What is that supposed to mean?"

"With how Martian speaks ... literally."

"Then get to walking, young man. I don't think I can wait till you're sixteen."

"Yes, mom," Cyrus said, smiling. "Now, I have a question for you."

"Shoot."

"Why are you here? You're obviously brilliant and really didn't need my help."

"You mean here in tutoring or here in San Diego?"

"Yes."

Auli'i chuckled. "Well, here in tutoring because I wasn't in school for the last two years. My family moved when my father got called on to be a governing chief. So, during that time, I learned a lot of things that were .. interesting but had very little to do with things like math, science or anything we've gone over together. So, I needed a refresher, and here I am. As to why I'm here in San Diego ... Putting it plainly, it was so I could escape my father."

Cyrus tilted his head with curiosity.

"My father is one of the three main chiefs that makes decisions for our people ... but we were outsiders coming in. It was very controversial my father being appointed as one of the chiefs of our nation. Suffice it to say, my family and I were treated pretty ruthlessly in attempts to get us to leave. Two years of this turned my father into a different person, and I wanted out. Instead of letting me go alone, like I had planned, my mom came with me instead ... she said I didn't have to do things alone and dropped everything to come with. I made her promise not to say anything if she decided to come, and that's what we did. She grabbed a bag of clothes, and we left then and there," said Auli'i, slightly embarrassed.

"Your mother is a good woman."

"Yeah ... She really is. Listen, I'm a little embarrassed, honestly, so don't you dare make fun of me for this, or I'll steal your wheelchair's battery pack and leave you stranded. OK?"

"You got it."

"Anyway, my father took me, my brother and sister out of school and to a different island when I was 12 and—"

"Wait, wait, wait ... You have a brother and sister?"

"Yes, I do. Now, shut up and let me finish."

"Sorry."

"When we were taken out of school, we moved to another island called Ni'ihau and were taught in the nation's 'ancient ways. At first, it was fascinating ... but it got old real quick. Mom and dad started fighting more. Everybody shunned us. I didn't want to live like that. So, I left."

She had a lot of tension on her face. Cyrus hurt seeing her like that.

"Why San Diego?" asked Cyrus.

"The house we are in right now belongs to my uncle. He's my mom's older brother. He would always tell us we had a place to stay if we decided to go to the mainland. My father and our nation forbid leaving the islands. Since they forbid it, I did it. So far, it's worked out pretty well."

"Your father ... is he ... bad?"

Auli'i paused and thought for a moment. "He's not a bad man, Cyrus. I love my father very much. He's very ... passionate about something I don't believe in, and I feel he was trying to force me to believe it. His priorities are mixed up. That's the best way I can put it." Silence filled the space. Not knowing what else to say, Cyrus changed the subject.

"I'm excited to try this Mahi-mahi. Your mother is definitely cooler than you."

"Well, I can cook just as good as her."

"I doubt that."

"Also," Auli'i pointed her finger right at Cyrus. "Give some effort by giving her a kiss on the cheek. She has been worrying that she is coming on too strong. Try. Make sure she feels some love back ... or else."

Auli'i made a fist at Cyrus, and he gulped.

"I will be watching."

"I'll be sure to put some chap stick on and pucker up. How loud do you want the smooch to be when I give her a kiss?"

Auli'i punched him in the arm.

"Ow!"

Tutoring ended at 11:30 on the last day. Cyrus and Auli'i said goodbye and thanked Ms. Dougle before they left. She smiled at their words of appreciation. Martin wasn't kidding when he said gratitude goes a long way.

The sun was shining and a light breeze was coming from the ocean. The perfect day to end tutoring and enjoy their freedom.

Martin was out front waiting.

"Aloha, Auli'i," said Martin with a grin.

Cyrus rolled his eyes hard.

"Aloha, Martian. You're dressed so nice for our lunch appointment!"

It was true. Martin wore a light blue shirt tucked into black chinos with a belt and black dress shoes shined to perfection.

"Well, shall we be on our way? Your mother did say around noon, correct?"

"That's right. We got 10 minutes so let's get going. Shoots summer tutoring!" Auli'i said giving the school the Shaka.

The drive after tutoring remained the same all summer ... seven minutes talking about Auli'i and Hawaii. Martin's questions were endless.

"Aloha means' hello, goodbye' and I love you?'"

"Yep. It also means something else. 'Alo' means 'face to face' or 'to share,' whereas 'ha' means 'the breath of life.' Aloha. It was, and still is, used in tandem with our traditional greeting where we embrace, put our heads together and inhale and then exhale deeply. We share our breath of life."

"Wow ..." said Cyrus and Martin in unison.

Auli i smiled. Hard to resist captivated listeners.

They rolled past the best donut shop in town. Cyrus loved the donut shop and so did Auli'i. Only now and then had Martin taken Cyrus there as a treat. Now that Cyrus had a friend, they went at least twice a week.

They pulled up to Auli'i and Kamalani's house. A little wall protected a tiny front yard while a pinkish hue splotched the walls of the house. Before Auli'i reached the door, it burst open and out came her mother. Smiling ear to ear, she embraced her daughter with a hug and a kiss to which Auli'i returned. Then, she pushed her aside and came towards Martin and Cyrus at a frightening speed. Cyrus could see where Auli'i had gotten her ninja skills.

"Oh honey, it is so nice to see you!"

"It's great to see you, too-"

Before he could finish his sentence, Kamalani swooped down and gave Cyrus a hug and smothered him in kisses. Cyrus peeked over Kamalani's shoulder and saw Auli'i pointing at him. Cyrus quickly gave Kamalani a kiss on the cheek with an audible 'smack'. Kamalani swooned, and Auli'i nodded in approval.

Finishing up, Kamalani turned her attention to Martin. Auli'i and Cyrus glanced at each other. They had a bet as to whether Martin would extend his hand. Every time Martin spoke to Kamalani, he had always stuck out a hand first to which Kamalani would ignore and give him a peck on the cheek and a hug. Auli'i said he would wise up and just accept it. Martin was a creature of habit so Cyrus bet he would still go for the handshake. Winner got to choose what they did the first day they hung out.

Cyrus made his way closer to Auli'i and looked around excitedly.

Birds chirped, cars drove by on the main drag and a cloaked man stood on the corner. Cyrus gave a double take and then returned his attention to Martin and Kamalani.

This is going to be good.

"It is so kind of you to invite us over for lunch, Mrs. Fualautoalasi," said Martin, extending his hand.

Completely ignoring the extended hand, Kamalani went in for the kill.

"Dang it," whispered Auli'i, putting her head into her hands.

Cyrus bobbed his head slightly. The moment Auli'i looked at him, Cyrus stuck out his tongue, and Auli'i made a fist at him.

"Sorry, Mr. Weatherford. We're huggers in this family ... And please, call me Kamalani."

"Oh, I noticed. We are very excited to be here, Kamalani."

"Well, come on in! The fish is ready and everything is hot, so let's eat! Auli'i, make them comfortable while I go grab the food for the table."

Cyrus continued to bob his head as he wheeled past Auli'i into their house. Auli'i looked at him blankly.

Cyrus whispered just loud enough for Auli'i to hear, "Winner, winner, chicken dinner."

"Weren't you listening? My mom said it was fish, not chicken."

Auli'i stuck out her tongue and locked the door behind them.

Cyrus saw a flicker of light behind him as they entered the house. Must have been his eyes adjusting:

The house was small but open. The walls were decorated with paintings of the ocean and islands. These oceans were much different from the one Cyrus saw everyday. I.B. was nice and dirty thanks to the Tijuana estuary that leaked into the ocean. The deep blues and vibrant greens of the photos brought the living room to life. The light from the windows and the bright lights inside made the home feel inviting.

Garlic and the smell of what Cyrus assumed was Mahi-mahi, marinated the room. It wasn't a strong fishy smell like Cyrus had expected. It smelled almost ... sweet. The table was set nice and neat.

In the center of the table was a jar of mysterious pinkish-orange liquid. Everything was new.

Kamalani brought out the plates filled with fish, rice and Okinawan sweet potato. The fish was cooked in a white sauce and garnished with green onions. The sweet potato blew Cyrus' mind.

It's purple!

The look of surprise made Kamalani smile. Mouths watering and stomachs grumbling, Kamalani impressed both Martin and Cyrus with a word of prayer.

It was the best fish Cyrus ever had, not too strong, with a slight sweetness balanced by a garlic kick. The Okinawan sweet potato was *really* good too. It had a nice chewy texture with a pleasant earthy-sweet taste.

Martin went on and on about how delicious it was and insisted she pass him the recipe. Kamalani basked in the glow of Martin's compliments. Cyrus chatted with Auli'i about their plans for the rest of the summer, constantly reminding her that he'd won the bet.

Life is pretty good.

"KAMALANI!!!" a thunderous voice bellowed from outside.

Martin jumped while both Kamalani and Auli'i's eyes filled with horror.

"AULI'I!!! I KNOW YOU'RE IN THERE!"

Cyrus had never seen Auli'i like this. She was visibly frightened and in disbelief.

"Auli'i ... Who is that?" asked Cyrus.

BANG BANG BANG.

The house shook from the force of the mystery man knocking.

Auli'i looked at her mother who had regained some of her courage.

Martin was already on his feet and in between the door and everyone else.

"Kamalani, what are we dealing with? Anything you can tell me will help," said Martin gravely.

BANG BANG BANG.

"It's my husband."

"OPEN THE DOOR!"

"He found us ..." Auli'i trailed off, looking at Kamalani in confusion.

BANG BANG BANG.

"Kamalani, if he is violent, I will defend," said Martin.

Martin had an expression Cyrus had never seen before. Martin didn't look worried or tense in the slightest. His shoulders were relaxed but his expression was lethal. He was completely focused on the door. The banging stopped. Not a sound could be heard. Cyrus dared not breathe it was so quiet.

Rapid footsteps approached the door. BANG!

The door burst from its hinges, revealing a mammoth of a man. He stood a couple inches shorter than Martin but definitely had him beat in girth. He had dark brown skin, long black hair and tree trunks for limbs. Behind the man stood what seemed to be a younger version of himself.

The man looked absolutely infuriated. His brow furrowed and his cheeks moved as he exhaled loudly, like a horse. The boy looked conflicted.

As soon as they got through the door, the large man marched straight to the living room, the man child following close behind.

Martin held his ground, not flinching when the man came face to face.

"I don't know who you are, but stay out of MY family affairs."

The man began to walk past Martin but before he could, Martin put his arm up, blocking his path.

In the calmest yet most dangerous way, Martin said, "If you have something to say, say it right here. We heard you from out there, they can hear you just fine right here."

A look of pure venom came from the man's eyes.

"Love, please," said Kamalani. "We will hear what you have to say, but please be calm. You're scaring us."

"LOVE?!" the man said incredulously. "You call me Love after leaving in the middle of the night taking MY daughter away from ME?!"

"Dad, it wasn't mom. I-"

"YOU DON'T GET TO SPEAK RIGHT NOW, AULI'I. I receive my new position leading our nation and you abandon me when I need you the most? YOU UP AND LEAVE?!"

Martin flinched. "Wait ... What did you say?" whispered Martin.

"For. The. Last. Time ... Stay out of my family affairs."

Martin's look of focus was replaced by intrigue.

"Don't blame mom! She didn't want me to go alone! I made her promise not to say anything, dad. I ... I just couldn't live isolated like that anymore. It was too much like a cult. You may believe in that nonsense, but I never did. I never had a choice!"

"NONSENSE?! CHOICE?! You have no idea what you're talking about! This way of life has been around for thousands of years. The Lumen Caligo is out there somewhere, right now! We are lucky to be a part of it."

"YOU felt lucky enough. The rest of us were just along for the ride!" yelled Auli'i back.

"Mongoose, I know Ni'ihau isn't Oahu, but it was a chance for—"

"You guys are from Ni'ihau?!" interjected Martin.

Martian is acting very out of character.

"This all makes sense now," he continued. "You guys are .."

"THAT'S IT, YOU ARE OUT OF HERE!" The mammoth of a man grabbed Martin's outstretched arm and began removing him from the house.

Cyrus gasped, suddenly feeling very helpless and worried for Martin. The man was easily twice Martin's weight.

Martin whirled around and a skirmish ensued. Both men moved impossibly fast, going toe to toe with each other. Kamalani started yelling for them to stop. The young boy began making his way towards the fight. Auli'i got up and, in her ninja way, got between the boy and the fight. Putting a hand to his face, she shook her head and scowled at the boy. He stopped in his tracks. Although he was much bigger than her, he seemed frightened of the expression she gave him.

In the blink of an eye, Martin had this Goliath of a man on the floor at his mercy. The man was face down with his hand twisted up behind him. Martin looked unfazed.

"I'm going to ask you again," started Martin, looking up at Kamalani. "Are you from Ni'ihau?"

"Yes, we came from Ni'ihau!" said Kamalani frantically.

"Who are you and what do you call yourselves?" asked Martin.

"HAWAIIANS, WHAT ELSE WOULD WE CALL OURSELVES?!" responded the man furiously.

Martin twisted the mans arm slightly, and the man winced.

"Think carefully before you respond. Who are you? What do you call yourselves? And what do you want with the Lumen Caligo?" asked Martin.

The man's eyes widened. Realization filled everyone's eyes in the room except for Cyrus. He had absolutely no idea what was going on.

The man's tone went calm.

"I am Manaia Fualautoalasi, and this is my son Kimo Fualautoalasi. To some, we are known as Terrams."

Martin released the man from his grip and stumbled back towards the dining room. Cyrus witnessed yet another expression he had never seen cross Martin's face ... shock— pure shock.

The man stood up quickly. He rotated his shoulder a few times with eyes that never left Martin. He was now the subject of interest.

"Now, I have a question for you," began the man. "Who are you and what do you call yourselves?"

Martin cupped his hands to his mouth and mumbled to himself. Cyrus could only make out a few sentences. "... this is too soon. I wanted him to wait until he was 16. How can I contain this? No ... It's too late, but ... no ... it is too late ... I'll have to go explain ..."

Martin looked at Cyrus intently. Worry filled his eyes.

"Hey! I'm talking to you. Don't make me ask you again. Who are you and what do you call yourselves?"

Martin looked at the ground, let out a long sigh and then began unbuttoning his fancy shirt.

"My people are known by many names, but our existence has nearly been erased in the memories of the outside world." Martin began removing his shirt ... there was a vest of some sort underneath.

"But to those who still know the ancient ways, we are known by a certain name."

The sound of ripping Velcro and ruffling filled the room. Facing towards Manaia, he let the shirt and vest drop to the floor. Cyrus jaw also dropped to the floor. Like a roll of wrapping paper being unraveled, two giant white wings unfurled from his torso and filled up the room.

I'm dreaming ... this is a dream ...

"I am Martin James Weatherford, and to some ... I am known as a Lumen."

Martin was glorious to behold. The wings seemed to be pulsating light from within. The feathers were individually highlighted and were as fascinating to look at individually as the wings were collectively. Each feather looked like a real-life Van Gogh brushstroke, the detail was so fine.

Manaia looked relieved but unsatisfied with the response. Pointing his sausage finger at Cyrus, he gruffly asked, "What about him? Your son?"

All eyes turned to Cyrus. Auli'i was looking Cyrus up and down, as if she had missed something.

"This is Cyrus Ganymede Weatherford and ..." Martin looked at Auli'i, paused and then said, " ... he is the Lumen Caligo."

Manaia let out an audible exhale of disbelief. "I don't believe you. Prove it."

Martin reached into his back pocket and extracted his wallet.

Carefully, he removed a single feather. It was small and detailed.

Martin then slowly rotated the feather, revealing the darkest black on one side and softest white on the other.

Kamalani fell to her knees and began crying. Auli'i cupped her mouth and both Kimo and Manaia fell to one knee with a strange hand gesture in between their eyes.

Cyrus had no idea how to react. There were wings, strange sounding words and tears following a conflict. This was too much for him to process.

He's had freakin' wings this whole time.

Nothing could surprise him now.

Manaia got up slowly from his kneeling position and Kimo followed suit. Turning to Martin, he asked in a humble tone, "May I approach?"

Martin nodded.

Manaia began walking toward Cyrus.

Cyrus gulped nervously. The man was much larger up close.

Leaning down to him, he took Cyrus' hand, interlaced their ring fingers and said, "We've waited for you for a long time, little one. Know that me and my family will always be loyal to you. I was blinded by my rage, but now I see it was fate that brought my wife and daughter here. Anything we can do to aid you, you can count on us."

"Umm... well... thank you very much, Mr. Fualautoalasi. I ... will ... keep that in mind." Cyrus was being treated like a king and he didn't know why.

Standing up, Manaia turned back to Martin.

"I must inform my nation. I am one of the three governing chiefs and hold sway. This will awaken my people to action. I will depart back to the islands with the news."

"No," said Martin. "There are too many with ill intentions within each of the governing bodies. He must remain a secret."

"I do not see why. These are glad tidings. Everyone will be thrilled to learn the Lumen Caligo lives!" Manaia said excitedly.

"NO. He doesn't even know about all of us."

Manaia and Kamalani audibly gasped. Kamalani had stopped her sobbing.

"Regardless, I will tell my people the Lumen Caligo lives. When my family returns back with me—"

"I am NOT going back," said Auli'i defiantly.

"Yes, you are," said her father with the same fire Auli'i had.

"NO. I'm not. I refuse to return to that black hole of an island. I'm staying right here."

"If I don't come back with you, your sister will pay the price of your abandonment with her life!"

Auli'i and Kamalani gasped. Great big tears welled up in Kamalani and Auli'i's eyes. Then Kimo issued his first words.

"After you guys left, the council met to decide how they would track you down. They were going to send Marquise to hunt you down and kill you, but we were able to convince them to allow us. Their only condition was they had to have Akela as collateral," said Kimo somberly.

"Not my baby..." said Kamalani sobbing.

"They gave us four fortnights. That was forty days ago," said Manaia.

"I told her to come. I begged her to come! But she insisted on staying to help daddy and tutu," sobbed Auli'i.

"Sailing back will take a month. We will have to send a godwit to let them know we have found you," said Manaia.

"Wait... there may be another way," said Martin.

All eyes turned to Martin.

"With the Lumen Caligo's permission, you may utilize modern technology, thus forgoing a sailing expedition. Fly back with me.

Leave your family with Cyrus, and I will help negotiate the release of this Akela. I presume she is your daughter?"

"Yes, my youngest. How will we justify my family not coming along? The rules may be harsh but they have preserved our way of life these past 300 years. You know this, Lumen."

"Swear your children to Cyrus."

Everyone froze.

"Swear them to Cyrus as the Virtus Latores, and the council will have no choice but to accept the new conditions."

"That might work.." said Manaia. "What if it fails? What's the back up plan?"

"Negotiate more aggressively," said Martin with a shrug.

Manaia and Kamalani looked at each other. Kamalani nodded and then Manaia extended his hand.

"Agreed."

Martin shook his hand firmly.

Turning to Kimo and Auli'i, Manaia and Martin gestured to Cyrus as they made their approach. Everyone gathered around Cyrus. He was surrounded.

"Now, you two are going to be sworn to Cyrus as his designated Virtus Latores. You know what that is, yes?" asked Martin.

Kimo and Auli'i looked at each other nervously, then back to Martin and nodded.

Martin clasped their hands with Cyrus, interlocking their ring fingers while the rest of their fingertips touched-almost like some sort of hand tepee. Kimo's meaty hand took Cyrus' left hand... Auli'i took hold of his right.

"You will repeat the oath in Latin. Repeat after me ... Et omne, quod ego dico et lux in tenebris et in griseo. Dum ultima die virtutis meae et iuvenes armigeri iurare praesidio."

They repeated it solemnly in unison. After they uttered the final words, they separated.

Turning back to the family, he said, "We leave immediately. Kamalani, I ask you move your stuff to our house tonight. I will advise our landlord of the situation. I will pack my stuff for this trip and purchase the tickets."

Kamalani nodded and immediately went to her room.

"Cyrus, give Manaia permission to fly by airplane."

"What?"

"Please, just do it," said Martin calmly.

"OK ... I give you permission to fly by plane."

Manaia smiled and bowed with his hands together and ring fingers bent.

"Meet me by the van. I must speak with Cyrus privately," said Martin to Manaia. Martin picked up the vest that covered his wings and the shirt he'd been wearing.

Manaia nodded, picked up the door he'd broke down, placed it next to the entrance and went outside.

"You two," Martin said, pointing to Auli'i and Kimo. "Come with me. I have some instructions for you."

Curiosity and confusion filled their faces. Cyrus moved his wheelchair forward. Martin put up a hand

"Not yet, Cyrus. You're after them."

Martin led Auli'i and Kimo to the kitchen. Cyrus peered into the kitchen. He couldn't hear what Martin was saying, but he could see the sibling's faces. Shock, disbelief and surprise filled their faces.

What was worse, they kept glancing over at Cyrus. It felt like middle school all over again... people talking about him behind his back.

This hurt more though. Cyrus cared about the people doing the talking.

Martin pointed to his back and then said something Cyrus couldn't hear. Both Auli'i and Kimo gasped in unison. Their gaze went straight to Cyrus with the most intense look of disbelief and pain. Auli'i and Kimo's eyes didn't stray from Cyrus this time. Kimo looked at him like he was the alien. Auli'i looked at him with the utmost compassion.

What is Martian saying?

Martin snapped his fingers and the siblings attention returned back to him. He expanded his chest and wings while pointing his finger at the siblings. The siblings nodded emphatically and then returned back to the dining room with Cyrus. Both of their eyes were glazed over and their mouths hung slightly open.

Auli'i gave Cyrus a hug and then followed Kamalani into her room.

"Martian ... I ... I'm so confused. What is going on?" asked Cyrus.

"Cyrus, I wouldn't know where to begin... since the short version would only leave you frustrated, I will leave the explaining to Ms. Palermo. I ..." Martin faltered. He never faltered when he spoke. "I need some time to gather my thoughts and explain. I will call Ms. Palermo right now to let her know."

Martin whipped out his phone and quickly put it up to his ear after finding Ms. Palermo's number.

"Martian, that isn't good enough. How do you have wings? How do ..." began Cyrus.

"Ms. Palermo? I am doing well, how about you? Forgive my bluntness, but I will cut right to the chase. It is time. I have to leave right now and will be back soon, but I need you to explain everything to Cyrus and ... yes, I mean everything. Ms. Palermo, I don't have time. I'm leaving as soon as I grab my things." Martin paused as Ms. Palermo rambled furiously in a muffled fury of words.

"Can you at least give me something?" whispered Cyrus.

Martin put his hand up softly. His focus was on the phone call.

After what seemed like 10 minutes, the muffled rant ceased.

"Ms. Palermo. I will assist where I can. I need you to remove the prosthetic skin. I've hidden as long as I could but now is the time. I trust in you and am forever grateful for everything you have done. I now ask that you do this for me. Do you understand?"

More muffled rants began, but this time Martin cut her off.

"Explain and remove the prosthetic skin. Understand?" said Martin seriously.

Cyrus could make out a muffled yes from Ms. Palermo.

"Thank you. I'll be at the house in seven minutes. You may ask questions while I pack," said Martin as he hung up.

"Martian, I want you to tell me whatever this is. Ms. Palermo always takes the scenic route," pleaded Cyrus desperately.

"This time you might enjoy the scenic route. You'll get more information about the day we found you and what we did to conceal you. Now, I really have to go."

He wrapped his arms and wings around Cyrus in what Cyrus could only describe as a 'double hug.'

"I love you, and when I have the words and composure, I will explain things. For now, be patient with Ms. P," Martin added with a sad smile.

"I love you too ... I mean ... wings! How could I have missed that all these years?" asked Cyrus as Martin let go and began walking towards the door.

Martin paused, turned around and with a warm smile said, "I am not the only one with wings in our household." With that, he was gone.

Fit hit the shan.

5

FIRST STEPS

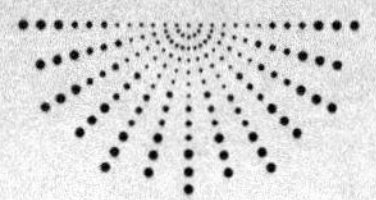

"**O**WWW! BE GENTLE!" SCREAMED Cyrus.

"If you didn't squirm so much IT WOULDN'T HURT!" Auli'i yelled back.

"Try and hold still, sweetheart ... it will be over soon," Ms. Palermo said soothingly.

"Almost there. Tough it out, big guy," added Kimo.

The pain was excruciating. Cyrus. Had. WINGS ... but they were wrapped around his torso, covered in graft-skin and smothered with some sort of adhesive. There was A LOT of adhesive.

It had especially freaked Cyrus out when he'd woken up and could wiggle his toes ... a week after Martin's sudden departure.

He could .. Wiggle ... His ... Toes. Cyrus joked that he should go into some church or give a TED talk. Auli'i egged him on. Kimo shrugged his shoulders. Ms. P said no. Along with the discovery of having wings, feeling had returned to Cyrus' entire body ... along with it, more aches and pains than any 11-year-old should have had.

Ms. P made him wait a week to take the skin off because they had just applied a fresh layer. She told him it would tear off actual flesh if they took it off now. That whole week was spent taking long baths and soaking to speed up the process.

Spleech.

Another piece of fake skin was removed and thrown into the growing pile in the bathroom corner. Maybe doing this at home instead of the hospital had been a bad idea... Cyrus didn't care. He didn't want to go back there. He always dreaded his monthly sessions.

Ms. Palermo protested at first but then gave in and got the necessary medical instruments to remove the skin that covered his wings and torso.

He had to take an hour long bath before this 'de-gluing' session.

Once it started, it was all hands on deck. If anyone had randomly walked in, it would have looked like a cannibalistic ritual. Tearing away the grafted skin from his hidden wings and actual skin was the stuff of nightmares. Good thing the Fualautoalasi's had strong stomachs.

"I think I'm gonna to be sick," said Kimo with a dry heave.

Maybe not all of them ...

Cyrus looked at him in pain and with a stern expression said, "Hey! You throw up in here, you clean it up with a spoon. Now, please help me end my literal metamorphic process."

Auli'i chuckled and held up her hand for a high five. "Teehee. Good one."

Despite the pain, Cyrus lifted his arm and gave her a high five.

He was too ecstatic that he could finally move to miss the chance, despite his pain.

On Martin's drugs, Cyrus had limited motor functions of his arms. Once the drugs had worn off, his video game skills went through the roof. One week off the injections and he could already wiggle his toes.

But that was tiring. His leg muscles were almost nonexistent. He had tried multiple times to walk and had fallen repeatedly. He thought Ms. P and the Fualautoalasi's would try and dissuade him from trying but they never did. But after the fourth bump in the night, they insisted Cyrus let them help him.

They were all very encouraging. They suggested he take it slow and, like an infant, learn to crawl before he could walk. That's exactly what Cyrus was doing, and it wore him out. Just crawling across the room he worked up a sweat. All those unused muscles in his body screamed in agony. The first time Cyrus successfully crawled from the kitchen to the front door without falling, genuine happiness came over him and he cried tears of joy. The Fualautoalasi's joined in and Ms. P bawled. It reminded Cyrus of how much she'd cried when she told him the story of how they found him. She really did go the scenic route.

"Then there was this letter from a friend of Martin's ... Oh, what was the name? I can't remember ... but after we read the letter and Martin inspected your body—you were pretty singed—we took you to the hospital where I worked and this is where I discovered what you and Martin were."

Cyrus sat captivated along with the Fualautoalasis.

"Martin made me swear before entering the hospital I would not tell a soul what he was or what you were. He then proceeded to show me his wings and yours. He explained he had come from a 'distant land' and would now take care of you. He said you were the most important person alive and people would come from everywhere to try and kill you if they knew where you were. Shocked and awe inspired, I agreed to his request ..but not because of the wings ... he had proven himself to be trustworthy the months leading up to your arrival."

"Why was I drugged? How does making me helpless make any sense if people would try and kill me?"

Ms. Palermo put her head down. Great big tears began to swell in her eyes.

"I ... I always hated that we did that to you," she sobbed. "M ... M ... M ... Martin insisted. H ... H ... H... He said it was for the best. That's all he ever said."

"What was it that I was being injected with?"

"That's just it ... It wasn't in our data base at all. I analyzed it for him at his request and it was nowhere to be found. I even cross referenced it through other hospitals and got nothing. Martin brought it with him from wherever he came from. When I asked him about it, all he told me was it was a powerful paralytic."

Cyrus pondered her words.

What on earth could drugging me for years possibly accomplish?

Cyrus returned his mind to the present. It had been two weeks since Martin had left with Manaia.

"Oh, here we go. I found a big chunk. This one's going to hurt, Cyrus," said Auli'i.

"Thanks for breaking it to me softly. It's not like I'm in enough pain," said Cyrus dryly.

"I'm going to pull it on three, OK?"

"OK, but please be gentle. I'm not wrapping paper around your presents," said Cyrus, eyes wide.

"OK, here we go."

"No, I'm serious, maybe go slow and painful rather than like a band-aid," pleaded Cyrus.

"One ..."

"Auli'i, we're friends and I want to keep it that way."

"Three!"

Sspleeech

Cyrus saw stars and gasped for air. His head slumped forward into the pillow Kamalani had placed on the toilet. All three of the Fualau-toalasis gasped, and Ms. Palermo shrieked.

Now do they realize they've gone too far?

Cyrus lifted his head with his hands and then gasped. Attached to the mixture of adhesive and skin graft was a single feather. One side was white as snow and seemed to be flickering a soft glow. The other side was blacker than obsidian with a shine. Everyone stared at the feather in awe. Cyrus couldn't believe he had something like that attached to him. It seemed inconceivable. Seeing that feather confirmed it wasn't a ruse.

"We should get scissors," said Auli'i.

"We should also do this under running water," said Kamalani.

"Put him in the shower again. Martin insisted we change the skin out every month or so. This shouldn't be much longer," said Ms. P.

"We should also be extra careful," said Kimo.

Cyrus looked at Kimo with eyes of gratitude. The large boy hadn't spoken very much since meeting Cyrus, but when he did, it was usually kind. Cyrus liked him more and more by the day.

"Yes, with emphasis on the extra careful. Guys, I'm not a toy. I'm having feeling in places I've never had. Be gentle ... please ..

Auli'i and Kimo helped him up. Cyrus put his arms around their shoulders and together they helped him take his first steps with exposed feathers .

Inside the shower, they put the water on warm and ran it continuously over his back and stomach. Slowly and methodically, they removed the membrane-like material off his back and then worked their way around his rib cage to his stomach. They discovered that his wings were wrapped around his torso one-and-a-half times.

Ms. P insisted she do the rest after watching Auli'i rip the piece off of Cyrus. She had Kimo and Auli'i support him while Kamalani handed her whatever tool she requested. Auli'i and Kimo had their eyes fixed on Cyrus. Even supported, standing with help was exhausting.

The last connecting point was at his stomach. Once Ms. P removed the membrane around his stomach, they would be able to unfurl his wings. The sensation was strange and he was seeing his wings and belly-button for the first time. He didn't know which one he was more excited for.

Snip. Thump.

Cyrus felt his entire torso droop, like a suspended rope bridge that had snapped. All of a sudden, he felt how heavy his wings were.

"I think that's it. Auli'i. Kimo. Each of you grab a wing and lead him to the living room," said Ms. P.

Auli'i turned the shower off and put his right wing over her shoulder. Kimo did the same with Cyrus' left. They slowly made their way out of the bathroom, dripping water the entire way. Cyrus was so exhausted he didn't even attempt a step. Kamalani had grabbed every towel and covered the entire living room floor.

As they reached the center of the living room, Auli'i and Kimo slowly lowered Cyrus down on top of the towels. As they laid him on his back, they slowly sprawled his wings. The white feathers softly brightened the room. The Fualautoalasi family looked at each other in amazement.

Slowly but surely, they unfurled his wings completely. As they reached 180°, Cyrus felt an excruciating pain.

"STOP! Ow!!! No more, no more ..."

Giant tears welled up and gushed from Cyrus' eyes. It was like trying to stretch a frozen rubber band. He'd thought his legs hurt when he'd tried using them, but this pain dwarfed that tenfold.

"What is it?! Cyrus, talk to us," said Ms. P coming out of the bathroom with her tools.

"Don ... don't ... don't st ... st ... st ...retch them," gasped Cyrus.

"Pain."

That was all Cyrus could say as tears ran down his face.

Auli'i stroked his face soothingly as tears welled up in her big brown eyes. Kimo patted him on the knee.

"OK ... You three," began Ms. Palermo sternly. "Foa-meow-colonoscopy, or however you say your name, DO NOT move Cyrus in any way without my approval these next couple of days. His muscles are atrophic and that goes for his wings. The slightest tweak will break something!"

"Ms ... P ... I ... don't ... want ... to ... stay ... still ... any ... more ..."

"Cyrus ... I know we haven't known each other very long and I can't imagine your pain. However, this pain .. if you will allow me a moment of optimism ... is good. You can use your entire body. It is painful now, but you have nowhere to go but up. I think I would endure any pain to keep that. You don't have to face it alone. We're here for you," said Kamalani, placing a hand on his face.

"Let's take it slow," said Kimo. "We can watch your shows while you do little exercises to build strength."

Cyrus began taking deep breaths.

"Cheee whooooo!!!" said Auli'i cheerfully. "You're basically learning everything from scratch. You need to follow the steps. First, learn how to crawl. Second, learn how to walk. Third, learn how to run. Then for you, you get to learn how to fly!"

Fly ...

Cyrus looked to his left and then to his right. His arms were tiny. His wings were skinny and frail. He really did look like a human chick-ling. He looked down and saw his real belly button for the first time.

I'm an outie.

He slumped his neck back onto the floor. Lifting his head was a workout for his abs. Cyrus still felt helpless. He had so far to go.

"I wish Martian would answer his phone. I have a couple million questions for him. Most starting with 'why' and 'how."

"We figured it out though, didn't we?" said Auli'i with a smile.

"I guess so ... Ms. Palermo, you staying for dinner tonight?" asked Cyrus.

"I would love to, dear. Let me hop over to my place to clean up and I'll shuffle back here in a hurry."

Kamalani whipped her head around to the clock ... 4:00 PM. "I am so behind preparing that lasagna!" said Kamalani, quickly making her way to the kitchen,

"Adieu," said Ms. Palermo with a curtsy as she left.

Why is it always Italian food when I have dinner with Ms. Palermo?

"Kimo, can you take a picture of me with my phone?" asked Cyrus.

"Uhhhh... I've never used a phone before," said Kimo, sheepishly.

Cyrus gawked hard. His jaw dropped and his eyes widened.

"You poor, poor child," said Cyrus. "Why?"

"It is forbidden. If you're a part of the jurandum, no modern technology..." said Auli'i, shrugging her shoulders.

Cyrus blinked rapidly.

"Show Kimo how to take a picture first. He'll like this," said Auli'i.

"It's really easy. Press this button on my phone and it will take a picture. Make sure to go as high as you can. I want to see what I look like."

"That's glass ... not a button."

Cyrus chuckled. "I suppose you're right. You can press the button on the glass or if it makes you feel better, this is the volume button. You can press this too and it will take the picture."

"You're giving me permission to use the phone?"

"More than that ... I'm asking you to."

Auli'i detected the sarcasm.

Kimo took the phone nervously and held it like a newborn. He stood above Cyrus and took one picture. He then handed the phone back to Cyrus with a sigh of relief. The photo was way off center.

"Kimo, let's try this again, but this time I want you to look at the screen when you take the picture. Do your best to put my body in the center. Here is the best part, though, Kimo ... I want you to take 20 pictures this time."

"You know we literally weren't allowed to have anything mod-ern' since the last Lumen Caligo disappeared in the late 1600's," said Auli'i, crossing her arms.

"Wait, seriously? I thought that was just a joke. And who's we?"

"Anyone who knew about the Lumen Caligo. If you do, you're a part of something called the jurandum or the oath, " said Kimo.

"Wait, what?"

Auli'i took the camera from Kimo and started taking pictures.

"Yeah, short version ... before the last Lumen Caligo disappeared, he made a rule that no one could use modern technology until the next one returned. Since he disappeared shortly after, it's been that way for over 300 years.. You're going to have to forgive us for staring at computer screens and phones like flies drawn to one of those zappy lights, but that's exactly what they are to us," said Auli'i.

"That's wild."

"You should have seen my mom's face when we decided to leave on a plane. That was wild."

"I wasn't the only one clenching the seats and my rea—" started Kamalani.

"The point is, everyone that knows about you has been anxiously awaiting for you to appear and most are on the verge of running away and joining modern society."

Auli'i smiled. Kimo took the phone back and kept snapping pictures.

"So, that's why you guys didn't watch TV or play video games?"

"Yep. Plus, we didn't know how to work it. At least now I do," said Auli'i, still smiling.

"Huh ... makes sense. Covid lock-downs must have been so boring for you two. What did you guys do? Stay at the beach from sun up to sun down?"

"Pretty much ... but that was nothing new," said Kimo.

"Well, I said it jokingly but now I feel kinda bad." Cyrus wiggled his toes. What a new sensation.

"It's OK. There is more to life than TV ... but since I've only known one without it, please make it my entire life while you gather your strength?" said Auli'i, putting her hands together in a begging position.

"Now, I just have to decide what show to indoctrinate you with after dinner," said Cyrus, stroking his chin.

"Oh, I'm so excited!" said Auli'i, throwing her hands up in the air.

"Do you guys need my permission for everything ... 'modern'? Wouldn't it be easier if I liberated everything for everyone?"

Kimo and Auli'i looked at each other and then back to Cyrus.

The clanging in the kitchen stopped and Kamalani peeked into the living room.

"I suppose you could ..." started Kimo.

"That would make it easier for you," said Auli'i.

"But would it be easier for everyone else?" asked Kamalani, coming out of the kitchen.

"Why wouldn't it?" asked Cyrus.

"The world essentially stopped in 1700 for the three nations. I don't recall the exact wording, but the decree halting all progress and interference with modern technology came about because of humanity's dependence of it and its tyranny with it. It was meant to be a shield so the three great nations could decide what course of action should be taken. However, shortly after the decree was made, the Lumen Caligo disappeared and the document stayed in effect. Anyone who used or learned about technology after 1700 was sentenced to death, no questions asked."

"Is that why Martian went back? To get you guys off of a death sentence?"

"Yes," said Auli'i. "What I thought was a maniacal religion turned out to be three nations under a 300 year house arrest. I still can't believe you of all people are the Lumen Caligo."

"Um, ouch …" said Cyrus, pretending to be offended. "You still haven't answered my question, Kamalani. Wouldn't lifting the ban across the board make things easier? Why would lifting this decree be a bad thing?"

"Think of the last 300 years and how much mankind has advanced … Let's suppose that all of that knowledge is water and this decree stopping all learning of this knowledge is a dam. Our people, along with the Lumens and the Caligos … they are the town on the other side of that dam. Safe to say that the dam is about to burst. If you let all the water come out at once, you will definitely wipe out the town.

But, if you let the water out gradually, you could stem the flow and prevent disaster. Many people's beliefs and ways of life have revolved entirely around you. Stem the flow. Learn our ways, and then teach us the modern world and all of its intricacies."

Cyrus dwelt on her words while he felt his entire body. It was all new to him. He lifted his arm and then let it fall to the ground with a clunk. He breathed deeply and felt his belly fill like a balloon and then let all the air out. He extended his arms just like his wings. They only reached about halfway. He wiggled his fingers and toes. What a freeing sensation. Auli'i and Kimo watched at first but then started pointing at different parts of his body and asking him to move them.

They then began showing him a couple simple movements. Shrugging shoulders was simple enough but it tired him out. While still laying on his back, the two siblings helped him hug his knees to his chest and then go one side to the other. His hips creaked from lack of use.

POP.

Pain and relief simultaneously hit him. The two Hawaiians helped him move his legs to the other side. Cyrus found that it was too much effort to do alone.

POP. POP. POP.

Bliss.

The siblings continued to show him the most basic movements all the while Kamalani was hard at work preparing the lasagna and garlic bread. The room permeated with the smell of delicious red sauce, meat and garlic and onion. It was mouth-watering.

There was a loud knock at the door.

"Guess who's back? Could you grab the door for me? My hands are full. I grabbed a couple a things to hopefully compliment the lasagna. At first, I wanted to bring some French bread but then I realized I didn't have any so I settled on some parmesan cheese that I think is still good.." Hyper-verbal Ms. Palermo had returned. She was a different person in social interaction than when she was Dr. Palermo.

She didn't like it when Cyrus called her doctor. She told him she had earned the title but didn't like how it sounded. Auli'i and Kimo helped Cyrus sit up with his back against the sofa. This time, he was sitting on the floor instead of in his chair. That felt strangely comforting.

Progress.

Ms. Palermo was still talking outside. She had somehow warped the conversation with herself to how she suspected that bleu cheese came from a French restaurant running out of regular cheese and trying to save face.

Kamalani went and opened the door and Ms. Palermo went straight to Cyrus.

"CYRUS!!!" screamed Ms. Palermo in delight.

Ms. Palermo went for a hug and lost her balance. Dread filled Cyrus as he realized he was about to have all of Ms. P squashing him. She caught herself somewhat on the couch but it was still a lot of weight on Cyrus.

OOOOF.

Kimo quickly came to the rescue and helped Ms. P off of Cyrus.

It lasted only a few moments but to Cyrus it felt like an eternity. The crazy thing was Ms. Palermo was still talking. It was a mix of apologies and trying to finish her thought. Cyrus gave up on trying to follow her story and focused on survival.

Need ... air ...

"... and that's how two peas in a pod came about!"

Cyrus had no idea what line of thought brought Ms. Palermo to say those things and frankly didn't care. He was focused on getting oxygen to his brain after being involuntarily suffocated.

"How are you holding up?" asked Ms. Palermo.

"Been better. It's ... nice ... to see you... again."

"Likewise! Anything new with you or Martin's hiatus to Hawai'i?" asked Ms. Palermo with a hula impersonation.

"Yeah, actually."

"Ohhh."

"I can wiggle my toes."

The parmesan cheese hit the floor, and Ms. Palermo stopped dancing. Her eyes widened, and her expression warped to one of shock.

"Yep... Watch this." Cyrus wiggled his toes happily.

Ms. Palermo had to support herself with the nearest cabinet.

"It's ... it's ... it's unbelievable."

"Yeah, I can almost walk, but I'm still too weak."

"From lack of use no doubt," said Ms. Palermo, adjusting her glasses and approaching Cyrus. She knelt down slowly and inspected Cyrus' feeble legs. Kimo stood behind her with his hands outstretched ... just in case.

"You haven't used most of your muscles for almost seven years, so they have shriveled up from lack of use. The mere fact that you can move this much astonishes me. Can you feel this?" Ms. Palermo pinched his right big toe.

"Ouch. Yes, yes ..."

"Fascinating. Can you rotate your ankle in a little circle?" With a lot of effort, Cyrus made one circle with his right foot.

After he completed it, Ms. Palermo clapped her hands excitedly.

"Marvelous! You will have to let me monitor your recovery process. Have you heard anything from our hula man Martin?"

"Nothing yet," said Cyrus a tad flustered.

"Oh? That's uncharacteristic of him."

"Yeah, it kind of is ..."

"Aloha! Ready for some lasagna, Ms. Palermo?" Kamalani asked with a ferocious hug and a kiss on the cheek. Ms. Palermo looked shocked and squished from the embrace.

Cyrus chuckled to himself. "Payback," he said under his breath.

"Welcome back, Ms. P," said Auli'i with a quick hug and kiss on the cheek.

"Lovely to be back, Ms. Auli'i," chirped Ms. Palermo returning the peck on the cheek.

Auli'i smiled and then lifted her eyebrows at Cyrus.

"I already helped you off Cyrus but hello, Aunty P," said Kimo with a kiss and a huge hug.

Ms. Palermo seemed delighted. She mouthed *Aunty P* as she was engulfed in a Kimo hug.

"Oh my goodness! It's like being hugged by a bear! Haha! Well, aren't you guys just the sweetest things."

"I'll take these to the kitchen, if you don't mind." Kamalani relieved Ms. Palermo of the cheese.

"Oh, why yes, of course!"

"I'll take your coat," said Auli'i.

"I didn't bring a coat," said Ms. Palermo, perplexed.

"I know. You live next door. It wouldn't make sense if you did," said Auli'i, running after her mother laughing.

Ms. Palermo put her pointer finger to her temple and tapped.

"Clever girl."

"Care to sit down, Ms. Palermo? Next to me this time." asked Cyrus.

"Oh, why thank you," replied Ms. Palermo with a curtsy.

"Ms. Palermo, I know you're an orthopedic surgeon and have helped Martian with my case for the last seven years ... Can I ask your opinion?"

Ms. Palermo nodded.

"How long do you think it will take for me to walk again?" Ms. Palermo was silent for a moment as she thought.

"Well," she began. "When patients break a bone-as opposed to rupturing a tendon-the recovery time differs greatly. Your situation focuses on everything. Bones, ligaments, tendons, muscles and joints. And I'm not talking about the type I caught one of my old tenants with. Who leaves that much meat just out in the open? Took me a week to get that wretched smell out of unit B. Kicked him out and kept his security deposit for violating my contract ..."

"Ms. Palermo ... How long?"

"It's hard to say, Cyrus, dear. On one hand, you shouldn't be moving that much and should gradually build up your strength over the course of a couple years. On the other hand, you should really speed this up before you hit puberty and permanent changes occur."

"I could be in puberty already," Cyrus said defensively.

"Honey, trust me. You're not," Ms. Palermo said with a laugh.

"I could be."

"Oh? Lift up your arm and show me the armpit hair." Cyrus looked down in defeat. He knew he hadn't started puberty.

He'd actively made fun of his classmates who had. Auli'i snickered in the kitchen. Cyrus felt his blood rush to his face.

"The point is this, Cyrus. You haven't used your body in years, so everything has been reduced to its bare minimum. I wish I could give you an accurate time table of when you'll be hopping and skipping around but the best advice I can give you is this ... Take it slow and ABOVE ALL ELSE, listen to your body. If it hurts, don't do it. If you're tired, rest. It's that simple."

"Thank you, Ms. Palermo."

"Dinner will be ready in fifteen minutes everybody! Kindly wash your hands and get those tummies ready!" Ms. Palermo rubbed her belly excitedly.

"Hey, Cyrus, want to try and walk to the bathroom with some help?" asked Kimo.

Ms. Palermo let out an audible gasp. Cyrus nodded. Cyrus liked the idea and wanted to test his limits.

"I'll help, too," said Auli'i.

Kimo went to his left side, Auli'i went to his right. Then, very carefully, they lifted him off the ground. Legs shaking and arms tired, Cyrus made one step forward and then another. On the third, his legs failed completely but Auli'i and Kimo were both there to catch him. They were holding his wings up, too.

Slowly and carefully, Cyrus moved his legs in very staggered steps, making his way towards the bathroom. Ms. Palermo and Kamalani had stopped what they were doing and stared in silent suspense. The hallway seemed so much longer now that Cyrus had to walk down it, but he was determined.

When they arrived, Ms. Palermo started clapping and Kamalani let out a loud 'Cheee Whooo.'

Still supporting Cyrus, Auli'i reached to turn on the faucet for him.

"No. Let me try," said Cyrus panting.

"Which side do you use?" asked Auli'i.

Cyrus had always used his right side more for controlling his chair and tablet. Now that he was gaining more control over his body, he wanted to learn his limits. He wanted to try both sides as often as possible.

"Can we switch off everyday? I want to get stronger."

Kimo and Auli'i looked at each other and nodded. Auli'i opened her mouth but before she could start, Kimo quickly said, "Ladies first."

Auli'i furrowed her brow and shot Kimo a dirty look before slowly lowering Cyrus' right arm to the faucet. Cyrus fumbled around for a bit until he finally got his hand on the faucet. He then twisted as hard as he could. Nothing. Panting, he tried again. Nothing. Kimo and Auli'i looked concerned but said nothing.

"I can do this."

With a laser focus, Cyrus put all his concentration on twisting the faucet. His exhalation became a hissing sound like a boiling teapot.

Just when he was at his limit, a burst of light, lasting no longer then the flash of a camera, pulsed from the inner part of his wings. The light reflected off of the mirror and momentarily blinded all three of them. It felt like a jolt of electricity leaving Cyrus.

"Cyrus, you OK dear?" asked Ms. Palermo from the living room.

Kimo and Auli'i were rubbing their eyes with their free hand and blinking rapidly from the unknown light source they had just experienced. Cyrus was more startled then anyone.

"Yea... yeah, we're fine. Just a bad fuse, I think. Be out in a minute!" said Cyrus.

"What on earth was that?!" hissed Auli'i.

"I don't know! I'm as shocked as you guys," hissed Cyrus back.

Cyrus slumped. Fatigue hit him, and it hit him hard.

"Cyrus," said Kimo, gently slapping his face. "Cyrus, Cyrus talk to us."

Panting, Cyrus came up with a gleeful smile on his face. The expression bewildered Kimo and Auli'i.

"I did it."

"What, blind us? Yeah, congratulations, glow stick," said Auli'i, a bit confused.

"Doesn't a glow stick count as 'new technology,' Auli'i?" Cyrus asked a bit amused

"I defected and now I'm back in. Cut me some slack."

"No ... he actually did it," said Kimo looking forward.

"What did you do that I don't know ..." started Auli'i looking where Kimo was.

With the silence came the sound of running water. All three of them watched water pour from the faucet. Everyone started laughing and celebrating. With Auli'i and Kimo's help, Cyrus slowly lowered his hands, and for the first time, he washed his own hands.

Cyrus got a little choked up. He was able to do something so small that he had been unable to do for so long. It was a small victory and Cyrus knew this, but the emotion that came from this success was overwhelming.

After he finished washing his hands, he turned to Auli'i and Kimo and said, "Guys, I know what were going to watch the next couple days and the best part is, it's based off of what just happened."

The two Fualautoalasis perked up.

"Two siblings in the most southern part of their country find and help a small boy who's been missing for a hundred years. During their first meeting, he blinds them with a bright light before they realize he's something the world hasn't seen for a long time and could be the key to saving the world."

"You really flatter yourself, don't you?" Auli'i rolled her eyes.

"Sounds good! What is it?" asked Kimo.

"The greatest animated show ever made and perhaps the greatest story written in the 21st century." Auli'i began to look excited.

"First, let's eat. Yip yip!" said Cyrus with a smile.

6

DEPARTURE

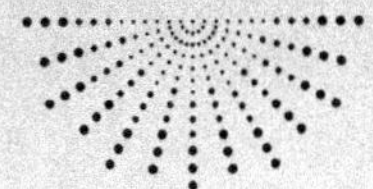

ULI'I HADN'T BLINKED IN five minutes. Kimo's hands covered his mouth. Kamalani did the same. Cyrus smiled with a nod of approval. The Fualautoalasis had been completely captivated by the series and were finally on the last episode. They'd started it two days prior, a season a day.

As the final moments unfolded and the credits began to roll, the Fualautoalasis clapped. Auli'i and Kamalani were in tears and Kimo was looking down.

Is he crying? Good, I'm glad I'm not the only one.

"That was incredible, Cyrus. Absolutely incredible," said Auli'i.

Kamalani hugged Auli'i and Cyrus on the couch.

"That was great. Thank you for making such a great selection," said Kamalani.

Cyrus lifted his arms over the Fualautoalasi ladies and hugged back. He had gotten used to their affection.

"This is the best version of this story. The live action, although good, wasn't up to par with this one. The fans realized they really liked the voice actors more than anything."

"There is a real life one?!" said Kimo, looking up.

69

"Two, actually. But we must never speak of the movie. It was a disgrace."

All three of them gasped.

"I know. You're pretty hard pressed to ruin a story of that caliber. Now, could we do something different for my little 'workout' tonight?"

Auli'i's eyes shined brightly in anticipation.

"I want to walk on the beach."

The Fualautoalasi family smiled, and Kimo let out a quick 'Chee whoo. It was 5 PM and the sun was still high in the sky.

Cyrus had spent the last three days crawling slowly from his room to the living room. The Fualautoalasi family had put every blanket and towel down on the hardwood floor to save Cyrus' knees but it was unavoidable. Cyrus had scrapes and bruises up and down his legs and arms from falling repeatedly. The first two days he must have lifted himself up at least a thousand times. It was the equivalent of doing one thousand mini push ups. That would take a toll on anyone. To someone who hadn't been using his limbs, the effect was compounded.

Not to mention his hip joints ached from crawling. A change of routine was needed.

The Fualautoalasis changed quickly and were out the door within five minutes of Cyrus' announcement. Cyrus thought he had a love for the ocean, but for the Fualautoalasis, the ocean was a part of them. Since the day they moved in, the Fualautoalasis had not missed a swim in the ocean.

"You going to swim, too?" asked Auli'i excitedly.

Cyrus pointed to the pair of shorts he had on. Cyrus didn't own a swimsuit, but his lightest pair of shorts would work.

"After I walk for a bit, will you guys teach me how to not drown?"

"Yeess!!!!" Auli'i jumped up and down.

Kimo let out another quiet 'chee whoo' while Kamalani smiled at the door.

"Well, let's move those okōles, we have about an hour and a half of sunshine left," said Kamalani.

Auli'i and Kimo put Cyrus' arms over their necks for support and made their way towards the beach. Cyrus had always been able to hear and see the ocean from the house and it had always brought him peace. Most rooms in his home faced the ocean, after all, especially the huge sliding glass door in the living room. Cyrus had never participated in beach time activities.

Sand castles, boogie boarding, burying your friends in the sand ... all of it seemed fun, but a long time ago Cyrus had closed off the possibility of actually doing them. It made him really sad watching people do what he wanted to do, knowing he wasn't physically able.

Having his options opened again really made Cyrus happy, but it was also brewing a storm inside of him. Why had Martin done this to him? Why had he taken away his ability to move? It was cruel ... not to mention it felt very unnecessary.

Martian has some serious explaining to do.

They reached where the sand and the ocean met. Cyrus looked around for a goal to walk towards.

"The pier," said Cyrus softly.

Imperial beach had a wonderful pier less than two hundred yards away from their place at Sea Coast Drive. There was a quaint little restaurant at the end that was decent at best, but made up for it with its view. The pier is where Martin and Cyrus had gone many times for a walk to see the sunset. Occasionally, they would get the fish and chips but usually they would go for the views and to see what people were catching. Lots of people went to the pier to fish.

"The pier," said Cyrus to Auli'i and Kimo. "Let me go."

"What?!" said Auli'i.

"Let me go."

Kimo gave an uneasy look. Auli'i was shaking her head.

"Let me go, I'll be fine. Just trust me."

Auli'i kept shaking her head. She hated every time Cyrus fell. The bruises up and down Cyrus' legs only added fuel to her fire.

She didn't like it. Seeing the look of determination on Cyrus' face, she relented.

"Ok ... But if you die, I'll kill you."

"That ... doesn't ... make ... sense ..." said Cyrus.

Slowly, both of the siblings came out from supporting Cyrus and let go. Cyrus was standing on his own two feet. The pier taunted him.

"We'll be right by your side," said Kimo assuredly.

Every muscle in Cyrus' legs trembled from stabilizing himself.

Cyrus took his first shaky step and then his second.

Phew ...

Then steps three and four, five and six, seven, eight, nine and ten. Confidence built with each step.

Twenty-one. Twenty-two. Twenty-th—

Cyrus snagged his toe on a small seaweed pile. There was no avoiding it, he was going down. He almost made it to twenty-three. MJ would be so disappointed.

Two sets of arms appeared out of nowhere and caught Cyrus.

Auli'i and Kimo, true to their word, were right next him, preventing another bruise from being added to his already extensive collection.

Cyrus panted from the effort and swiveled his head around to see how far he had gotten. He had made it from his house to the 'ART' sign stairwell.

Not bad.

"Thanks guys. I would have eaten sand for sure." The siblings put Cyrus back on his feet and then stepped back.

"We're right behind you," said Kimo.

"You got this," said Auli'i.

Cyrus continued his trek to the pier on his own. Being a weekday, there were considerably less people than usual. It was going to be a fantastic day if he could make it to the pier on his own two legs.

Cyrus breathed in deeply and then took his next step. Slowly and surely, Cyrus made his way towards the belly of the pier. Cyrus stumbled three more times, never hitting the ground. Auli'i and Kimo were there every single time.

Then, after 15 minutes of focused effort, Cyrus made it to the pier. Euphoria came over him.

"Yeah!!!!" said Auli'i loudly.

"Chhhhheeeeee Whoooooo!!!!" Kimo's volume was earth shattering. It was the first time he had heard Kimo go all out. Auli'i followed suit.

"Chhhhheeeee Whoooooo!!!"

"Chhhhheeeee Whoooooo!!!! went Kamalani, a little bit further off.

"I'm going to walk to the other side," said Cyrus. He was determined to pass his goal. Right as Cyrus passed the last pillar of the pier to the other side, he put his hands in the air in jubilation ... bad idea.

The shift in weight threw off his balance and his right foot tripped over his left. He was going down. Thank goodness for Auli'i and Kimo. Cyrus closed his eyes, waiting for the four hands to catch him before he hit the sand ... they never came.

SPLAT! Cyrus' face hit the sand.

The Chee Whoo's stopped immediately.

"Oh gosh, Cyrus!" Auli'i rushed to his side.

"Oh sole ..." said Kimo, scampering over.

The siblings helped Cyrus up with apologetic looks. Cyrus came up laughing ... loud, happy laughter. The two siblings looked surprised at first but then smiled in relief and joined in the laughter.

Cyrus was spent. He had walked further than he ever had in his life. He wanted to walk more. The progress he had experienced in the last three weeks was addicting but Ms. Palermo's words rung in his head.

Take it slow and listen to your body.

Right now his body ached from being used and was asking for a break. However, he'd also promised he would go in the ocean with Auli'i. Cyrus sighed. He was a little apprehensive about going in the water, but he wanted to keep his promise.

Maybe I can just float.

Imperial Beach was not known for its huge waves. It was pretty flat most of the time and the water was almost always a nice brown color.

"Cyrus! You still going to try and swim with us?" asked Auli'i.

"Depends. Will your sinking prevention be as affective as preventing me from falling?"

Kamalani snorted. Kimo and Auli'i shook their heads, suppressing smirks. Cyrus smiled triumphantly.

Subtle jab. Witty delivery. Hearty laughter from a third party. Nailed it.

Kimo grabbed Cyrus, threw him over his shoulder and started walking into the ocean like a DK cargo carry. Auli'i followed behind cackling.

"Not so tough now, huh?" said Kimo with a smile.

Cyrus started feeling queasy. He had eaten a decent amount for dinner and was going into the ocean for the first time with four working limbs. Now he was being rocked back and forth by a huge man-child. This was not how he'd imagined his first time in the ocean.

Kimo was about waist deep. With a little flick, Kimo flipped Cyrus' legs over his shoulder towards the open ocean. Horror and vertigo hit Cyrus simultaneously.

Free falling for a split second, Cyrus' legs were the first thing to enter into the ocean. Silence. Cyrus was underwater. Had Cyrus not had salt water up his nose and in his ears, the silence might have been nice ... but Cyrus didn't know how to swim. Panic began to fill Cyrus. Someone's arms encircled him and pulled him out of the water.

Panting rapidly, Cyrus wiped the water from his eyes and peeked to see who his savior was. It was Auli'i.

"I'm so sorry. Kimo, you scared him!"

"You OK, Cyrus? I wanted to introduce you to the ocean in a way you'd never forget."

"Yeah, I'm fine. I was just worried about the added weight with my wings and sinking."

"Yeah ... I probably should have thought of that," said Kimo sheepishly.

Cyrus' heart rate stabilized. In the comforting arms of Auli'i, he took in some new sensations. The chilly dark water seeped through his clothes, giving way to goosebumps up and down his neck and arms.

The waves melodically sang to Cyrus almost like they were welcoming him to the ocean. With each wave gurgling by, the sounds reminded him of a bubble.

"Can you hang onto me while I go under? Next wave?" asked Cyrus.

Auli'i nodded. She repositioned Cyrus so he was floating on his stomach. As the next wave approached, the sound built like a stampede. Cyrus narrowed his focus despite his growing fear. The wave was five seconds away from impact.

You got this, and even if you don't, Auli'i does.

Cyrus inhaled and closed his eyes. Auli'i gave Cyrus a gentle push under the wave and the sensation of water rushing over him completely eclipsed all of Cyrus' senses. The current underneath the water went in every direction and the salty mixture entered through his nose.

Uh oh.

Flailing to the surface, Cyrus ejected salt water from his mouth and nose. Coughing and snorting, his eyes stung from the pain. Auli'i gently lifted Cyrus out of the water and back into her arms.

"I have you. I have you. Don't worry. I have you."

Cyrus composed himself, wiping away the water and snot coming from his face.

Goodness, it's everywhere.

"This is why you're my favorite. You keep me from drowning rather than attempting to."

"So," started Kimo. "What do you think of the world's biggest ocean?"

"Salty, scratchy and stinky. I love it."

Cracking an infectious smile, Cyrus slowly opened his now red eyes. The sun was setting and the water glowed. Cyrus' wings were now sticking out of his shirt by his waist.

"How do your wings feel?" asked Auli'i.

"Not bad, actually. I thought they would be heavier."

Cyrus sat up a little and adjusted. When he'd been under the water, he'd felt significantly lighter.

Maybe ...

"Hey, how many people are around us?"

Kimo and Auli'i swiveled their heads around. They were some of the last ones in the ocean. Most were on the beach admiring the sunset.

"Almost no one ... Why?" asked Kimo.

"I want to spread my wings."

The siblings froze.

"Too open, Cyrus. Don't forget there are people on the pier, too," said Auli'i.

"Yeah, but what if we went under the pier and opened them?"

Kimo and Auli'i pouted their lips and rocked their heads side to side.

"Could work ... " said Kimo.

"Yeah, seems safest," said Auli'i. "Why don't you just wait till we get home? That's the safest option."

"Yeah, but it feels easier with the water! Plus, I don't think the tub will fit me, you know?"

"Fine, but we're floating you over there like driftwood," said Auli'i.

She gave Cyrus the horsey smile, and together with Kimo, they floated Cyrus over to the pier. Every time a wave approached, Auli'i would gently lift him so he didn't get a face full of water. Kamalani followed from the beach.

Reaching the belly of the pier, Kimo helped remove Cyrus' shirt and put his feet on the ground. The water was shallow enough where he could stabilize himself with his arms.

Kimo and Auli'i quickly did a double take of their surroundings and then slowly unfurled Cyrus' wings.

Cyrus grimaced. The strain was still there but significantly less. As they reached the same level of unfurling from a couple days ago, Kimo and Auli'i let go.

Cyrus leaned into the water, letting it support him and his wings. Cyrus was on all fours facing the beach. One twitch in the left wing. One in his right.

My gosh... I can move them.

It felt natural, like an extra set of arms. They were definitely a part of him. The realization that they were there and were as integral to him as his arms and legs was starting to hit him. However, they felt more foreign. Like someone learning how to use a sword or a tennis racket for the first time. They were blunt instruments attached to his back for the time being, until he mastered them.

"Cyrus ..." said Aulii.

"Wow ..." said Kimo.

Cyrus tilted his head to either side. The reflection of sunlit water illuminated his darker feathers. The detail was absolutely mesmerizing. You could see each feather outlined in silver like a branch of a tree with no leaves. The shine came and went with the moving water.

Auli'i and Kamalani gasped as their eyes went up and down Cyrus wing span.

Kimo mouthed, *"Wow."*

The waves gently splashed onto the shore. Cyrus closed his eyes. The moment felt reverent.

What peace ...

Kamalani fumbled through the beach bag she'd brought.

"Cyrus ... I'm going to take a picture."

Cyrus smiled. He had taught her the shortcut on his phone to access the camera yesterday.

VMMMMMM. VMMMMMM. VMMMMMM.

Cyrus sat up. He knew that sound, even on silent. He had a notification.

"Kamalani, can I see my phone? Kimo. Auli'i. Can you help me up and then cover me?"

The Fualautoalasis made quick work of lifting, drying and covering Cyrus. Once Cyrus had dry digits, he tapped his screen. 10 missed calls and six messages. All from Martin.

"SHOOOT!"

"What?! What happened?" asked Auli'i.

Cyrus flashed the phone screen in their direction. Instant interest.

They were both peering over his shoulder in seconds.

"What did he say?" asked Kimo.

"My baby OK?" asked Kamalani.

"Guys, let me read the messages and call him back. Hang on."

Cyrus are you there?

Cyrus I really need you to pick up.

I don't have a lot of time or cell service.

I'm just getting to Kauai.

Cyrus seriously please pick up. This is urgent.

Call me the moment you see these. I have one hour.

The messages were twenty minutes old. Cyrus went to missed calls and clicked on *Martian*. Putting the phone to his ear, the phone let out its first monotone ring. Cyrus was nervous. He had no idea what to expect.

Click

"Cyrus! Can you hear me?"

"Yeah, I can. Martian, you OK?"

"Yes, I'm fine. Listen, the council of Akhet didn't rule in Manaia's favor so they sentenced his daughter Akela to death as punishment. They're carrying out the sentence Sunday."

Cyrus was really glad he hadn't put the call on speaker.

"Oh my ..." He immediately stopped.

The three Fualautoalasis looked at him anxiously.

Come on, man. Keep it together.

"Yes, but the plot thickens. At Manaia's request, I've been asked to 'abduct' her before that happens and bring her with me to IB."

"Oh my goodness. Do uh ... do you need something?"

"Yes, I need you to buy two flights from Oahu to San Diego leaving Saturday at 6 PM."

"What happened to your wallet?"

"Confiscated. Luckily, I buried my phone in Kauai."

"Huh ... Well done."

"You know the three fake flowers in the kitchen window?"

"Yeah ..."

"Under the blue one I have an emergency credit card. It's white. Use that, and keep it with you."

"OK. Blue flower. Got it."

"Now, Manaia told the council California is where he went to find Auli'i and Kamalani and although that is vague, I am still worried IB may be compromised."

Cyrus gulped and kept a straight face. Three sets of eyes were on him.

"What ... What needs to be done?"

"Until I know for certain it isn't, I want you to leave IB. Leave with Auli'i and Kimo. Ask Kamalani to stay until I make it back. I want you far away from IB until I know for certain our location is safe."

"Where? I've never been outside San Diego."

"I'm not sure, Cyrus. I've kept a low profile in IB ever since I left ..."

Martin stopped mid-sentence. Cyrus could tell he regretted saying that much.

"Left what? Your home? Martian ... were you going to say your home?"

"I ..."

"Martian, please answer me."

"Yes... My home."

"Where is your home, Martian?"

Cyrus heard Martin exhale slowly before a quick inhale.

"A place called Aeolia."

"What?"

"Aeolia. It's the Lumen capital. It's ... it's a couple hundred miles southwest of Bermuda."

Cyrus opened his mouth to speak and then closed it again. "Wh... wh ... what?"

"Cyrus, focus. Bermuda. British Territory off the East Coast of the US... but that is the last place on earth I would have you go to."

"Why? That's your home. Is it that bad?"

"It's not safe, Cyrus. Your very existence is seen as a threat to some. I don't know if your mother ..."

Heart beating and adrenaline pumping, Cyrus couldn't believe what he'd heard.

"What ..."

"Cyrus..."

"Martian, what about my mother?"

Silence filled the air except for Kimo's steps transitioning from sand to cement.

"That's where your mother is."

"Name."

"What?"

"Name! What's my mother's name!"

Martin was silent. The Fualautoalasis looked worried.

"MARTIAN. WHAT IS MY MOTHER'S NAME?"

"Her name is Marcella."

"Marcella ..."

"Yes."

"I'm going to Aeolia."

The three Polynesians stopped dead in their tracks and looked at Cyrus like he had said a bad word.

"Cyrus, please don't. I'm begging you. It's too dangerous. Wait for me, and we'll go in due time."

"Due time?! DUE TIME?! All those years I asked about my parents and you always responded 'wait til you're 16' and 'you adopted me outright. Now you have the audacity to tell me not to go see her?!"

"Cyrus, please. I know it seems like I did this out of spite, but believe me, I did it to protect you."

"Oh? Same as making me a quadriplegic? Was that to protect me, too?"

"YES."

Cyrus fell silent. As upset as he was, how Martin responded cut him to his core.

"Cyrus, don't think for a moment I enjoyed your pain or keeping you in the dark ... but you have no idea the wheels that are turning because of your existence. I did what I did for the bigger picture. I did what I did with the end game in mind. I did what I did ... TO. PROTECT. YOU."

Cyrus breathed deeply.

"All will be explained soon, but you really need to trust me."

"Then take me to my mom. If you know where she is and she's not opposed to seeing me, you have to take me to her. There's no argument."

"There are several, actually, but I do understand your desire to see her."

"Not a desire. A necessity."

Martin went silent for a moment.

"I'm going to extend an olive branch, OK?" began Martin.

"O ... OK."

"In my room, in my sock drawer, in the back right corner, I have a letter from your mother. Take that and read it. It's not much, but it's what you were left with."

Cyrus' head was spinning.

"Left with?"

"Yes, when Ms. Palermo and I found you on the doorstep."

"Are you kidding me? On the doorstep like some knockoff wizard story?"

Martin let out a little chuckle.

"Yes, except no wizards or witches. Sorry."

"I would have taken a lightening scar over a wheelchair any day of the week."

Auli'i and Kamalani's faces oozed sympathy. Kimo gave a couple supportive pats. Cyrus was brimming with questions.

"I'm assuming she has wings?"

"Yes."

"White?"

"Yes, she's a Lumen, like me."

"What else can you tell me about her?"

"A lot, Cyrus, but I can't do that right now. My time is up and I have to get back to Ni'ihau before they notice I'm gone. The cloud cover is passing so listen closely. Get your passport from my room, pack everything you need in a backpack and leave tomorrow. You will meet your mother under one condition."

Cyrus inhaled and then mumbled for Martin to continue.

"You let me take you. I too have some questions for her." Cyrus furrowed his brow in confusion.

What does Martian want to ask my mother?

"OK. I can agree to that."

"Get on it right away, Cyrus. Do NOT dilly dally. I am turning my phone off and burying it again, so don't expect to hear from me until I get back to San Diego. Keep Auli'i and Kimo close while you travel. They can push you around in your wheelchair and explain more about the Lumens."

"I'm walking already."

"What?! Really?! That's ... that's fantastic!!!"

"Yeah, we pulled that synthetic skin off, too. You have a lot of explaining to do."

"I know and I will, but right now is not the moment. My focus is the life of Akela. Now, repeat back to me everything you must do before I hang up."

Cyrus groaned. It was just like when he got home schooled during the Covid lock down.

"Get the white credit card from the fake blue flower pot. Buy two tickets from Oahu to San Diego. Dive into your sock drawer for a letter from my mother. Pack everything I need into one backpack, including my passport. Buy the first flight to Bermuda with Auli'i and Kimo."

The two siblings did a double take. Kamalani stopped dead in her tracks.

"Very good. Last thing. Go and stay on the west side of the island. Ms. Palermo can help you with reservations. Once you get there, look for a man by the name of Jorge Worley in Hogs Bay. He should still be the active post on Bermuda. If you don't hear from me in one week, you go with him, understood?"

"Understood."

"Again, that's Jorge Worley."

"OK, let me write it down ..." Cyrus put his phone on speaker and opened his notes app.

"G."

"J, corrected Martin.

"J?"

"J."

"OK ..."

"J-O-R-G-E. W-O-R-L-E-Y."

"Wouldn't that be pronounced 'Jorge' instead of 'Jorge'?"

"No, it's pronounced 'Jorge'."

"OK ... We'll find him." Cyrus took the phone back off speaker.

"One week. You hear nothing from me, you go with him. Understood?"

Cyrus audibly gulped. This more serious Martin was intense.

"Understood."

"Reassure Kamalani that I will do everything in my power to save her youngest. Please thank Ms. Palermo for all she has done as well. I love you. May your light illuminate the darkness," Martin said with a softer tone.

"Love you, too. Good luck, and come back with Akela, OK?"

"I will."

Click.

Cyrus looked at his phone in disbelief.

I know nothing.

Cyrus looked up to see three sets of Hawaiian eyes glued to him. They had arrived back at the apartment.

"Let's go inside. We have a lot to do."

THE LEGEND OF THE LUMEN CALIGO

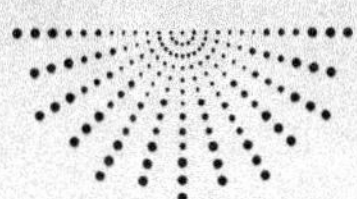

OH MY GOSH, OH MY GOSH, OH MY GOSH! Cyrus clutched the armrest and exhaled rapidly. The weight on his chest with the roar of the accelerating engine was overstimulating.

Auli'i reached over and grabbed Cyrus' left hand. She gave a small smile and nodded. Cyrus nodded back and then looked at Kimo.

Visible drops of sweat were beading down his face. He licked his lips nervously and stared straight ahead, blinking furiously. Cyrus had forgotten it was Kimo's first time on a plane too. Cyrus released his death grip on the arm rest, reached over and patted Kimo on the shoulder. Kimo whipped his head towards Cyrus. Seeing the fear in Cyrus' eyes made Kimo forget his own. He quickly composed himself and relaxed. Kimo then took Cyrus by the right hand and together they ascended.

"Ladies and gentlemen, this is your captain speaking. We have reached a cruising altitude of thirty-five thousand feet. Blue skies and a nice tailwind today, our estimated arrival will be 4:10 PM in Atlanta. Sit back, relax and enjoy the flight, and as always, we would like to thank you for flying with ..."

Cyrus tuned the rest out. They were thirty-five thousand feet up in the air. *Wow.*

I wonder how high I will be able to fly?

Kimo was releasing his death grip on the arm rest.

"I was pretty nervous the first time, too," said Auli'i. "The second time is a lot more fun. Take off is amazing!"

"I don't know, Auli'i," said Kimo. "Using modern technology has been great up until this moment. I prefer my feet on the ground or legs in the sea. I wasn't built for this."

"He's scared of heights," whispered Auli'i to Cyrus. "This way is faster though, Kimo. Just like mom and I coming from Hawaii. Not everyone wants to sail across the ocean."

Cyrus jaw dropped. "You sailed from Hawai'i to San Diego?!"

Kimo nodded.

"With your dad?"

Kimo nodded again.

"Just you two?"

One more nod

Cyrus put his hands to his head and imitated an explosion. "How long did it take?"

"Twelve days."

Auli'i nodded and then held up her two hands and imitated an explosion next to her temples. She then held them out flat in the air.

"Six hour flight with mom," said Auli'i looking to her left hand. "Or twelve days at sea with dad?" she said looking to her right.

"Well it wasn't like I had choice. You and mom left us, thinking there wouldn't be consequences when there were. Did you even stop to think about Akela when you left?"

Auli'i's expression went dark. Kimo forgot his fear of heights and quickly discovered a new one. Auli'i pointed her finger directly at Kimo.

"You know ... YOU KNOW we tried to convince her to come," hissed Auli'i. "She is daddy's little girl and tutu's favorite. We asked her to come and she said no. Unlike dad, we respected her choice and let her stay rather than FORCING her to come with! Being trapped on Ni'ihau, away from her family and in that environment, was NOT good for her. So don't you DARE go throwing out accusations, and more importantly, don't you ever bring this up to her. She already feels enough guilt for NOT coming. If you're upset you didn't get the invitation, why don't you just come out and SAY IT!"

Cyrus stayed as still as he could as Auli'i's finger retracted back into her personal space. Cyrus could see Kimo turn his body away out of the corner of his eye. The silence hung in the air like a dense perfume.

Cyrus furiously thought of what to say. Martin's words came to mind.

They can explain more about the Lumens.

Cyrus gulped. He was going to have to break the silence.

"So ... uh ..." started Cyrus. "Martian said you guys could explain more about the Lumens to me ..." Kimo and Auli'i remained silent.

"I don't know anything about myself or Lumens or you guys ...

Still silence.

"Guys ... it's going to be a long flight. I'm not telling you to kiss and make up, but I'd rather learn a couple things about who I am than sit in silence between you two?

The siblings flashed a quick glance at each other and then back to Cyrus.

"Plus, if you do wind up fighting, I don't think I would survive the encounter." Stonewall.

Cyrus looked down and went quiet. Grabbing his phone, he plugged in his headphones and hit shuffle on an 80's playlist he'd downloaded before the flight. His attempts to distract the two siblings had been shot down and frankly, Cyrus felt embarrassed.

Auli'i touched his shoulder. Her eyes were full of emotion and she was chuckling softly. She wasn't crying but those eyes were definitely dewy.

"Kimo, I'm sorry you had to get along without us and felt like we abandoned you. I missed my twin tremendously."

Kimo was chuckling, too. The moment Auli'i uttered those words, his expression went soft.

Cyrus did a double take.

TWINS?!

Auli'i and Kimo reached over Cyrus and embraced. Cyrus, caught in the middle again, refused to spectate. Lifting his arms over the twins, he joined the embrace.

"Group hug," said Cyrus. "So, when were you going to tell me you guys were twins?"

The three of them sat up with smiles.

"You mean, you couldn't tell?" asked Kimo.

"No! Absolutely not. What happened? Did you eat your lunch and then hers growing up?"

Auli'i snorted. Covering her mouth she let out a muffled laugh. Kimo raised an eyebrow.

"Tough talk from a little guy, huh? Didn't you learn anything from the beach yesterday?"

"Yeah, I did actually. Never expect a Hawaiian to catch you at the finish line." Kimo snorted and Auli'i's muffled laugh became audibly louder. Cyrus smiled. He was glad they could laugh despite the situation they were in. Kimo noogied Cyrus on the head.

"Sorry we ignored you earlier. As you can see, we are not the perfect Virtus Latores. We will try our best though," said Kimo.

"OK, stop ... All these words. 'Virtus Latores', 'Lumen', 'Caligo'... What are all these things? What are you guys called that have no wings? I should have asked sooner, but I was still wrapping my head around the fact that I could walk and had wings."

Auli'i gave a forced laugh. "Haha! Right?! That series was crazy?!" Cyrus looked at her confused. Kimo joined in.

"It sure was, huh, sis?" laughed Kimo in agreement.

Cyrus whipped his head back and forth in confusion.

Auli'i grabbed Cyrus by the face, brought him in close and whispered, "There are people around us."

Cyrus gulped

Right ...

"Cyrus, let me tell you a story," began Kimo a little loud. "The story is called, 'The Legend of the Lumen Caligo and remember, it's PURELY fictional."

Cyrus looked up the rows of the plane.

Should I be worried we're being watched?

"Once upon a time," he started with a smirk. "There was someone called the Lumen Caligo."

"OK, OK... no need to milk it. If you're going to tell the story, at least tell it correctly. Start over," demanded Auli'i.

"Fine." Kimo sat up straight, squared his shoulders towards Cyrus and leaned in. Auli'i followed suit so they were all inches away from each other. Kimo then inhaled and began.

"There are three types of people on this earth in which we reside. There are Lumens, white winged individuals that, like the light they are named after, pursue truth, knowledge and superiority of the skies. There are Caligos, masters of navigating and discerning the darkness in the world, whose wings are as black as night. Then there are the Terrams," said Kimo motioning to Auli'i and himself. "Maintainers of virtue and a seafaring folk, their creativity knows no bounds. Yet, in the cracks of history, there were whispers of another ... one who always led mankind into a time of prosperity, technological advances and extreme growth. His title, lost on the lips of history, was ..."

"The Lumen Caligo," interjected Auli'i. "Every 350 years there was one born whose beauty and uniqueness dwarfed all of the people of the earth. One who understood both black and white, earth and skies, light and darkness ... and with that knowledge, united the peoples of the earth into unparalleled progression. After all, a united world with a common goal knows no limitations."

"From the great pyramids in Egypt to the Meso-American civilizations that mysteriously vanished, at the center of all of these been the influence and leadership of the Lumen Caligo," Kimo continued. "Now, what makes this Lumen Caligo so special? The Lumen Caligo is the outward embodiment of all people. The battle between light and dark that resides within us all. With vibrant white on one side of the feathers and a deep black on the other, the Lumen Caligo acts as an intermediary between those of the skies and those of the earth. A balancer for those who dwell in darkness and those who are blinded by the light. The link from the past born again to lead us to a better future. Cyrus ... you are all these things. You are the Lumen Caligo."

Cyrus sat entranced by the story. Gulping nervously he asked, "I'm the only one?"

Auli'i and Kimo nodded.

"You guys are ... um ... Terrams?"

Both nodded.

"What about everyone else? On this plane for example ... what do you call them?"

"We refer to them as the Civilized. Terrams know and actively participate with The Lumen Caligo. We are part of the jurandum, or the oath to follow the Lumen Caligo. We know the history and follow the rules and protocols. At least most of us," said Kimo, flashing a smirk in Auli'i's direction.

Auli'i made a face at Kimo.

"The Civilized are everyone on this plane. They are completely ignorant of your existence. They are outside the jurandum. Due to that, they can use modern technology."

"OK, why can't you use modern technology? You just said the Lumen Caligos of the past led you to 'unparalleled advancements'. What changed? Why do you act like the Amish now?"

"That's the last Lumen Caligo's doing," said Auli'i. "Before the last Lumen Caligo vanished, the three nations were at the brink of war. Lumens, Caligos and Terrams were all up in arms against each other. To prevent war, the last Lumen Caligo gave the three nations strict orders to return and stay in their own domains until a solution was reached. This order is known as the Isolation Order."

"Only," Kimo continued. "The Lumen Caligo vanished... so, it was decided that in order to prevent all out war, the three nations would remain separate from one another and await the return of the Lumen Caligo. The Hawaiian islands are our home but the most sacred island is the island of Ni'ihau. That is where the temple is located. Our ancestors saw wisdom in the Isolation Order and returned. Our family has inhabited the islands ever since."

"Ni'ihau is the Hawaiian name of the island though. To those within the jurandum, we call it Akhet," said Auli'i.

"Akhet? Like a sneeze?"

"That's not funny."

"Sorry."

"Aside from returning and staying in our domains," said Kimo.

"The three nations were also instructed to abstain from ALL technology dating after 1700 AD ... under penalty of death."

"Death? So, you guys in this plane with me right now. Anyone finds out and you get the axe?"

"No," said Auli'i. "The Isolation Order specifies that only the Lumen Caligo can lift the ban. It just never said *how*. Remember the discussion we had with my mom?"

"I do. So, Akela... is she taking the fall because you interacted with modern technology to leave or because you abandoned ship?"

"It's because I left. The Lumen Caligo, along with the three nations, have always been at the forefront of advancement in society. However, secrecy has been the tool of choice. One of the last details of the Isolation Order was also the most strict. The three nations are not allowed to venture outside of their domains. Any deserter is immediately sentenced to death."

"So, the only reason Akela is still alive is because your father is one of the chiefs?"

"Yes ... the only reason," said Kimo. "If it wasn't for that fact, she probably would have been executed immediately. My father is many things ... persuasive is one of them. You should have seen him in front of everyone back home. It was something to behold."

"He really is ..." Auli'i confirmed with a slight smile.

"Could have fooled me with that dramatic entrance of his back in IB," said Cyrus with a chuckle. "Your dad is one of the chiefs ... is it just three?"

"Yes," answered Auli'i. "The Terram nation is governed by three high chiefs. Our father is a descendant of one of the oldest Terram families responsible for the financial wellbeing of all Terrams. None of them ascended to the title of chief. Our ancestors fulfilled their role and made ends meet but there was never a surplus ... Until my father tried a different approach and did incredibly well."

"He found a way to capitalize on the booming tourist scene," Kimo added. "He wrote scripts, taught many traditional Polynesian dances and made them funny on top of that. Among the Civilized and the Terrams, our father is a legend. Most of the luaus he made still thrive across the islands. He met our mother at one of the luaus and married her, even though she was a Civilized."

"Mom was a hula girl," said Auli'i with a nudge.

"Ohhhh ...Was she now ... Haha! Are you guys allowed to marry people outside of the jurandum?"

"Well ... that's one of the reasons why our family was shunned. Sure, they speak highly of us and enjoy the money, but there are many gunning for my father and his position. Marrying our mother, a Civilized, is a bit of a grey area. Some still view it as a direct violation of the Isolation Order. Even after she became a part of the jurandum, they doubted our family. I don't even want to get into the stories of how much they complained about him breaking the Isolation Order because of the luaus. They even put him on trial for use of modern technology," said Kimo, shaking his head.

"Why?"

"Microphones," responded Auli'i. "Regardless of dad's restrictions, he was wildly successful and actually created a reserve for the Terrams. The truth is, the other chiefs complaining and accusing him of breaking the Isolation Order turned out to be the best thing for him and our nation. He swore not to use any modern technology (including microphones) and outsourced the part of MC. This gave him more time to focus on creating more luau's. The more luau's he created, the more successful he became. The more successful he became, the more he made for the Terram Nation."

"OK ... everybody loves money and success. Why are you guys 'outcasts' when you've contributed so much?"

"Envy. The Fualautoalasi family has only ever been in charge of the financial wellbeing of the Terrams. During my father's success, one of the three high chiefs named Manoa summoned my father to Ni'ihau. Manoa and my father were very close since Manoa had been my grandfather's best friend. He was on his deathbed and did something that hasn't happened in 300 years ... Our father was given the mantle of chief. Manoa... gave our father and the Fualautoalasi family ... his position ... over ALL of his own sons, nephews and grandchildren."

"Oh man ... That must have stirred the hornets nest."

"You have no idea. Manoa died a week later, and we moved to Ni'ihau a week after that."

"When did this happen?"

"Right before the pandemic," said Kimo.

"You guys probably weren't the most popular kids in town, were you?"

Kimo and Auli'i shook their heads.

"That's why it was so hard on mom," said Auli'i. "She had friends, family and access to technology. When she married our father, she had to give it all up and be around people who scorned her. That's why our situation is so messed up. When they find out we are bound to you as the Virtus Latores, they're going to flip."

"You guys keep saying 'Virtus Lator'. Explain."

"Every Lumen Caligo usually selects one person from each nation to teach him what that nation specializes in along with the inner workings so they can navigate the cultural and political intricacies," explained Kimo.

"Oh. So, I get two Terrams for the price of one?"

"Lucky you," said Auli'i returning the sarcasm.

"What is it you guys 'specialize' in? What am I to learn from you?"

"That all depends on you," said Kimo. "What we have to teach you is control over your body, both on land and in the water."

"Yeah, and I'll teach you how to make some humble pie if this 'I'm the Lumen Caligo,' starts to go to your head," said Auli'i punching Cyrus in the arm.

"Don't forget the sugar in that pie of yours," said Cyrus, rubbing his arm.

Auli'i laughed and then wrapped her arms around Cyrus. Cyrus blushed.

"Virtus Lator means bearer of strength and virtue," said Kimo.

"Our job is to train and protect both of these. Being sworn to the Lumen Caligo is the highest honor you can receive in this life. Over the course of history, the Latores have had more influence over their nations than the proper rulers. In fact, when the Lumen Caligo passes away, it is usually the families of the Latores that become the governing bodies of each nation."

"So, what am I supposed to learn from the other two nations? The white wings and the black wings?"

"First," said Auli'i. "You should call them what they are. Refer to the white wings as Lumens and the black wings as Caligos."

"Man, political correctness, too?" said Cyrus.

"No," said Auli'i. "What people want to be called is political correctness. What people are is just a fact."

"Then why do you call it Ni'ihau instead of Akhet?

"Because Ni'ihau is the Hawaiian name of the island and that's what I grew up calling it. They are interchangeable for us Terrams. The Lumens and Caligos will call it Akhet, no doubt, but Ni'ihau is how I knew it before learning about the jurandum."

"Fair point."

"You should announce us as Terrams, too. Specifically, Terram Virtus Latores. That will provide us with some protection under the Lumen Caligo title," added Kimo.

"Protection?"

"It's been 300 years... if the other two nations are anything like what we saw on Ni'ihau, then they won't be friendly," said Auli'i.

"OK, so back to my question. What am I supposed to learn from the Lumens and the Caligos?"

"We don't know..." started Kimo. "Mother taught us about our connection with the earth and the sea. Father focused on physical strength and our mana within. If I had to guess, it has to be something involved with flying."

"Great deductive skills, Kimo. I would have never guessed the people with wings would be the ones to teach Cyrus how to fly. I thought that was our job," said Auli'i, touting her head and gawking.

"Oh shut up," said Kimo.

"Do I have to go to them or can I just have them come to me like you guys did? Not gonna lie, much easier that way."

Kimo cracked a smile.

"From what we were taught while we were on Ni'ihau," said Auli'i.

"You have to go to each location and abolish the Isolation Order the previous Lumen Caligo set in place. That goes for our islands."

"I'm all for going to Hawaii. That's a bucket list location for me."

"Cyrus," said Auli'i. "I'm as excited to show you my home as you are to see it ... but please don't make the same mistake I did and not take this seriously. This world that my family and I were introduced to ... I thought it was a made up cult with an elaborate back story. Seeing you and Martian with my own two eyes has changed things considerably. What I once took as 'story time' has now turned into 'story of my life'. Don't underestimate your importance."

Cyrus looked down. Things really were changing beyond what he could have ever expected. To think that almost two months ago he was in a wheelchair meeting Auli'i for the first time.

"One more thing I want to tell you," said Kimo. "When we were being taught the tales of the Lumen Caligo and how they intertwined with mankind's achievements, the elders always referred to you to as the 'hummingbird of history'." Auli'i did a double take.

"And ..." said Cyrus.

"And it never made sense to me. I figured I should tell you since you've been learning all of the titles and whatnot."

"Hummingbird of history? ... I'll take it flying backwards is going to be my signature move." Cyrus threw out some energetic punches.

Auli'i and Kimo looked at Cyrus with an expression of, 'What the ...'

"What? You don't like my Bruce Lee punches?"

"Those were punches?" said Kimo.

"Those punches could use some work," said Auli'i with a smile.

Cyrus smiled back.

"So, I have to figure this Lumen Caligo stuff out on my own?"

"You have us, don't you?" said Auli'i.

"Exactly! Plus, I would imagine each nation has their own written record of the Lumen Caligo just like we have ours," said Kimo looking at Auli'i.

"I checked out when I got to Ni'ihau, so I only remember bits and pieces," said Auli'i.

"I enjoyed learning about it. Even if Auli'i made fun of me for it," said Kimo.

"Yeah ... I was not the nicest person. I thought it was all a sham and I was annoyed for leaving our friends and family. You studied the Lumen Caligo, I left home and found him. Call it even?"

"Fair enough. There is so much to learn. I'll have to dive into the written history when we get back," said Kimo.

"Do you guys think it is safe to go back to Ni'ihau?" asked Cyrus.

Kimo and Auli'i looked at each other. Auli'i held up her hand and gave the fifty-fifty gesture.

"We'll see when we talk with Martian again," said Kimo. "Each nation has its own record of the world. Our history is an oral one, traditionally passed down through chants. However, when it came to teaching us, the elders did have scroll looking things they read off of."

There's that word again.

Cyrus thought of Martin and Ms. Palermo at his graduation.

"Well... it's a start," said Cyrus. "Keep an eye out for 'scroll looking things' when we make our way to Ni'ihau."

"You know what I wonder ..." said Auli'i.

"What's that?" asked Cyrus.

"Is everyone going to be white skinned and white winged like Martian ... or are there different colors of skin with white wings?" Cyrus and Kimo thought for a moment. It would be interesting to see people contrasting their wings like Cyrus did.

"You know what I wonder ..." said Cyrus. "What does my mother look like?"

Cyrus turned his phone to selfie mode. Light brown skin with freckles all across his face. Curly dark brown hair with copper high-lights, and his eyes. Those two different colored eyes. He desperately wanted to know which eye came from where.

"I didn't ask yesterday, but what did the letter say?" asked Auli'i.

Cyrus reached into his pocket, opened it and read it out loud to the twins.

"Short and sweet, huh?" said Auli'i.

"Yeah..." said Kimo. "But incredibly vague at the same time."

"You gonna ask her about it?" asked Auli'i.

"I'm going to ask her a lot of things ..." replied Cyrus.

"Like what?"

"Why? When? Who's my father? When was this 'right time' she mentioned? Didn't she want me?" Cyrus' voice cracked.

Auli'i wrapped her arms around him. Kimo did the same. Cyrus hated it when he cried. It was embarrassing, and he didn't like making a scene.

Why though? Why had she left him with Martian?

The emotions swirled inside Cyrus like a brewing storm. Between being told he could walk and his mother was alive, he didn't know which one shocked him more.

The embrace from the twins comforted him. The constant hugs, noogies and playful punches to the arm had really added an extra layer of comfort he didn't know he needed.

"Cyrus," whispered Kimo. "Forgive your mother."

8

BERMUDA

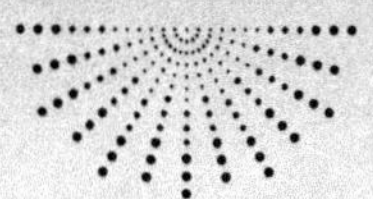

THE SUN BLAZED ABOVE as they exited the Bermuda airport. An ocean breeze enveloped the young travelers, filling their noses with a salty aroma.

Kimo waved down a taxi, and they made their way to the west side of the island. The teal water and the white sand made the ocean look absolutely breathtaking. (Much different from the brown water I.B. was known for back home.) Cyrus had found a deal online for a resort and promptly had Ms. P book it with the white credit card Martin had provided. Under normal circumstances, he would have researched more into it, but given the situation, it was good enough.

After the pandemic, the hospitality and tourism industry had offered generous discounts to incentivize travel. It worked, to a degree, but people were cautious. Things hadn't fully gone back to normal. Auli'i and Kimo said the same thing had happened in Hawaii.

Water was on both sides as they made their way west towards their hotel. Questions filled their heads concerning the beautiful new place in which they had just arrived. Fortunately, they had a very social cab driver who introduced himself as Michael. Like the majority of the population, Michael was a dark-skinned fellow. His accent was as if an American had had a love baby with a Brit in the Caribbean. It was hypnotic and pleasing to the ear.

"We're passing through Hogs Bay right now. The reason it has the name 'Hogs Bay' is because of the herds of wild hogs the Spanish explorers left behind in the 1600's. Is this your guys first time to Bermuda?"

They snapped out of their trance.

"Yes! This is our first time here. It really reminds me of our home. We're from Hawai'i," said Auli'i sweetly.

"Chingas! You're from Hawai'i, huh? Always wanted to visit there me self. This must all be a spitting image, then?"

"More like a mirror's reflection in the Atlantic," said Kimo. "Your home really is beautiful. I'm excited to explore the ocean once we reach the resort."

"Just mind the reef. You don't need me to tell you, but the reef can be very unforgiving. What about you, young sir. What part of the world do you come from?"

"I ... uh ... I come from San Diego, actually."

"Another beautiful place I've heard good things about. I'm green with envy of you three. Traveling the world at such a young age. You guys on vacation then?"

"Yes! Yes we are. We're actually meeting up with someone here on the island. He should be here in a couple days," said Cyrus.

"Huh ... well, if you guys or your friends need a ride anywhere— or just want some information about this paradise away from home— here's my card."

Cyrus took it with a smile and slipped it into his pocket next to his mom's letter.

They arrived at the resort. Cloud white buildings contrasted the green landscape and blue ocean. Feelings of comfort surged through the three. It felt inviting.

The lobby was pleasantly breezy. Kimo carried the bags while Auli'i checked into the hotel with Cyrus. When they reached the room, all three of them flopped on the bed.

"We made it ..." sighed Cyrus.

"My back is killing me. Do they make those seats on the plane for midgets? That head rest was digging into my shoulders," said Kimo, massaging himself.

"Maybe if you weren't 10 feet tall ... Cyrus and I were quite comfortable," said Auli'i.

"Shrimps...

"I wasn't that comfortable. I never want to sit again after being confined to a wheelchair for no good reason."

Auli'i turned around to lay on her stomach and looked at Cyrus inquisitively.

"Why do you think he did that to you?"

Cyrus shrugged. "One of the thousand questions I have for him when I see him again."

"Did you seriously not know you had wings this whole time? I mean, come on ... They're attached to you, for crying out loud," said Kimo, turning around onto his stomach.

Cyrus furrowed his brow and with a little effort, turned around and faced the twins.

"No. I didn't know they were attached to me. In my earliest memories, I was already in a wheelchair. I don't remember learning how to walk as a toddler. I remember learning how to control my wheelchair and computers. That's it."

The twins looked at each other and then back to Cyrus.

"What about showers and baths? Didn't you realize something was up, then?" asked Kimo.

Cyrus felt his blood rush to his face.

"Cyrus... you don't have to answer that. My brother ..." said Auli'i, punching Kimo in the arm. "Doesn't know how to ease into things."

"I'm sorry, Cyrus. I didn't mean to embarrass you. I just find the whole situation... odd. Ma bad brudah."

"It's fine ... No harm, no foul ... The truth is, I didn't notice anything strange. I didn't have any feeling in my limbs except my hands and I attributed my pot belly to no exercise. The ... 'artificial skin' — or whatever you want to call the stuff you peeled off of me-looked real enough ... Not to mention, every month or so, I would go to the hospital where I would get a check up with Ms. P, that they called

'mini surgeries. They always put me under ... I bet that's when they would change the skin."

"What about your belly button? It definitely looked weird with the fake skin covering it," asked Auli'i.

"I didn't really spend a lot of time inspecting my own body. My mobility was limited to just below the elbows and I was always under the watchful eye of Martian and my teachers. Even in my spare time on my bed, it's not like I could stand up and look in the mirror. I guess I just had different things on my mind. I tried not to think about it and Martian did everything to distract me from the despair if I did."

"Fair point. I'm curious what his thoughts were doing that to you and how he convinced Ms. Palermo," said Auli'i.

"Speaking of Ms. Palermo, weren't you supposed to call her when we landed?" said Kimo.

"Shoot! You're right. Let me give her a call and then we'll make a plan of attack."

Whipping out his phone, Cyrus hit the number two. The call didn't even make it past the first ring.

"Hello, hello! Cyrus, can you hear me?! Hello?! Can you hear me?"

"Hi, Ms. P! Yep, I can hear you loud and clear. We made it safe and sound to Bermuda. The ocean is beaut—"

"Oh, I'm so glad you're safe! I was worried about you! I mean I know you have Auli'i and Kimo and they are great travel companions, but goodness me, I just couldn't help myself! With you walking and all these changes coming at once it has just been one thing after another.

Plus, you know how fond I am of you and Martin. It just hasn't been the same with both of you gone! Your presence, our weekly dinners, Martin's subtle and not so subtle humor ... it's just ... I realized how much you guys have become a part of my life and I was never one for family, having thrown myself into my work, but I must say, you two have really taken over a piece of my heart. It reminds me of this play I saw a couple years ago when"

"Ms. Palermo!" She would have gone on forever had he not interjected. Cyrus had to focus her attention. "I miss you, too. Don't worry about me, we will be back soon. I wanted to see how Kamalani was holding up, if you've heard anything from Martian, and more importantly, I wanted to talk to you about my recovery."

"Oh, of course, darling! Kamalani is doing just great, she and I have really bonded and I'm actually right here next to her if you wanted to say hi, she has been taking being left alone rather rough, the poor girl."

Cyrus pressed a couple buttons on his phone and turned the phone call into a video call.

The twins will appreciate this.

"Kimo, Auli'i, get over here."

The twins stopped what they were doing and jumped onto the bed with Cyrus. Cyrus felt like he was experiencing an earth quake when Kimo jumped on.

"Ms. P, I turned the call into a video chat. Bring the phone away from your ear and press accept."

"Oh! Good idea, Cyrus. Oh, you've always been such a considerate child. Martin taught you so well! What a good boy you are!"

Cyrus rolled his eyes and the twins starting laughing. Auli'i, patted him on the head and began talking to him like he was a dog.

"Who's a good boy? Who's a good boy? You are! Yes, you are!"

"Get away from me, you weirdo." Kimo let out a hearty laugh.

The phone chimed, confirming the video call and the three kids were looking right up Ms. Palermo's nose.

Why do boomers always put their phone so close and at such unflattering angles?

"Hi!!!" Ms. Palermo excitedly waved.

"Hi!" said the three in unison.

Ms. Palermo then shifted the camera towards Kamalani whose face lit up. Her eyes were puffy and red.

"Oh, my babies! You guys OK? You eat enough?"

"Yeah, mom, the plane had a meal and we're going to scout out a couple restaurants after we unpack," said Auli'i with a smile.

"Even filled me up, mom. Not as good as your Ahi, though. Promise you'll cook when we get back?"

"Oh, of course. I'll find some taro and make some poi. I miss your smiling faces and my heart is happy seeing them through the phone.

Have you heard anything else from Martin concerning Akela?"

"Nothing yet, mom, but it should be soon. The moment we do, we'll let you know. We're in this really nice resort right by the ocean. The water here reminds me of when you would take us to Waimeia Bay. It's so clear," said Auli'i.

"Aww ... You always loved that beach. You'll have to show Waimeia to Cyrus when you guys make it out there. If he has the courage, you ll have to jump off the rock with him, too."

"Even if he doesn't have it..." said Auli'i with a smirk. "He's still going to jump."

Kamalani let out a chuckle. Kimo nodded with approval.

"Arlene, you are also invited, should you make your way out to Hawai'i," said Kamalani to Ms. Palermo.

Auli'i mouthed, 'That's her name?'

"Oh, that would be lovely! Hawai'i has always been a place I've longed to see with my own two eyes. The beaches and the pineapples, it seems like its own paradise on earth. Not to mention, if everyone is even half as nice as your family, I will feel right at home! I must reject the offer to jump off of this rock you speak of. I'm terrified of heights. No can do ..."

"Ms. Palermo, changing the subject a little bit, not much has changed since you inspected me except for me being really shifty on the plane. I found sitting that long uncomfortable, if you can believe it." Ms. Palermo dialed in her focus. When it came to the medical stuff, she was always on it.

"I can believe that, Cyrus dear. All the changes these past couple weeks have made you tired and sore. Your body is not only adjusting to this new movement, it's hungering for more. You are a boy, after all, and like most boys your age, sitting still tends to be a challenge. You have pent up energy and a desire to move. That's great! But please remember my advice, and take it slow. You need to keep doing your stretches every night like you were doing here, understood?"

"Every night."

"Is Kimo helping?"

"Every night Aunty. P," said Kimo giving her the thumbs up.

"Good. Continue doing those every night before you lie down for bed. Consistency is key. Overall, how do you feel? I still think you shouldn't be taking things so fast, Cyrus dear."

"I'm doing fine, Ms. Palermo. I just feel stir crazy and achy at the same time. Overall, though, I'm just so happy to be moving."

"OK ... please don't do anything drastic. Your body right now is like an elastic band. Put it through something too strenuous, you could snap and hurt yourself. Promise me you'll be extra careful?" She raised her eyebrow and pointed at Cyrus on the other end of the screen.

Cyrus gave a smile that only Ms. Palermo could get out of him.

"I promise."

"Also, be careful in Bermuda. I just watched a documentary about all the disappearances that have occurred over the years, and oh, it just made me worry that much more. Ships and planes disappearing into thin air and all the wild theories swirling about. Between Kamalani missing her babies and me missing you, we've been a ball of nerves and emotions. All of the theater in the world couldn't have prepared me for all these em-mo-mo-tions..." blubbered Ms. Palermo.

"Ms. P ... Ms. P ... Ms. P ... It's OK! It will be a quick trip. At the very latest, we will be back when school starts. You're not going to rent our spot to anyone else, will you?"

"Heavens, no! I would never."

"Good ... because I can't see me living anywhere else. Please don't cry, Ms. P."

Ms. Palermo closed her eyes, took a deep breath and recomposed herself. She then dramatically put her hands to her face and swirled them while she changed her expression to a strong one. The twins chuckled. Never a dull moment. Kamalani then took the phone from Ms. Palermo.

"OK ... We'll let you guys go unpack. You be safe, and don't go getting into trouble, ya hear me? Love you wit all ma heart." Kamalani blew a kiss.

"We anxiously await your return. Be brave like Hercules and swift like Hermes ... and do your stretches or there'll be hell to pay ... like Hades," said Ms. Palermo facetiously.

"Wow... Going through a new phase of reading, Ms. Palermo?" asked Cyrus.

"Oh, you know me so well. The Greek tragedies ... I can't get enough of them. Alright. Off with you. Love you, and be safe."

"BBBYYYEEE!" said the three in unison.

Beep beep.

"Well, what do we do now?" asked Auli'i.

Cyrus checked the time on his phone. It was 7:53 PM and the sun was going down.

"How about we go see the sunset from the beach and then make a plan for these next couple days. Sunset is in half an hour."

"Perfect! Let's go."

"Alright!" said Kimo.

The three changed and headed down to the beach in front of the hotel. The breeze was absolutely delicious. The white sand was warm on their toes and soft to the touch. Every step was like stepping onto a soft cloud. Cyrus found himself becoming tired quickly.

Kimo sprinted ahead full speed and, like an Olympic long jumper, catapulted himself head first into the ocean. Auli'i let out a suppressed 'Chee who' as she supported Cyrus. Slowly but surely, Cyrus made his way to the ocean.

Yellow and red painted the sky, contrasting against the teal blue ocean. Cyrus had never seen a blue as blue as his left eye. It seemed to pulsate light. Some shades of the ocean came close. The waves frothed as they crashed onto the shore making a sizzling sound comparable to a newly opened soda can. The water was warm.

Cyrus let out a long sigh. The ocean was home. No matter what part of the world he was in. Home.

Auli'i let out a small chuckle. Cyrus felt her eyes on him.

"You OK there? You seem like you're in your own little world," said Auli'i with a smile.

"Yeah... Sorry. I kinda got lost in how beautiful it is here. Minus Kimo and his whale reenactments."

Kimo was frolicking in the waves shamelessly. He let out a series of dolphin noises while looking at Auli'i and Cyrus ... a big stupid grin across his face.

"Don't be sorry. I'm glad you love the ocean. We couldn't be friends if you didn't."

"Really?"

"Really..." she said with a wicked smile.

"EEHEEHHHHEEHHHEEEEE," went Kimo again.

"Hey! Wanna-be-dolphin ... Get over here and enjoy the sunset," said Auli'i. Kimo sloshed out of the ocean and threw himself on Auli'i and Cyrus.

"Nooooooo!"

"Get off lolo!"

Kimo let out another hearty laugh and let go of his two now wet victims.

The three got comfortable and watched as the sun slowly set. The only sounds were the crashing waves. Slowly but surely, the sun made its repeating journey towards the horizon. A thousand colors displayed themselves in a frenzy with the last bit of light. Cyrus, Auli'i and Kimo held their peace as they watched the sun. The sun setting on the ocean's horizon was a holy ceremony the three had grown up with ... peace whispered to their souls.

As the sun descended below the horizon, Kimo broke the silence.

"OK. What's our plan?"

"Pretty straight forward. We need to find this mysterious Jorge Worley, Martian mentioned. Then we wait for Martian to join us while I build my strength and endurance. Preferably on a secluded beach so I can stretch my wings a little bit."

"You still get winded pretty quickly," said Kimo.

"Well, being in a wheelchair his whole life might have something to do with that."

"Ha. Ha," said Kimo.

"Let's sleep in tomorrow, do some stretches and then go to Hogs Bay and ask around. We can come back to the resort around dinner time. We'll adjust our plan depending on the information we receive," said Cyrus.

"What if we can't find this guy, Cyrus? How long did you reserve the hotel for?" asked Auli'i.

"A week. I would like to think that it won't take Martian that long to contact us. If it does ... Well.. Let's just cross that bridge when we get to it. My main goal is to meet my mother. With or without Martian."

The twins raised their eyebrows.

"We should wait for Martian, Cyrus. We don't know what were walking into," said Auli'i.

"Yeah ... None of us have ever met a Lumen besides Martian before. We don't know if they're going to treat us with hostility or not," said Kimo.

"But I'm the Lumen Caligo, aren't I? Based off of how you guys reacted and what you've told me, I should be welcomed with open arms. Or, open wings?" said Cyrus with a half smirk.

Auli'i rolled her eyes and suppressed a smile.

"Yes! They will welcome you Cyrus ... but will they welcome us? You're not going there alone. From what we saw back in Nihau, the tribe mentality still dominates the Terram nation. I'm worried it will be the same thing in Aeolia. We shouldn't rush into this," said Auli'i.

"I'm not rushing into this! Auli'i, try and understand ... I found out where my mother lives 2 days ago. I need to meet her."

"And you can't wait a couple more days? Cyrus, you said it your-self. We need a plan. No pun intended, but we shouldn't just wing it.

Not until we've explored our options."

"Yeah ... I guess you're right."

"Then be proactive and do the little things. If you plan on creating balance as the Lumen Caligo, better start practicing now. What's that saying? Dreams without plans are just dreams. Little things, Cyrus ... do the little things."

"I will ... But you can't blame me for wanting to see my mother as soon as possible ... That is my priority. That is why we're here in Bermuda."

"You can give yourself whatever excuse to convince yourself not to be prepared. Rush into it, if you really want to. I've given you my advice and told you what I think. At the end of the day, you are the Lumen Caligo, and we are the Virtus Latores. We will follow your lead and respect your decision. Just remember that before this role was assigned to me, I did it because we were friends ... Don't forget that."

"I ..." started Cyrus. He tried to formulate a counter argument. but couldn't think of anything.

She was right, of course, but Cyrus hated that. Like a puppy with his tail in between his legs, Cyrus nodded his head and motioned towards the hotel. There was silence between the three while they made their way from the beach. The moment they stepped into the hotel, Kimo spoke up.

"Hey guys, you want to know the best part about this resort, besides the beach?"

Both Auli'i and Cyrus looked at Kimo with bewilderment.

"Continental breakfast..." said Kimo with a huge smile. "I read about it while you were booking the resort."

"You know... you can be really random sometimes, Mr. Dolphin," said Cyrus as they got into the elevator.

"What can I say? I found my porpoise."

Groans and laughter erupted as the elevator doors closed.

9

MAURÍCIO

WHAT A BUST. Six Days had past since they'd begun looking for the mysterious Jorge Worley fellow. They had received six days of perplexed looks, shoulder shrugs and 'I don't knows. The days were hot and the weather was extra humid. Every time Cyrus stepped outside, he felt like he was melting. Walking around this much, even with the twins helping him, had exhausted him.

Two days prior, he'd had the great pleasure of experiencing his first muscle cramp. It was the worst pain he had ever felt ... until his second cramp. It was agonizing. Cyrus would rather listen to Ms. P talk about every musical she'd ever seen alphabetically than experience that again.

Cyrus cried unapologetic tears of pain as his body turned against him.

Kimo went and bought two bunches of bananas while Auli'i stayed by his side.

"Better than being in a wheelchair, right?" said Auli'i with a pained smile.

True ...

They had called it early that day to give Cyrus time to recover. They focused on stretching and resting while they watched a western on TV. The twins were machines. Even in the hot sun, they didn't seem phased. When Cyrus pointed this out, they shrugged it off and said they'd grown up in similar weather. Warm and humid.

Cyrus began feeling the effects of having his wings wrapped around his torso a lot more. They seemed to insulate him, and as the day went on, they would droop further and further below his waist. Getting home and releasing his wings from their cotton prison was incredibly refreshing.

The strength in his wings was increasing as was his range of motion. Cyrus could completely span his wings and hold that pose for 10 seconds. He kept forgetting to breathe when he did it, though.

The twins were incredibly supportive but he still felt bad having them help him all the time. With Martin, it was no problem because that's how he had grown up. With these two, Cyrus felt embarrassed.

Every time he brought it up or thanked them excessively, they would both tell him to shut up and that it was their pleasure to help him. He would then get a lecture from Auli'i about how he needed to stop being so hard on himself and that he had made leaps and bounds in a couple weeks. Literally.

It was a Friday, and the twins had officially dubbed it, 'Aloha Friday.' The three of them decided 'Aloha Friday' would be the last thorough day of searching, and they would then take the weekend off.

This time, they would do something different. Instead of traversing Hogs Bay and the west side of the island, they would try the east. A couple of sailors said there were more boats over on that side.

Martin had yet to contact them, and Ms. Palermo and Kamalani hadn't received word on their end either. Kamalani was worried sick. Cyrus held it in, but he was too.

Martian should have reached out by now.

His flight was the following evening, and if he was successful leaving the island, the first thing he would do would be to text or call Cyrus. It was the complete radio silence that wasn't normal. Cyrus tried to justify it when they video chatted with Ms. Palermo and Kamalani, but deep down he knew something was up. Every time he tried to call, it would go straight to voice mail.

"Alright! Breakfast, and then off we go! Kimo, get up, lazy-head!" boomed Auli'i.

"Uhhhhh." Kimo rolled over.

Cyrus supported himself on a chair and stretched his back, legs and wings simultaneously. Bliss. Morning wake up stretches were becoming his favorite ritual.

"Kimo, get your overgrown okōli out of bed or I'ma go for your ribs," said Auli'i.

"Mmmuhnnhhhnn."

Pop!

Cyrus' left wing felt better. Cyrus was making little circles with his left wing and left leg.

"I'm not playing," said Auli'i.

Pop!

Cyrus rotated his neck as he wrapped up his morning stretches.

"WHAT ARE YOU DOING?!! GET OFF, GET OFF!! I'M UP, SEE? I'M UP!" screamed Kimo.

Cyrus jumped from surprise. He turned around to see Kimo backed into the corner while Auli'i crouched on the bed like a frog. She pointed her hands at Kimo like guns while she laughed maniacally. Kimo looked authentically scared. No grogginess there.

"Do I have to use my death pokes anymore?"

"I SAID, I'M UP!" Kimo wiped away what little sleep his eyes had left.

"You sure?"

"YES."

"Alright then." Auli'i holstered her finger guns.

"You really are the evil twin," said Kimo.

"You know you love me." Auli'i blew a kiss.

"Mmmhm …"

Cyrus chuckled to himself.

They made their way to the continental breakfast downstairs and stuffed their faces. Sausage, eggs, bacon and a make your own waffle station dotted the buffet line. Waffles had quickly become a favorite of the twins. They had never had waffles or maple syrup before and loved both. Cyrus made a game of finding out how much real-world exposure the twins had had before they moved to Ni'ihau. Waffles, surprisingly, had not made the list.

Seeing the twins experience things Cyrus took for granted fascinated him. Simple waffles and old western movies brought them such joy. The fact they weren't embarrassed was so refreshing. It was a 180 degree shift from the kids he went to school with. Most kids would rather look cool than learn. It was another reason why he'd felt like he didn't fit in. He wanted to know as much as he could about the world around him.

"How are the waffles?" asked Cyrus.

"Mmmmmmmmm," hummed Auli'i and Kimo in unison, their mouths incredibly full.

Cyrus cracked a smile.

"Shyyyrus ..." said Kimo with a mouth full of waffles. "Howshs

uheii guhnna geshhet tto vah eshhhe shifide ovv vah ishllanv vooodai?"

Cyrus raised an eyebrow and looked at Kimo incredulously.

"Was that Hawaiian for oink oink?" said Cyrus.

Auli'i snorted a mixture or orange juice and waffles from her nose. "Auli'i!!! Gross!"

Kimo chomped his food ferociously while laughing, swallowed and then tried again.

"How we gonna get to the other side of the island today?"

Cyrus was wiping the Auli'i spray from the table. Auli'i blushed from embarrassment but kept laughing. He then whipped out his backpack and flashed the card Michael had given them a week ago.

"I'm going to call that taxi driver we had the other day."

"The one with the cool accent?" asked Kimo.

"They all have cool accents," said Auli'i wiping her mouth.

"Michael was just the first one we heard."

"Yeah. That guy. I'm going to call him."

"What if he doesn't answer?" asked Kimo.

"Then we call another taxi, catch an Über or a Lyft." They gave Cyrus confused eyes. "What?"

"New words. Explain them, please," said Auli'i.

"Ah ... Uber and Lyft are like taxi services you can access on your phone."

"Got it."

"While you guys munch away, I'm going to call."

Cyrus input the number into his phone and pushed the green call button. On the third ring, Michael picked up.

"Michael Simmons taxi services, how can I assist you today?"

"Michael, it's err ummm, it's Cyrus. You picked us up from the airport last week and I was wondering if we could uhhh ... employ your services?"

Kimo and Auli'i bust out laughing.

"What?" mouthed Cyrus.

"I would love to. Could you be more specific which kids? I drive a lot of people around, Mr. Cyrus. It is my job, after all."

"Oh, yeah. I'm from San Diego and the other two are the Hawaiian hyenas you hear in the background."

Cyrus couldn't understand why the twins were laughing.

"Sure thing. I can be over in half an hour. Would that work?"

"Yeah! We'll meet you out front."

"See you soon."

Click.

"What is so funny?"

"You," said Auli'i. "You get all nervous and trip over your words. It's as comical as it is cute."

"Minus the cute part for me," said Kimo with a smile.

"Ha. Ha. We have half an hour until Michael gets here. Finish up. Let's get what we need and head out."

Kimo and Auli'i quickly wolfed down what they had on their plates, stuffed a bunch of granola bars and fruit into their pockets and headed up to the room with Cyrus. They packed what they had into a backpack ... water, Cyrus' charger and all the food they'd scrounged from the continental breakfast. It was an efficient way to hold down their hunger during the day until dinner.

Michael was right on time. His silver van pulled up to the entrance, and he greeted the three kids with a smile.

"Aloha! Long time no see," he said.

"Aloha!" replied the twins.

"Nice to see you again Michael," said Auli'i.

"We missed ya," said Kimo with a smile.

Michael let out a hearty laugh. "I must have made quite the impression. Well, hop in and tell me where you'd like to go."

Kimo and Auli'i helped Cyrus into the car and then settled in themselves.

"Where to?"

"Michael, we're actually looking for someone," started Cyrus. "His name is Jorge Worley, and we were told he would be in Hogs Bay, but after looking these past five days, he was nowhere to be found ... We were out of ideas, so we figured we would search a different part of the island. Do you know where we could start?"

"Hmmmm.. Can't say I've heard of a Jorge Worley on the island. Does he own a boat?"

"We don't know. We told you everything we know."

"Why are you looking for this mystery man?"

"Well, my ..." Cyrus paused as he contemplated his next words. "Dad told me to find him while he made his way over here. He is a family friend, of some sort. Anyway .... anything would help."

"Hmmmm... Well I don't think I'm much use to you guys. I haven't the faintest idea who that is," said Michael with a shrug. "But I know someone who might. He's the old harbor master that's dealt with the comings and goings of people for the past 30 years. He just retired and enjoys the isolation. Normally, I wouldn't recommend going to see him, but he's been talking about sailing to Hawai'i for years now and think he might be inclined to help ya."

"OK. It's a start. Can you take us there?" asked Auli'i.

"Let me give him a call first."

Michael took his phone from the dash and manually input a number. The phone rang twice, and then a deep voice answered.

"Oi, Ace boy, you up and at it?" asked Michael.

Rapid muffled speaking followed.

"Yeah, I know. I figured you might actually sleep in once in a while now that you're nice and cozy in retirement ... Ha! You're not wrong. I can't wait ta be where you're at. A couple more years, I'll be sitting at home just like you ... Listen, I've met some folks from Hawai'i that are looking for someone they can't seem to find and, what? ... Yeah, I said Hawai'i ... Br ... bring em over? Oh, well that didn't take a lot of convincing, now did it. I was expecting you to put up more of a fight, old boy. Must be the old age ... OK. Yeah. We'll be there in about twenty minutes. Thanks. See you soon. Bye."

Michael turned to the three youngsters and smiled.

"Let's be off, then."

Michael put the car into gear and drove away from the resort.

"Do you guys get that a lot?" asked Michael.

"What?" asked Auli'i.

"Interest in who you are just because you're from Hawai'i?"

"Yeah, we do. Fortunately for us, it has led to meeting some great people," said Auli'i, looking at Cyrus.

"Now, before we get there, let me tell you something," began Michael. "The old harbor masters name is Maurício. He is a sailor at heart and can be a little rough around the edges. The man has no filter whatsoever, so keep that in mind. You've been warned."

"Sounds like dad ..." said Auli'i.

Kimo smirked. "If that's the case, then we'll get along just fine." The drive was as breathtaking as ever. The vibrant blue ocean and soft fluffy clouds dotted the horizon. Reggae played on the radio, adding to the ambiance. Michael's car turned onto a rough dirt road and shook everyone inside. It was like a nice massage after all their exploring.

Trees dotted the path as they made their way to meet the mysterious Maurício. Eventually, the trees stopped, and they entered a clearing with a small white house and a white sail boat with blue trim. You could see the other side of the harbor where they had been searching the past five days. The air was still and quiet. Birds sang and a faint whisper from the wind made its way through the trees. If there was anywhere to retire, this man had chosen the most ideal spot.

Michael turned off the car, and all four of them got out.

"I figured I would go greet the ol' boy real quick since it's been a while, if that's OK with you," said Michael.

"Of course!" said Auli'i.

The four of them walked up to the house. As Michael raised his fist to knock, the door swung open. A burley brown man stood before them. Standing at least six feet tall, he had a thick mustache and a balding hairline. He wore a wife-beater, swimming trunks and flip flops. His belly protruded out like a giant bowling ball, exposing a bit of skin.

Buddha would be jealous of that belly for sure.

"Look what the wind blew in. Come here, Ace boy, it's great to see ya!" bellowed Maurício. He embraced Michael in a back breaking hug

"Uhhh. I've been trying to get that kink out my back for a month. One bear hug from you and it's gone. Maybe I should hire you as my chiropractor," said Michael.

Maurício let out a booming laugh. "T'll certainly charge you less.

Well, chingas! You brought me some authentic Hawaiians. Did you season them on the way? I'm starving!"

Cyrus gulped.

"Come now, you don't want to frighten them."

"Of course I do! This world can be a cruel place. I want to see if they can hold their own. Ever heard the tale of Hansel and Gretel?"

"From the looks of things, your house isn't made of gingerbread," said Auli'i. "Not to mention, you could use a diet."

Cyrus and Kimo's jaws dropped. Michael looked back at her in horror and Maurício looked seriously at Auli'i.

"Are you calling me fat?" He walked up to Auli'i and menacingly stood over her.

Auli'i looked back defiantly at Maurício. Kimo and Cyrus stood shoulder to shoulder with her.

"Well, I certainly wouldn't describe you as thin," said Auli'i, doing the quotation marks with her fingers.

Maurício stared at Auli'i and slowly put his face right in front of hers. Auli'i looked as determined as ever and held his gaze. Cyrus was getting anxious from the building tension.

Finally, when the two were basically nose to nose, Maurício took a deep breath and then let out an even heartier laugh.

"Now that's some spunk, little one. I'm Maurício. Who might you be?" he asked, extending his hand

"Auli'i Fualautoalasi," she said, hesitantly taking his hand.

"Aloha, Auli'i! What a beautiful name. It sounds like you're singing me a song."

Auli'i gave a forced smile. Cyrus could tell her defenses were still up.

"And this is ..."

"Kimo Fualautoalasi. I'm Auli'i's brother."

"Not nearly as beautiful as her. Clearly she got all the looks but you ... clearly got all the brawn."

Maurício had an uncommonly deep voice. Its very utterance commanded respect. This was a man used to being listened to.

"Now, this doesn't look like a Hawaiian to me, but what do I know.

State your name and where you're from," said Maurício, turning to Cyrus.

"C-C-Cyrus Weatherford ... from California.

"Say it like you have a backbone," boomed Maurício.

"Cyrus Weatherford from California!" shouted Cyrus louder than he probably needed to.

"Thats's better. California, aye? Never been there either. You lot are an exotic one. What can I do you for?"

"Were looking for a man by the name of Jorge Worley," Aul'i said. "We've spoken to half the island already, yet no one knows who he is. We were hoping it might be different with you." Maurício's face contorted into a skeptical scowl.

"Now, how would three kids from the other side of the world come to know about Jorge Worley?"

Kimo widened his stance as if he was preparing for an attack.

"We were told to look for him. He is who we were told to talk to about Aeolia and—"

"Let me stop yeh right there. Ace boy, you mind waiting in the car. I need to talk to these kiddos in private, and then I'll send them right back to you to take them home."

Michael looked confused at the request but promptly let himself out and returned to his car. Maurício peered over his shoulder to make sure he was in the car and out of ear shot. He then turned to Kimo, Auli'i and Cyrus and beckoned them to follow him. They walked into the living room with a big brown-leather couch cracked from exposure to the salt air and a matching recliner.

"Sit."

The three of them sat. Kimo did not put his back against the cushions. He was on edge and ready. Maurício noticed.

"I'm not going to pull anything with you, don't you worry," said Maurício in an oddly comforting tone. "Now, which one of yeh has wings?"

Their eyes bulged.

"Ahhh ... So one of you does. If I were to guess, it would be the small one from California. I've only seen one of yeh ... and it was when they whisked Jorge away fight'n and screaming. He mentioned this Aeolia place before they took 'em."

"So, you knew him? How long ago was he taken?" asked Cyrus.

"Two years ago."

"What did you do?" asked Auli'i.

"What would you do?"

"Figure out what I knew and what I didn't. Then try and fill in the gaps."

"As smart as yeh are beautiful. Deadly combination ... Well, that's exactly what I did. Jorge was a special case on this island. The reason you couldn't find anyone who knew him was because he specifically asked me not to mention him or keep him in the books when he came to port. He paid handsomely for it."

"He bribed you?" asked Cyrus with a look of surprise.

"Bribe is a strong word. He lined my pockets, and in return, 1 was quiet. Always in gold, too. He did that for years while I was port master, and I never questioned nor cared what he did. The reason being ... he never did nothing. He would have me buy his groceries, he would never leave his ship and only in the last six months did he start coming over to my place fer a drink."

"Was he a Lumen?" asked Kimo.

"Lumen ... Is that what you're called? I would have thought angels."

Kimo stood up, turned around and lifted his shirt. After revealing his back, he turned back around.

"I'm a human. Were not the 'angels, but we are looking for them. It is very important we find them. They have Cyrus' mother."

Both Cyrus and Auli'i turned to Kimo with a look of surprise. It was an interesting angle to lead with. Maurício snapped his eyes towards Cyrus with sympathy. Maybe he wasn't just a grizzly old sailor.

"Then your situation isn't so different from Jorge's," he said with a sad undertone. "A couple hours before Jorge was taken, he approached me with a proposition. Now, Jorge was always calm and collected. But the night he came to my house, he was frantic. He went on about his daughter. Said 'they' had her in the triangle. He then went on about the 'Lumens' and how it was his job to keep Bermuda secure and how this was some outpost ... I thought the man had a case of boat fever, to be honest."

"But ... he then said he needed my help saving her. That she, along with hundreds of others, were stuck, 'enslaved in the middle of the triangle,' as he put it. As port master, I've seen my fair share of disappearances. People leave and don't make it to their destination. But hundreds enslaved? The man was either crazy or knew a lot more than he let on, since the center of the triangle is notorious for disappearances, which is why us sailors avoid it .. It lives up to its nickname..."

"Which is?" asked Kimo.

"The devil's triangle."

Cyrus audibly gulped.

"Haven't you heard the stories? Just in the last century, yer home, the states, has lost more ships and planes than anyone else. I've come near the center once. My instruments went haywire, GPS completely useless and the fog was as thick as pea soup."

"Well..." began Auli'i. "We need to get there. Will you take us?" Direct and to the point. Maurício raised an eyebrow.

"After everything I just told you, the first thing you want to do is try and get there?" he said, shaking his head. "I don't think so. Not worth the risk."

"What about helping out your friend Jorge?" asked Cyrus. "Don't you want to find him and see these Lumens?"

"Jorge was a stand up guy but to risk my neck and come out of retirement is a tall order."

"We could show you around the islands when you come visit," said Kimo. "Kaiwi channel can be dangerous and I know it better than anyone. All we need is your help."

Maurício rolled his eyes. "That's if I decide to make the trip out there. I may have expressed interest but not that much."

Cyrus looked over at Auli'i who sat cool and composed. She casually crossed her legs and leaned forward.

"If you don't have the courage to help us, could you please indicate someone who does?"

Maurício slowly sat up straight. A soft smile touched his lips.

"Listen closely, young lady. Yes, I do know others who would be willing to brave the seas, if I asked them. I will not, however, ask them based off of your feeble attempt at reverse psychology."

"What will you do it for, then?"

"I'm not sure I want to. I have a comfortable life and worked hard for it. All that is left for me is a life of leisure and satisfying my curiosity about the world around me."

Cyrus stood up. Wincing in pain, he removed his shirt and let his wings unfold. With all his might, he opened his wings to their maximum width. Maurício's eyes bulged and he involuntarily retreated into The Lumen Caligo his seat. Cyrus let his wings fall to his side and began to fall from all the exertion. Kimo caught him in a flash. Cyrus sat down again and looked straight at Maurício.

"I have had these my whole life but only found out about them less than a month ago. I have been confined to a wheelchair thinking I had a terminal illness only to find out it was full-body sedation. My mother, whom 1 also didn't know existed until a week ago, is now somewhere in the middle of the Bermuda Triangle along with more people that supposedly look like me." Cyrus had fire in his eyes.

"You say you want your curiosity of the world to be satisfied? Well, I NEED to find my mother! I don't know who or what I am ... I can barely walk. Yet, I still stumble forward because I know EXACTLY what 1 want. You have been the only person who has been remotely useful, and now you say you're 'not sure if you want to? Curiosity or leisure, Maurício? Choose one. Will you help us?! If not you, point us to someone who can!"

The waves crashed onto the sand outside. Seagulls called in the distance. The faint wisp of the wind seeped through the cracks of the house. Maurício looked at Cyrus in terror. His eyes rolled back and forth, right wing to left. Gradually, he composed himself and looked up with weathered focus.

"Tomorrow. 0500. We leave. Don't. Be. Late."

10
SEAFARERS IN A PINCH

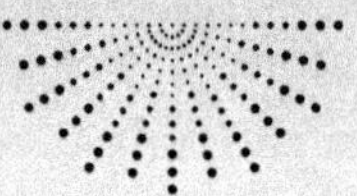

WITH EVERY RISE AND DIP, Cyrus' stomach performed gymnastics. It was the first time Cyrus had been on a boat. They had been sailing for two days and Cyrus still hadn't adjusted. Kimo and Auli'i seemed to soak up every movement, every spray of the sea and every word Maurício spoke.

Bessy ... That was what Maurício had named his boat. Cyrus had laughed out loud when Mauricio told them, to which Maurício shot him a dirty look.

Bessy ... What a funny name.

Cyrus thought of a cow on a farm.

Good ol Bessy.

It didn't get old.

Bessy was a sailboat that also had a pretty hefty engine. Sailboat wasn't even the correct name for the boat. "Bavarian Yacht," according to Maurício. It seemed nicer than what he should have had. After the stories Maurício had been telling, it became apparent that obtaining this yacht had been his sole mission in life. All of his money and time went into maintaining her. Maurício had no children or family. His love was traveling and sailing. That was it.

Maurício was proud of Bessy. She was the equivalent to his child.

A 65-foot Bavarian yacht with a comfortable cabin and a meticulously cared for exterior. The boat was all white with a deep blue trim that looked worn but clean—like a pair of leather shoes that were worn every day and shined every night. The boat was sturdy, and you could tell its captain knew its every detail.

The past couple days had been just as informative for Maurício. He asked Cyrus question after question about his wings, how they felt and if he could fly. Not only that, but also about the Lumens and what Cyrus was called since he had black on the other side of his wings. Cyrus, with the help of the twins, was able to answer all of his questions and fill him in. Explaining 'Lumen Caligo to Maurício had been humorous because of the way he said it with that deep voice.

After Maurício learned those words, he almost exclusively called Cyrus 'Lumen Caligo' after that.

Cyrus had called Ms. P and Kamalani the night before they had set sail with Maurício. Ms. P hated everything about the idea of them journeying into the Bermuda Triangle with someone they had just met and tirelessly tried to convince them to wait. Cyrus had his mind made up though. All was quiet from Martin still. In the end, Ms. P and Kamalani wished them luck and sent their love along with a laundry list of 'be carefuls'.

The sun dipped just above the horizon. There were minutes left in the day. A thin haze began to form as the sun said its final farewell.

"We are getting close to the center of the triangle" said Maurício.

"Anything wrong with the instruments?" asked Kimo.

"Nothing yet. This haze though ... It has me worried. Never underestimate the ocean. It could be the start of something. Guards up. Eyes peeled."

The twins gathered with Cyrus on the starboard side of the bow to enjoy the sunset. With the encroaching haze, the water seemed to be on fire. It looked like lava on the bottom with a layer of fresh snow on top. The ocean never ceased to amaze Cyrus. The sun slowly faded over the horizon... the wet fire subsided. Darkness began creeping into the world.

"OK. Now, the instruments are glitching," said Maurício with a tinge of worry.

"The current is slightly picking up, too," said Kimo, peering over the railing.

"You sure about this, Cyrus? It's not too late to turn around," said Maurício with all seriousness.

Cyrus looked at the glitching instruments, the thickening haze and the darkening sky. He thought of only one thing ... meeting his mother.

"We stay on course. I'll stay in the cabin with you," said Cyrus with conviction.

Maurício nodded and returned his attention back to the controls.

"Expect the unexpected. Here we go."

Maurício hit the flood light at the front of the yacht and tightly gripped the helm.

"Current is still steady in a southwest direction," yelled Kimo.

Auli'i joined Maurício and Cyrus in the cabin. She seemed worried. A stark contrast to the joy she had displayed the past two days at sea.

"Do you think the Lumens will attack us once they spot us?" asked Auli'i.

Probably. Cyrus thought to himself.

"I think we'll be fine," said Cyrus. "If they revere the Lumen Caligo as much as you've told me, they'll welcome us rather than attack."

"This fear I have ... It's just like when we fled from Ni'ihau. I feel on high alert. Every splash of a wave I think someone is coming for me."

With considerable effort, Cyrus extended his arm and his wing and put them over Auli'i's shoulder.

"You're under the Lumen Caligo's protection, miss. There is nothing to fear," said Cyrus in his best British accent.

Auli'i cracked a smile, shook her head and then leaned into Cyrus for comfort. Cyrus felt his cheeks go hot.

"The instruments are useless now. Even the compass is going in circles. We're getting some intense electromagnetic interference.

Kimo! Keep a close eye on the current! That's what we're using to stay on course now!"

"Aye aye, captain!"

"The haze is now a full-blown fog," said Cyrus.

"A keen observation, Mr. Lumen Caligo. I couldn't help but over-hear Auli'i's question, but I would like a straight answer. Will we be attacked when we get close enough?" asked Maurício.

Cyrus looked up and shrugged. "This is just as new for me as it is for you. Like I said though, if they hold me in such high regard because I am the 'Lumen Caligo', then no."

"Current is picking up!" Kimo yelled.

"By Saint John, he's right," said Maurício.

Cyrus felt the increase in speed. Auli'i looked up with worry. Kimo went back and forth from the port to the starboard, constantly leaning over to see the water. The fog was growing increasingly thick. The instruments were going haywire. Maurício turned on the engine and turned off the flood light. All of the sudden, a voice split through the eerie night.

"TURN BACK IMMEDIATELY. YOU HAVE VENTURED INTO SACRED WATERS."

They froze. They couldn't pinpoint where the voice was coming from. Maurício looked at Cyrus with a look of surprise like he hadn't actually expected to find something out there. He shifted the controls and kept going forward.

"I SAY AGAIN, TURN BACK. THIS IS YOUR FINAL WARNING."

"Into the unknown?" asked Maurício.

"Into the unknown," responded Cyrus.

"Kimo, tell them we're here on purpose," said Auli'i.

"We seek Aeolia!" said Kimo.

Silence. The current splashed against the boat. The wind whistled.

"I say again, we seek A—"

THUD!

Something landed on the roof of the cabin. Kimo froze in his tracks and slowly backed up.

THUD! THUD!

Two more. Auli'i's eyes widened and Maurício grabbed a handgun from behind the helm.

"If they dented Bessy, there will be hell to pay," muttered Maurício.

The strangers voice spoke, "You have ventured too far. State your purpose before we commandeer this ship."

"Oh, hell no. Auli'i take the helm. Cyrus, with me." Mauricio stepped outside of the cabin. Cyrus slipped on a jacket and followed Maurício. As Maurício took his first step, an arrow struck where his next step was going to be.

"YOU STAY THERE!"

There was a blur of motion, and then three Lumens surrounded them. One was in front of Kimo, the second was by Auli'i and the third stood before Maurício and Cyrus at the entrance of the cabin.

Dark cloaks covered them from head-to-toe, their wings folded behind them. All were pointing nocked arrows.

"You were given fair warning," said the mysterious voice. It wasn't coming from the three in front of them but seemed to come from above.

Cyrus looked up. A slow flapping sound became louder and louder. Then, like a phantom, he saw it. Huge white wings attached to a man who descended gradually until he landed in the middle of Bessy.

"I am Ori, son of Lucius. Why did you not turn back? How do you know about Aeolia? Speak quickly."

"We have business in Aeolia. We seek Marcella," said Cyrus.

"*Lady* Marcella. You must not know her well if you chose to forgo her title. Your insolence is not helping your case. What business do you have with her?"

"A personal one. She is not expecting us. However, I assure you our business with her is of the utmost importance!"

"Do you take me as a fool? What kind of guard would I be if I were to waltz a bunch of strangers into the presence of Lumen royalty? You could be assassins. You could be diseased. There are standards to entry."

Maurício sighed loudly. "He is the Lumen Caligo! Can we skip the formalities and get this show on the road. I feel Bessy picking up speed and with no bearing of where we are, I don't want to sink her."

The waves quieted. The wind itself seemed to stop.

"It can't be ..." whispered the Lumen guard closest to Cyrus.

All eyes were on him. The leader flapped his wings erratically, breaking the silence. Up and down his eyes scanned.

"The penalty for impersonating the Lumen Caligo is death. Is what he says true? Are you the Lumen Caligo?"

The ship lurched forward. The current was growing faster and the fog thickened.

Cyrus removed his jacket and let his wings unfurl. The wind had just enough bite to make him shiver. All four of the Lumens gasped and approached Cyrus in awe. They circled him, reaching out their hands to stroke his wings softly. They whispered, "It can't be," and "I never thought it would happen in my lifetime." Then, after they had walked a couple circles around him, they turned to each other and began whispering in an impromptu meeting. Cyrus took a moment to rest his wings.

He couldn't see the bow of the ship anymore. The fog and the speed at which they traveled had increased. Maurício had snuck back into the cabin and was furiously banging on the equipment, trying to will it back to life. Kimo and Auli'i were staring at the Lumens. Their wings poked out slightly just behind their necks. The white wings almost had a glow to them, even in the pale fog. Looking at his own wings, Cyrus noticed that they glowed a little bit more. He peered over his shoulder, and to his surprise, it was somewhat difficult to see the dark side of his wings. They seemed to absorb any and all light. Had they not been attached to him and three inches away from his face, he might have missed them.

"It is decided," began Ori. "We will guide this ship to our port island Luna, and then we will escort you..." Ori pointed at Cyrus. ...before the high council on Aeolia. The rest of you will remain on Luna until you have been assigned a labor task."

Dread crept into Cyrus. He looked over to Auli'i and Kimo who both mirrored the anxiety Cyrus felt.

Auli'i stepped forward with a fierce look in her eye.

"We will accompany the Lumen Caligo to Aeolia."

Ori circled Auli'i, his eyes inspecting her back. Once satisfied, he returned to the forefront of the other Lumens.

"No Terram has set foot in Aeolia for over 300 years. The last one was Sir Kaimana and he was—"

"The Virtus Lator to the Lumen Caligo? Yes, we know. Now, who do you think we are?" Auli'i gestured between herself and Kimo.

"You or the woman?" said Ori to Kimo.

"Both of us," interjected Auli'i. "Virtus means strength and virtue. We both have the mantle of Virtus Lator appointed to us from the Lumen Caligo. A mantle we ask that you honor and respect!"

"You must hail from Akhet," said Ori, looking at Kimo more closely now. The guards behind Ori sneered.

Ori looked to Cyrus for confirmation, to which he gave a nod.

"What about the commander of this vessel? Is he also a Virtus Lator?" asked one of the guards. There was obvious irony in his voice. The other guards snickered. Ori remained unchanged but allowed the question to hang in the air. This time it was Cyrus who spoke up.

"No. He is a sailor and our guide. He volunteered his time and vessel to escort the Lumen Caligo to Aeolia. I ask that he be treated with respect and allowed to return back to Bermuda when he pleases."

"I can only promise he will be treated with respect. Our laws prohibit leaving once you arrive. If you hadn't noticed, the current is too. strong now. He couldn't get out even if he tried. He is caught in the swirling eye. Now, let's be quick. We don't have much time. Have your captain follow my lieutenant's lead. I will fly ahead to scout a path."

With that, Ori and two of the Lumens whooshed off the ship and disappeared into the night. The third guard flew ahead of the ship in view. His wings acted as a beacon to follow as shimmers of light reflected off of them with each flap.

Maurício kicked everyone out of the cabin 'to concentrate. It reminded Cyrus of how Martin would turn down the music when they were driving and got closer to a new location. It helped him 'see better. Cyrus wondered where he was at that moment.

The current continued to speed up. They followed the Lumen guard for what seemed an eternity. All three of them stay glued to the constant flapping of his wings. Seeing a Lumen in action was something that excited Cyrus.

I'll learn how to run first before I learn how to fly ... I still haven't mastered walking.

The current carried them faster and faster until the four Lumens made a reverse letter I,' curving them to the left. Maurício upped the engines power.

"Interesting …"said Cyrus.

"What?" asked Kimo.

"They were in a line. One could see the other just in front of them, kind of like an assembly line."

"Impressive."

"Smart," said Auli'i.

"Common sense," said Maurício, overhearing them.

'Common sense isn't so common'. That was one of Martian's favorite sayings.

The fog began to thin. At the same time, the sound of moving water grew louder. Then, like pulling back a curtain, the fog cleared.

Cyrus, Auli'i and Kimo audibly gasped. All around them, islands flickered with lights from torches. Like Christmas lights from afar, the lights danced with the wind. The most eye catching of them all was the biggest island in the middle. It towered above them. They arched their necks upward to take it all in. It was like a giant wall, blocking everything behind it. Cyrus shivered.

Ori and his three guards continued to guide the boat to the left as the current picked up speed. The Lumens guided them closer and closer until they reached a nearby island with flickering lights.

Two of the Lumens landed on the island in a narrow strip between more shadows. The closer they drew to the island, the more the shadows became shapes. Then, the shapes became distinguishable. Auli'i gasped.

"Ships ..." said Kimo.

Abandoned ships across the beach as far as they could see in the light of a crescent moon. No dock. No people. Just ships of all sizes.

Cyrus felt like he had just entered a scene from a horror movie.

"I'm not stranding my boat here. Kids, jump off and ask them if there is a dock on the island. I don't want to scratch Bessy up," barked Maurício.

Kimo and Auli'i immediately moved toward Cyrus and the edge.

Cyrus froze in fear. He had 'swam' in the ocean during the day but jumping into the ocean in the dark night... that was terrifying.

Without a word, Kimo jumped into the ocean, completely vanishing under the water. He reappeared and beckoned for Cyrus to jump.

Cyrus looked at Auli'i in terror. Auli'i clasped hands with Cyrus, and before he could think about it, Auli'i tugged Cyrus over the edge. The water was warm. Cyrus lost sight of everything in the darkness. Fear pumped through his very being. Then, a split second after he'd landed into the water, Kimo's strong hands caught him.

"Sole! That's bright!" said Kimo.

A light encircled the water around them. Cyrus looked up at the ship but noticed it wasn't the flood light. The light was coming from Cyrus. Cyrus looked at his drenched wings. The white side of his feathers pulsed a soft warm light. The water seemed to react with the light Cyrus emulated and spread out in an expanding circle. Auli'i and Kimo's faces were easily visible with this newly ignited source of light. They looked at Cyrus with surprise and awe.

Kimo and Auli'i swam to shore, dragging Cyrus with them.

Cyrus had tried to be useful and paddle but quickly tired out. The high from his adrenaline was ebbing away.

Is the light taking up some of my energy, too?

The twins helped Cyrus get to his feet as they reached the sand. Cyrus rubbed his eyes clear and looked up to see the four Lumens looking at him with absolute awe. They slowly approached him as if he were a sleeping baby. Ori spoke first.

"Although there are still tests to verify your claim as the Lumen Caligo, I, for one, believe you without a shadow of a doubt." Ori clasped his hands together and bowed with the same strange gesture Auli'i and Kimo's father had done-ring fingers bent together, the rest outstretched. It was very peculiar.

Cyrus nodded, too tired and wet to attempt the gesture. Kimo stepped forward.

"Do you have a dock? Maurício is asking."

"He'll have to anchor here. We don't have any docks and as you can see in the moonlight, we don't have much space. We have already started sending a couple of the wooden ships into the eye to make space."

What the heck is this eye Ori keeps talking about? Cyrus thought to himself.

Kimo turned to leave.

"I wouldn't try to swim, if I were you. You're lucky enough that you made it when you jumped off the boat. I'll send one of my lieu-tenants."

He motioned to one of the Lumens who whooshed towards Maurício. Watching Ori and the guards fly had been fascinating.

The control they had over their bodies was something else. When they flew forward, they assumed a superman-like position. When they hovered in the air, they went into a vertical position like they were about to stand. Standing ... something Cyrus still had difficulty with. Flying seemed like a far away dream. His body was so weak and frail, it was hard to imagine getting to the point where his wings weren't glorified ankle weights attached to his back.

The floodlight got closer and closer to shore until the boat ran aground. Maurício cut the engines and then hopped off his beloved Bessy. He must have misjudged the distance in the darkness because as he hit the ground he went headfirst into knee-high water. Spitting and cursing, he quickly got up and made his way to the group, wide-eyed and on edge.

"This current is unnatural. What is causing it?" asked Maurício.

Ori looked annoyed. "The great eye, as I have been saying. You cannot see it very well during the nighttime, but during the day ... it will all make sense. Now, more guards are on the way to fly you three up to Aeolia. While we wait, whatever possessions you two bear from the outside world, I ask you to give to me," said Ori looking only at Auli'i and Kimo.

"Why not me?" asked Cyrus.

"You are the Lumen Caligo. You are the exception to the rule. After all, you were the one who made it."

Auli'i and Kimo complied without question. This surprised Cyrus.

All Auli'i had on her person was a bracelet and some sea shells she'd collected in Bermuda. Kimo pulled out some sand and a banana peel. The rest of their stuff, including Cyrus', was on the boat.

"What about me? When will I get my transport to this Aeolia?" asked Maurício.

Ori gave a sideways glance to the guards. "You will remain here. I will only bring the Lumen Caligo and the two Terrams who invoked the Virtus Lator. If Cyrus' claim turns out to be true, all Latores bound to the Lumen Caligo have an exemption to certain laws prohibiting entrance to our citadel."

"So, I'm just going to sit around twiddling my thumbs until you get back?"

"No," said one of the guards with a smirk. "You will be assigned work from one of our taskmasters until we decide what to do with you." Cyrus really didn't like the sound of that. Maurício backed away slowly.

"The guards are arriving. Do you need anything? Once we go to Aeolia, you may be there awhile," said Ori.

In the dark sky, Cyrus could see four more Lumens coming from above.

"I do, actually. Will you be flying me to the city?" asked Cyrus.

"Would you like me to?"

"Yes. But first, could you please take me back to the boat. I want to grab some things."

The air suddenly turned colder. Ori perked up and inhaled deeply.

"Let's be quick. Rain is coming. Flying will be difficult enough carrying you. No need to add more weight."

With that, Ori spread his wings open, startling everyone, and rushed forward, grabbing Cyrus away from Auli'i.

"Cyrus!" she shouted.

"I'm all good! I'll see you in Aeolia!"

The twins vanished in the dark. In quick succession, Ori leveled out and lowered onto Bessy.

What a rush.

"What do you need, Lumen Caligo? Point and I will retrieve it."

"Green ... backpack ... cabin," panted Cyrus.

Ori was almost as fast on foot as he was in the air. In a flash, he went into the cabin, grabbed the bag and handed it to Cyrus.

"A word of caution, if I may, Lumen Caligo?"

Cyrus nodded.

"You are the bridge between many things. One of them is light and darkness. In our culture, we associate light and darkness with knowledge and wisdom. We have kept ourselves in the dark since the Isolation Order was made. We have had no advancements come from the outside world that we haven't immediately disposed of. In these past 300 years or so, we have grown accustomed to being in darkness ..." Cyrus nodded his head, intrigued.

"My point is this ... Don't shine a light so bright that it blinds those living in the dark ... Take it slow— a little bit at a time. People are naturally resistant to change."

Cyrus put the backpack on and nodded.

"Make sure you hang on ... We're going up."

Aeolia ... Mother ... Here I come.

THE ATRIUM

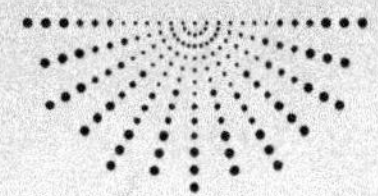

ORI CRADLED CYRUS, and with a whoosh, accelerated into the air back toward the beach. Ori whistled as they flew over and the other Lumens launched into the air with Kimo and Auli'i. It was a sight to behold.

Auli'i was carried by a tall Lumen while four Lumens carried Kimo by each of his limbs. He looked like a tied hog. Cyrus chuckled.

As they flew over, Cyrus heard a commotion. Cyrus could just make out Maurício running back towards his boat, three Lumens chasing him.

"Cyrus! CYRUS! CYR—" They swarmed Maurício.

Panic filled Cyrus. In all of this, he had neglected Maurício.

"Stop! Don't hurt him!" screamed Cyrus. It was futile over the wind. Maurício fought the other Lumens as the scene faded from view. Cyrus squirmed in Ori's arms, trying to catch another glimpse but the darkness engulfed the scene.

"What will happen to him?!"

"Just what they said ... He will be assigned to a taskmaster and put to work."

"Work? What kind of work?"

"Crop yielding, weaving, tool making, fishing ... Those tend to be the usual tasks assigned."

"What's the unusual?"

"Maintenance on the spire," he responded with a serious look.

"Do I even want to know?"

Ori shook his head.

"When you say taskmaster... Is Maurício a slave now?"

"Lumen Caligo. Cyrus ... May I suggest you prepare yourself emotionally and mentally to enter Aeolia. Shortly, you will be summoned before the three dukes of Aeolia. Arch Duke Winston Weatherford will be most pleased to receive you to our city."

Cyrus tongue caught in his throat, and he started coughing. Ori patted him on the back.

"No dying in my arms, OK?" said Ori with a smirk.

Cyrus recomposed himself.

Ori ascended at a gradual angle. They entered a cloud and Cyrus shivered as the moisture gathered all around him. Cyrus wrapped his wings around his body. The sound of moving water grew softer as they flew higher.

"We're about to arrive, hang on tight."

As they exited the cloud, Ori barrel rolled and flapped his wings in quick succession. Discombobulated, Cyrus looked forward and gasped. The cloud had cleared revealing what looked like a mountain in the sky. On this mountain was a city that seemed to have been cut out of stone. Giant bonfires illuminated the extremities of the mountain on each side. Gazing upward as high as he could crane his neck, Cyrus saw what looked like a lighthouse at the top of the city.

An enormous bonfire filled the center of the tower as clouds circled like vultures.

They continued to fly upward into the higher part of Aeolia where, even in the moonlight, you could tell it was better taken care of and more illustrious than the lower part of the island. Underneath the lighthouse were an array of beautiful buildings sculpted from the mountain. They reminded Cyrus of the Ancient Greece section from 6th grade.

Guess public school isn't completely useless.

Cyrus could see a couple blurs of white circling the city. Suddenly, Cyrus heard a *whoosh* and on their right appeared another Lumen. He wore a contraption around his eyes that looked like goggles. His wings were in a thin black cloth that masked their white glow. Everything he wore was black, which had aided in his sudden appearance.

"Captain Ori. Back from the perimeter so soon? What have you got there?"

"Good evening, Herald. I carry precious cargo that requires immediate attention from the dukes."

"It is the middle of the night, Captain Ori. Can this wait until morning?"

"It probably could ... but I don't think the dukes will want to. Now, what I am going to tell you must only be told to the dukes personally- not their butlers, not their wives ... the dukes only. Do you understand?"

Herald nodded

"Behold, the Lumen Caligo has arrived."

Herald gasped and swerved in the air. "Is it true?!"

Cyrus slowly uncurled himself. The light side of his wings contrasted against the dark side. Herald's mouth gaped open and his eyes shifted back and forth rapidly like he couldn't take it in fast enough.

He lifted his goggles to make sure.

"I'll get right on it, Captain. We will meet you in the Atrium." With a huge flap of his wings, Herald zoomed ahead and quickly faded into the maze of Aeolia.

"Will everyone be this amazed to see me?"

"Most likely. You are the Lumen Caligo, after all. Now, hang on tight."

They rapidly approached a bonfire towards the top where the architecture was most elaborate. Cyrus could not wait to see this place in the light.

Ori swooped down, and then, like the sails on Bessy, he opened his wings and caught all the wind to come to a soft landing. Small droplets of rain began to splat on the stone surface that seemed to gleam with a silver sheen. Cyrus looked up and saw the clouds move swiftly across the sky, covering what little light was coming from the stars and the moon. The wind howled and the rain began to fall more steadily.

Cyrus heard a thud behind him and quickly whirled around to see Kimo standing up quickly after being dropped. The four Lumens put their hands on their knees and panted deeply.

How much does Kimo weigh?

The other Lumen landed softly next to Cyrus, gently setting Auli'i down. He made the bent-finger greeting and then whispered something to Auli'i.

His face was shadowed by his cloak. The moment he finished, he flew off into the night sky. Auli'i looked around wide-eyed. Kimo did the same.

"How was your flight?" asked Cyrus.

"Serene," said Auli'i.

"Agonizing," said Kimo, shaking his head. "They dropped me ... twice."

Ori turned and headed straight toward the four panting Lumens.

Cyrus couldn't hear the hushed reprimand, but from the looks on their faces ... It wasn't pleasant.

Auli'i slipped something into Cyrus' hand. Cyrus felt a small piece of paper. Auli'i and Kimo leaned in close to Cyrus.

"What's it say?" asked Auli'i softly.

Pretend you don't know me.

Cyrus' heart beat a little faster as he inspected the hand writing. Auli and Kimo looked at Cyrus with anticipation. They were all thinking the same thing.

As soon as Ori finished whatever he was saying, he quickly pointed his finger upwards and the four Lumens quickly disappeared into the night sky. Ori rapidly approached the three and beckoned them follow him. Cyrus stuffed the paper deep into his pocket.

The rain began to pick up even more. Cyrus felt himself growing heavier as his wings got wetter. The altitude was slightly higher, too, so Cyrus shivered from the cold. Auli'i wrapped her arms around Cyrus. Kimo wrapped his arms around Auli'i.

"Forgive the delay. Those were our newest perimeter guards. If I didn't correct them right then and there, they wouldn't have learned a thing. Now, please follow me and let's get out of this rain."

Ori's pace was brisk initially but he slowed down when he perceived Cyrus progressively walking slower. Auli'i and Kimo supported him on both sides.

"Are you injured, Lumen Caligo?"

"You could say I'm recovering.. "

The rain picked up, the wind howled and the bonfires flickered and hissed.

"What did the Lumen carrying you say?" asked Cyrus under his breath.

"Right pocket. When the guards aren't looking," whispered Auli'i.

"That's it?"

Auli'i nodded as she looked around, taking in the surroundings.

Everything was carved out of white-ish grey stone. The deeper they walked into the city, the more elaborate the architecture became. The road was leading them to a looming shadow with the giant lighthouse.

They appeared to be walking on a cobblestone road. It had intricate swirls carved into each individual stone. The pattern looked vine-like and each art engraving connected all the stones on the road, forming a hypnotic symmetrical design.

The surrounding building's designs were just as impressive. Large stone pillars supported what Cyrus could only describe as a Greek temple. The archways just below the roofs displayed carved murals that Cyrus could only see if there was a bonfire close by. He assumed that each one had a unique set of figurines and stories associated with the carvings.

Well-kept vines slithered down some buildings, giving them an enhanced feel of luxury and care. They matched the look of the cobblestone road. The deeper they went, the more elaborate the carvings and the vines became.

They reached a clearing where the buildings stopped and an imposing edifice stood in front of them. Directly under it was the lighthouse-looking structure. Cyrus looked back behind him and noticed they had essentially reached the mountain's peak. Everything revolved around this building. Looking back, Cyrus could see a gradual curve. It was like they were on top of a sphere.

The main entrance was guarded by two Lumens dressed extravagantly. They had long, flowing white cloaks all the way down to the ground with hoods that covered their faces completely. All along their cloaks, feathers adorned the edges. The feathers were laid in an intricate pattern that created what looked like triangles at the edge. However, as Cyrus approached, it almost seemed like an optical illusion. The triangles turned into circles from a different angle. It was fascinating.

Their wings fully outstretched to the sky while holding a solid silver spear that was as tall as their wings— easily 7 feet tall. Cyrus wondered how they were able to hold that pose. He couldn't get his wings that high. Even outstretching them as far as he could, he was only able to hold the pose for a couple of seconds. Holding that pose must have been exhausting.

The Atrium was perfectly round. Cyrus could see two other entries from afar. One on the right, and the other on the left. Each had two guards in front dressed in the same attire.

They approached the guards closest to them. They guarded an entryway made of stone. It confused Cyrus as he looked for a knob or keyhole that would get them inside.

"Halt."

Cyrus couldn't tell which one had spoken.

"State your purpose for entering the Atrium during the witching hour," said a different voice.

"A meeting of the utmost importance between the head dukes of Aeolia and ... the Lumen Caligo."

The wings of one of the guards faltered for a split second, and Cyrus heard a soft gasp.

"Proof is required for access to the Atrium during the witching hour," said the first voice.

Cyrus finally pinpointed who was talking. It was the guard on the left.

Ori stood to the side and gestured to Cyrus. Cyrus slowly walked forward and looked from the guard on the left to the guard on the right. Everything was silent except for the patter of the rain against the silver cobblestone road.

With effort, Cyrus unfurled his wings. As his wings unsheathed themselves, the white on the inside of his wings shone through. With as much effort as he could muster, he extended his wet wings and lifted them as high as he could. He did a quick circle also revealing the black on the backside of his wings. Cyrus felt his temple vein throb.

"Breathe, Cyrus..." whispered Auli'i.

Cyrus exhaled loudly and felt dizzy. He faced the guards once more after doing a full circle showing both the back and the front of his wings. His wings pulsated a light like the flash of a camera before his wings dropped and he lost his balance. The guards looked on in complete and utter disbelief. Auli'i and Kimo were immediately at his side to catch him.

Mental note. Thank Kimo and Auli'i more.

They truly were great friends, and he would be bruised head to toe if it weren't for their watchful eyes and quick hands.

Cyrus breathed heavily and then looked back up at the guards.

Their wings remained up in high alert but they had dropped to one knee in reverent respect. Both had their spear resting against their torso while making the bent ring-finger gesture.

They spoke in unison, the emotion audible, "Lumen Caligo, to which this Atrium was built, light the way. Be our sword. Be our hilt."

They stood up, grabbed their spears and inserted them into two holes by the doorway. Both of them turned and whistled a tune to the other guards who, from afar, appeared to be doing the same thing. It seemed like a cadence. The guards turned their spears perfectly in sync. It was as pleasant to the ears as it was mesmerizing to watch.

The left guard turned his spear clockwise while the guard on the right turned his counterclockwise. As they turned, there were a series of pops and clicks like a key in an old lock. Cyrus could hardly believe his eyes. It was like another optical illusion. Either the lighthouse was rotating or the entire land mass they were standing on was rotating The lighthouse began to get taller and taller as the entrance spun faster and faster.

Finally, it began to slow. A giant opening began to appear where the wall of stone had been. Slowly, it filled the entire entrance and came to a loud thud. A series of rapid whistles filled the air and the two guards reversed the way they twisted their spears and removed them. The other guards in the distance did the same.

Heavy panting filled the air between the two guards. Their wings never dropped. The two guards stood up tall and then beckoned to Cyrus. Kimo and Auli'i helped Cyrus move forward.

"NO!" said one of the guards defiantly. "The Lumen Caligo must enter on his own and then invite those he deems worthy!"

Cyrus nodded to Kimo and Auli'i, then stood on his own two feet. The two guards stepped aside in unison while making the bent ring finger gesture. They lowered their wings as he passed.

The hallway was about 10 feet long and he could see that the inside of the Atrium was already well lit. Cyrus' jaw dropped as he entered.

The Atrium was an enormous full dome. The entire Atrium was covered in beautifully painted scenes. There were paintings of Lumens with golden covered wings holding long spears and swords in battle.

They flew high in the sky with wings outstretched and shoulders wide and strong.

Mirrors decorated each scene, illuminating and enhancing them.

There was a radiant sun glowing brightly above every depiction.

Even the entire floor was one giant mural of the sun with its flaming rays extending to all three entrances.

The light that filled the room was a warm glow. Upon further inspection, Cyrus saw that light was coming from the top of the Atrium. He could visibly see rays of light trickling down, bouncing from one end of the Atrium to the other. It took him a little while but Cyrus finally had the *aha* moment.

The bonfire that was above them was surrounded by mirrors pointing in every direction. The mirrors were angled downward in such a way that the mirrors below would reflect the light to the other mirrors below them. The light filling the room was relatively dim compared to a room lit by electricity. But for the dead of night, in the middle of the Atlantic, it was impressive.

The light converged into the center of the Atrium where there was a circular crystal slab. In the middle of the slab were four cylindrical spires protruding from the ground with platforms on top. They were perfectly round, exhibiting flawless workmanship. Each one was a different height that gradually led to the highest point at the center. All of them were translucent.

The smell was earthy and the air felt electric. Cyrus' arm hairs stood on edge.

"Cyrus..." came Auli'i's voice from afar. "Invite us in. Mahalo."

Right.

"The Lumen Caligo formally invites Auli'i and Kimo Fualautoalasi, Virtus Latores to the Lumen Caligo, to enter the Atrium of Aeolia." Cyrus' voice echoed, carrying to every inch of space and seemed to rise up until it dissipated through the flames of the bonfire above him.

Talk about an acoustically pleasing venue.

The guards outside made a synchronized clang with their spears, and then Cyrus heard Kimo and Auli'i's footsteps rapidly approach from the hall. The moment they cleared the hallway, they stopped and gasped.

Cyrus didn't know what to do next except admire the paintings sprawled across the Atrium walls. Even in the paintings, that odd hand gesture was made. Cyrus wanted some answers.

"The Lumen Caligo formally invites Captain Ori to enter the Atrium."

Another synchronized clang from the spears rang out followed by footsteps. Ori emerged, lowered his hood and bowed his head with eyes closed and made the bent ring finger gesture. Cyrus mimicked the hand gesture as Ori approached.

"Ori, what is this called and what does it mean?" asked Cyrus.

Ori seemed surprised at Cyrus' question. "It is the Omniscius Salutatio or the 'all-knowing greeting. It is done in various degrees. One hand is sufficient for all Lumens, Caligos or Terrams. Two hands are customary towards the Lumen Caligo or someone of high rank in our society. It's usually done as an apology or, in your case, to show immense respect to an individual."

Kimo and Auli'i gathered around Ori.

"Each finger represents the different nations of the world. The thumb represents the Terrams, the flightless people who know of our ways. They may be wingless but, like the thumb on my hand, they are strong and dexterous.

Cyrus looked at Kimo and Auli'i who shrugged. This seemed to be new information for them as well.

"The pointer finger represents the Caligos. It is believed that there was darkness before there was light. Just like we hold up our pointer finger to gesture the number one, it is believed that the Caligos were the first people to be born with the gift of flight." Ori lifted his middle and pointer fingers.

"The middle finger represents my nation, the Lumens. The tallest of the fingers, it represents the heavens and the sun from which we receive the light of day. It is from this light— physical and metaphorical— that we strive to rise up and be a standard for all other nations to see."

Ori pointed to his pinky.

"The pinky represents all human beings that are not a part of, or unaware, of our nations. Those outside the jurandum. This comprises the majority of humanity. They remain separate from the Terrams, the Caligos and the Lumens by design. The only thing that connects us to them ..." said Ori now pointing at his bent ring finger, "is the Lumen Caligo."

"Why is that finger bent?" asked Cyrus.

"Out of respect. It has been said since the days of the Egyptians, that the ring finger contains the vena amoris. This vein goes from the ring finger all the way to the heart. This vein only exists in Lumens, Caligos and you ... It is why wedding rings are worn on the ring finger. You represent the light and the darkness within every person's heart. You are the embodiment of good and evil. Your very existence is meant to guide all of humanity towards the lofty goal of world order and balance. Our physical selves and our body language can convey more respect than any amount of words. We have bowed the ring finger as a sign of respect since the first Lumen Caligo and we will bow it until the last."

Ori put both of his hands to his forehead in the Omniscius Salutatio and bowed

Cyrus put his right hand up awkwardly in front of himself and half curtsied. Kimo snorted. Auli'i giggled. Cyrus felt his face flush. Ori looked up.

"If I may, Lumen Caligo, for you to return the greeting, simply put your left hand into the Omniscius Salutatio and place it under your chin like this. If you wish to convey respect, you will accompany the Omniscius Salutatio with a bow. The lower the bow, the more respect you show."

Cyrus tried again. He put his left hand under his chin in the Omniscius Salutatio and bowed at a 45° angle towards Ori. Ori quickly resumed his bow at a full 90°.

"PERMISSION TO ENTER THE ATRIUM!" boomed a voice from one of the other entrances.

All four of them whipped around, startled by the voice.

"Ask who seeks entrance," whispered Ori. "Also, you need to get to the top of that pillar." Ori pointed at the tallest pillar.

"Why?" asked Cyrus.

"It was built for the Lumen Caligo to address Lumens in the Atrium."

"Do I have to?"

"It has been foretold."

"Like a prophecy?" Cyrus asked with a hint of sarcasm.

"Yes."

Cyrus gave a sigh. There was no way he could get up there on his own.

"Fly me up there, please."

Ori nodded and grabbed Cyrus by the shoulders. With two hard flaps of his wings, Ori rose up into the sky and placed Cyrus gently on the top pillar. There was a small slit in the center of the spire that went about three feet deep. Ori promptly returned to the ground and looked up at Cyrus and smiled. He then looked at the twins.

"The bottom pillar is for the Virtus Latores. In the past, it has usually been one but I think there is enough room for the both of you. Go, join Cyrus on the pillars so the dukes will know of your status."

The twins scurried to the shortest pillar. It was about two feet taller than Kimo. Kimo lifted Auli'i up and then Auli'i pulled on Kimo with all her might until Kimo made it to the top of the pillar as well. Cyrus suspected that wasn't the first time they had done something like that.

"WHO SEEKS ENTRY INTO THE ATRIUM?" yelled Cyrus.

"Arch Duke Winston Weatherford with escort," said the voice.

"High Duke Gabriel Bradford with escort," said another on the other entrance.

"Duke Fredrick Evynwood with escort," said a third voice from the entrance they had just come through.

Cyrus looked at Ori.

"Grant permission to all parties," he whispered.

"PERMISSION GRANTED TO ALL PARTIES!"

The melodic echo swirled around them once more.

Synchronized clangs from the spears rung throughout the Atrium, adding to the swirling noises that seemed to harmonize throughout the dome. Footsteps slowly approached from all sides.

The three dukes came into view, each in a lavish robe. The Arch Duke seemed to have solid gold decorating his robe while the other two had silver. Their wings were sprawled out wide with their arms opened skyward, like they were praising Cyrus. The duke's faces were exposed while their escorts had their hoods up. Smiles adorned the duke's faces.

Duke Gabriel Bradford was a tall red-headed man with an equally red beard. He stood tall and proud above everyone in the room. Along with the silver lining on his clothes, he had a scarlet sash around his waist.

Duke Fredrick Evynwood was a short and rounder man with pudgy cheeks. He wore a serious expression and cradled his neck up high as if he were trying to squeeze every inch of height from his round frame.

Arch Duke Winston Weatherford had a tanner look to him, compared to the pale skin of the other dukes. His eyes were slightly slanted and his head was shaved and wrinkled with age. He seemed to ooze confidence and walked like a man accustomed to power.

Their smiles grew increasingly more excited as they approached the center pillars. Cyrus looked at Auli'i and Kimo who clearly had their guards up as much as him. Cyrus decided he would run with this whole 'prophecy' charade.

Cyrus unfurled his wings and made another full 360° turn. He exhaled softly but forcefully as he held out his arms and wings. The dukes and their escorts halted. The duke's expression had turned from smiles to looks of awe. The Arch Duke smiled even more intently.

The dukes made the Omniscius Salutatio with both hands and bowed deeply. The escorts removed their hoods and exposed their faces. Duke Fredrick Evynwood's had a shaved head covered in swirling tattoos. Cold blue eyes adorned his face. He bowed.

Duke Gabriel Bradford's escort was a short brunette teenager with piercing green eyes that glowed like emeralds. She bowed.

Arch Duke Winston Weatherford's escort had a familiar jaw line, blue eyes and freckles on his left cheek that formed a perfect triangle.

Cyrus' eyes widened and the twins softly gasped as their eyes met his.

He then bowed.

Martian ...

12

THE DUKES

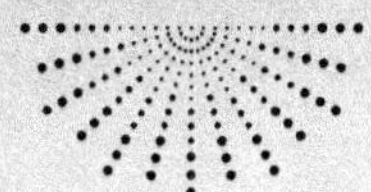

"L UMEN CALIGO. WE HONOR YOUR presence here in the Atrium of Aeolia, our humble city among the clouds. May I have the honor of your name?" said Arch Duke Winston putting both hands into the Omniscius Salutatio. Martin followed suit and bowed deeply.

"Uhh ... Cyrus ... Cyrus Ganymede." Cyrus returned the Omniscius Salutatio with a 45° bow. He felt himself struggling to contain his emotions.

Why didn't Martian contact me? Where has he been this whole time? Why is he next to the Arch Duke? Why do they have the same last name?

"Osiris? Like the Egyptian God of the underworld?"

"Not quite. My name is Cyrus ... just Cyrus. It uhh ... is special and has many meanings."

Cyrus felt Kimo and Auli'i's eyes fall upon him. He knew what had left his mouth was not eloquent at all. Cyrus had no idea what to say so he decided to focus on the twins.

"These are my Virtus Latores. Kimo and Auli'i Fualautoalasi from the Hawaiian islands."

All three of the dukes and their escorts turned to the twins and with one hand, they made the Omniscius Salutatio. Their bow was substantially less, especially the green eyed girl who only inclined her head slightly.

Kimo and Auli'i returned the gesture. Kimo couldn't quite get his finger to bend completely so it stuck out at a 90° angle. Auli'i's finger trembled.

"Is the raven close by?" asked Arch Duke Winston, looking up and around the Atrium.

Cyrus looked directly at Martin. He had no idea how to answer or what that even meant. Martin's expression remained neutral, but ever so slightly, he nodded his head.

"Well ..." He decided to use a technique Martin was extremely

good at ... redirection. "He is out there somewhere, however, that is not the primary concern right now. I would like to get to know you a little bit better."

"Right you are! Allow us to formally introduce ourselves. I am Arch Duke Winston Weatherford of Aeolia and its surrounding provinces, leader and caretaker of the Lumens in your absence, my liege. With me, I have my eldest son, Sir Martin Weatherford, who has recently returned to us after 12 years of diligent service abroad. His return was followed by good fortune as you arrived shortly after."

Cyrus choked a little bit.

"I am High Duke Gabriel Bradford," said the red-headed Duke charismatically. His voice boomed throughout the Atrium. Cyrus instantly liked him. "I am the high general of the Lumen Air Force and commander of the duke's escorts and the Lumen Caligo's protective unit. I also enforce the Isolation Order issued by the former Lumen Caligo. With me, is Lady Marianne Evynwood, daughter of Duke Fredrick Evynwood and the second youngest to ever be permitted into the LC protective unit. Second only to the great and terrible Sir Martin Weatherford."

Admiration was very clear between the two. Martin returned the gesture with a deep bow and single handed Omniscius Salutatio.

"I am Duke Fredrick Evynwood." His voice was high pitched and squealy. "Auxiliary to Arch Duke Winston Weatherford as well as the chief accountant of the royal Lumen treasury and director of resources on Acolia. With me, is my escort Karlovic Jocovic, who's ancestor, Vladimir Jocovic, served as the Lumen Lator to the previous Lumen Caligo." Duke Fredrick gave a wide smile that rippled across his face as he bowed in Cyrus' direction. Karlovic stared at Cyrus coldly as he bowed and gave the Omniscius Salutatio.

Cyrus was getting whiplash with all of the names and how many times they would bow and make the Omniscius Salutatio— a sign he had trouble saying let alone making. Thank goodness for Ori's crash course.

Cyrus made the Omniscius Salutatio and gestured to each duke in the order they had presented themselves. He racked his brain for the best way to approach the situation. Water dripped from his wings and he could hear the rain and thunder raging outside. Cyrus felt exhausted so he decided to keep them talking about themselves.

"Thank you so much for receiving me. I confess, I am rather ignorant in the ways of the Lumens which is why I have journeyed from uhhhh... afar to learn. Tell me, what is your expectation of me?"

There was a murmur of approval from all three of the dukes, and Arch Duke Winston spoke first.

"Tell me this, Lumen Caligo... You have your Virtus Latores from Akhet, or, as you call them, 'The Hawaiian islands' but did you come from Akhet? Where do you come from?"

Cyrus looked passed Arch Duke Winston to Martin. His face strained and looked urgent. It was the, 'keep your mouth shut' look. It reminded him of the eggplant incident with Ms. Palermo.

"I met the twins on my journey across the United States by sheer chance. Some may call it fate. But no, I have not been to Hawai'i ... or, as you call it ... Akhet."

"As we call it or they do ... Whoever landed there first gets to name it, don't you agree, Lumen Caligo?"

The question felt like a trap. With how little Cyrus knew, his only option was to agree-but he didn't want to.

"It depends on who resides there at the time. Generally, yes. First one there gets to do the naming."

"Our ancestors passed through those great islands thousands of years ago and gave them the name which all Lumens, Caligos and Terrams know it by ... Akhet. Names are a powerful thing, Lumen Caligo. It is how we inform or confuse the world," the Arch Duke said with a smile.

"Now, to answer your question," interjected High Duke Gabriel Bradford as he shot the Arch Duke a serious look.

"Yes, yes ... Forgive my geographical semantics. My intent was only to inform." The Arch Duke bowed his head and took a small step backward.

"What we expect of you, great and noble Lumen Caligo, is a heading," began High Duke Gabriel. "The last word of the previous Lumen Caligo was the Isolation Order. Everyone under the jurandum was ordered to return to their designated lands to wait and regroup until the next Lumen Caligo was born. All outside knowledge, culture and thinking was to remain separate from us so we could preserve our way of life. Are you familiar with the histories of your past selves, Lumen Caligo?"

Cyrus shook his head.

"Well ... Allow me to tell you about the one prior to you. 350 years ago, the three great nations were at the brink of war with each other. Sir Francis Etherington, the Lumen Caligo from a generation past, worked tirelessly to build peace between the Lumens, Caligos and Terrams. At every turn, his efforts were thwarted and in an effort to preserve as much life as possible, he issued a decree called the Isolation Order."

Cyrus looked at Auli'i and Kimo. They were as enthralled in the story as he was.

"The only problem was, no instruction ever came. Sir Francis Etherington vanished without a trace, leaving the three nations in a standstill and very much divided. Although this is the 'short ver-sion' of the story, I tell it to you, Lumen Caligo, so you can begin to understand your history. Your arrival marks the beginning of a new era for us. Your arrival, I hope, signifies the rebuilding of our great nations. Closing the rift that has permeated us for so long."

"The wound runs deep," said the high pitched voice of Duke

Fredrick. He cleared his throat and continued. "Let us not forget the negligence of the Caligos as our history has shown. The Lumen Caligo's shadow must always be a stone's throw away, if not closer. The lack of this is what led to the previous Lumen Caligo's disappearance."

"Yes, but time heals all wounds, wouldn't you say, Duke Fredrick?" asked Arch Duke Winston.

"But of course ... Arch Duke Winston ... of course!" squealed Duke Fredrick nervously.

"Let us not forget our own inability... The Lumen Lator failed in his duty just as the Caligo Lator and Virtus Lator did in theirs. All three have paid an extraordinarily high price," said High Duke Gabriel towards Duke Fredrick.

High Duke Gabriel glanced over at Duke Fredrick with a look of disapproval and then glanced at Duke Fredrick's escort. Pity filled his eyes.

"Hair represents spiritual strength amongst us Lumens," began High Duke Gabriel. "The Jacovic family is the only family who shaves their heads in the entire kingdom. They then have the mothers tattoo their child's heads every month, starting at the first month of life. The practice continues until their 18th birthday. Then, and only then, are their mothers no longer obligated to perform the penance practice."

Arch Duke Winston and Duke Fredrick bowed their heads.

Cyrus glanced over at Karlovic. His eyes remained unchanged: cold, penetrating and focused.

Does he even blink?

"Who began the practice?" asked Cyrus, looking in Karlovic's direction. Cyrus was frankly scared of the man.

"My great-great-great grandfather ... After the Virtus Lator disappeared and the Caligo Lator killed himself," said Karlovic flatly. His voice was as cold as his look. It seemed to physically make the room colder with how it hissed.

"The Jacovic family has a very straight forward philosophy. They have endured generations because of it. Karlovic is also the one who trained Lady Marianne. If you wouldn't mind, my lady, could you teach the Lumen Caligo the Jacovic moto?" asked Duke Fredrick.

The young lady nodded and stepped forward. She was small and looked a little older than Cyrus. The fierce green eyes mimicked those of Karlovic.

"Life is pain. The strongest welcome it," she said. Her voice was raspy but still feminine. She quickly stepped back after she'd finished.

Her eyes never strayed from Cyrus but remained unflinchingly focused. Cyrus didn't know who was scarier... her or Karlovic. Probably Karlovic. He was bigger and foreboding. Cyrus couldn't take him in a fight ...

But Kimo could.

"Life is not all pain, though," began High Duke Gabriel. "It is also meant to be enjoyed. Otherwise, what reason do we have to work hard?"

Duke Fredrick puffed up as big as he could.

"If I may ..." began Arch Duke Winston. Everyone fell silent. "Our entire world has anxiously awaited your return. I am somewhat fond of surprises, so with, and only with, the agreement of everyone in this room, I have a proposal."

Everyone's eyes shifted to Arch Duke Winston-even Lady Marianne's.

"We hold a city wide celebration three days from today. Not a single soul is to know that the Lumen Caligo has arrived. When the celebration begins, we reveal your arrival. This will permit you to recover your strength after a taxing journey and to see the city as one of us... uninterrupted from the masses who will no doubt swarm you."

The dukes turned to their escorts and began muttering. Martin leaned forward and whispered something in the ear of the Arch Duke.

His FATHER.

The Arch Duke opened his eyes and nodded. Martin turned his back and promptly went out the way he'd come.

The muttering settled down and they each nodded. High Duke Gabriel spoke first.

"I, High Duke Gabriel Bradford, do agree to this idea and pledge my help in organizing the royal guard to protect the Lumen Caligo.

You will be assigned one of the duke's personal escorts to assist and protect you during your time here. If I may, I would like to recommend my personal guard, Lady Marianne Evynwood. Her age would facilitate the Lumen Caligo's ability to remain incognito given that she is of a similar age and size. Your ability to roam around Aeolia will remain largely unhindered given, of course, you hide your wings," he said with a smile.

"I, Duke Fredrick Evynwood, do also pledge my support. I will organize our resources for a great feast. I do also support High Duke Gabriel's designation of my daughter, Lady Marianne, as the Lumen Caligo's personal body guard," he said, making the Omniscius Salutatio in High Duke Gabriel's direction. It was the first time they'd seemed to be in agreement on something.

"Very well," began Arch Duke Winston. "Sir Martin has already begun his rounds with all the guards who came into contact with the Lumen Caligo. They will not speak of anything that has happened here tonight. As for my pledge ... I pledge my presence at the party, a formal invitation to all Lumens and an unforgettable day when the moment arrives." With that, Arch Duke Winston clapped his hands twice and nodded his head with approval. Everyone in the Atrium did the same.

Cyrus heard footsteps approaching.

Martian finished already? That was quick.

He leaned in and whispered in Arch Duke Winston's ear. In response, he furrowed his thin white eyebrows and then nodded.

"Now," began Arch Duke Winston. "I believe that is enough excitement for one night. With your permission, Lumen Caligo, I would like to adjourn this meeting."

Cyrus' legs had been quivering for some time. He had never had to stand this long on his own and everything felt heavy. His legs, his wings ... his eyes ...

"Yes! That would be err ... excellent. Thank you all for receiving me to Aeolia, and I look forward to seeing you during my stay."

"Please, stop by my manor before the feast, Lumen Caligo," began High Duke Gabriel. "It would be an honor to show you around and speak with you further." He made the Omniscius Salutatio, whispered some instructions to Lady Marianne and then made his exit. Lady Marianne stayed where she was, eyes fixed on Cyrus.

"Please, also stop by my manor," began Duke Fredrick. "With my daughter as escort, she may also serve as the Lumen Lat-"

"You forget your place, Duke Fredrick! Do not attempt to sway the Lumen Caligo. Allow yourself to be swayed by him! The trials and the Lumen Caligo are the only things that have a say on who will be the Lumen Lator!" said Arch Duke Winston crossly.

"I meant no ill-will, your greatness! Forgive this sleight. I meant no harm!" squealed Duke Fredrick, making the Omniscius Salutatio with both hands towards Arch Duke Winston.

Arch Duke Winston casually turned his head back towards Cyrus.

"Be weary of those trying to influence you, Lumen Caligo. Within you is the greatest treasure in existence. Your power threatens and influences men to do things they normally would not do. Should you ever need help perceiving such things, I would be happy to oblige. Stop by at your leisure. Sir Martin will show you the way once he hands me off to his replacement."

Arch Duke Winston made the Omniscius Salutatio with both hands and then turned around and left the way he had entered. Martin followed. In the last sliver of light before he exited the Atrium, Martin glanced behind his shoulder and made eye contact with Cyrus. His facial muscles softened into a smile for just a moment. Then he was gone.

Cyrus felt faint. He was utterly spent. Kimo looked up and beckoned him down. Cyrus outstretched his arms and threw all his weight off the side of the crystal pillar towards Kimo. Sudden flapping and a jolt grabbed Cyrus out of the air. The body was much smaller and couldn't hold Cyrus' weight for long. With a sudden maneuver and a flurry of flaps, Cyrus landed not so softly on the cold hard floor of the Atrium. Standing above him were those green piercing eyes ... Lady Marianne.

She was huffing and puffing from all the effort. She had straight white teeth and defined lips. Freckles dotted her face and strands of blonde hair mixed with her brunette ones. She was taller than Cyrus but shorter than Auli'i. The quickness with which she had nabbed Cyrus out of the air was dizzying.

"Don't ... Be ... Reckless," said Lady Marianne. Her voice reminded him of Martin when he was annoyed. Clear. Concise. Impossible to misunderstand.

"He wasn't," said Kimo behind her. "He was relying on his Virtus Lator."

Lady Marianne stood up slowly and turned to face Kimo. Cyrus could no longer see her face ... but he could see Kimo's.

"An unwise choice. The Lumen Caligo should never descend to any of us. We should strive to reach him."

"If you understood our bond, you would understand that his willingness to trust us outweighs the risk of injury," said Auli'i.

"Leave it to the Terrams to have two Latores as opposed to one," scoffed Lady Marianne. "A testament of your nation's weakness on full display." Lady Marianne turned back to Cyrus.

Auli'i began to tie her hair up and walk towards Lady Marianne.

"No, no, no ..." said Kimo, coming between them. "She's not worth it, sis. Let it go."

"GET OUT OF THE WAY!" Auli'i's voice reverberated across the Atrium.

Lady Marianne turned back toward Auli'i with a smile on her face.

"As much as I would love to deal with whatever you think you could do to me, violence within the Atrium is punishable by limb severance or wing clippings."

Auli'i acted as though she hadn't heard and kept trying to get around Kimo with little success.

"Unless ... The Lumen Caligo grants exemption to this rule." Both Auli'i and Lady Marianne fixed their eyes on Cyrus.

"Enough!" said Ori.

Cyrus breathed a sigh of relief. He had forgotten Ori was still there.

"It has been a long night for all of us. I will help escort the Lumen Caligo and the Virtus Latores to their chambers and we will all sleep to regain our senses. Idle threats during the witching hour do not become you, Lady Marianne."

With a sudden ruffle of feathers, Lady Marianne was at Ori's throat, a knife drawn.

"You forget your place ..." said Lady Marianne.

Ori didn't flinch. "You yourself stated the law. No violence is to be had within the Atrium. Lumen Caligo, what does this look like?"

"Violence," Cyrus said flatly.

Lady Marianne sheathed her blade in a flash.

"It was a warning."

"A threat. Yes, I know," said Ori, walking past her nonchalantly.

Her green eyes made Cyrus shiver.

"Now ... let's be on our way," began Lady Marianne. "I'll run point. Terrams, you surround the Lumen Caligo. Captain Ori, you bring up the rear."

Captain Ori nodded. "Let's go ..."

Lady Marianne made her way towards the exit on the far right side of the room, a different exit than they had entered. Cyrus relied heavily on Kimo for support. His entire body felt very heavy from standing by himself that long. Auli'i looked worriedly at Cyrus and then suspiciously at Lady Marianne.

As they walked away from the center of the Atrium, Lady Marianne lifted her hood up and bent her wings in a folded v-like shape on her back. Her wings wrapped around her sides, almost to the front. Cyrus wondered why and mimicked her as best he could. He cringed in pain.

The pattering of the rain grew closer and closer. They reached the corridor leading to the outside where three cloaked Lumens waited for them. Each held two white umbrellas, one for themselves and one, presumably, for Cyrus and gang. The umbrellas seemed really out of place.

When were umbrellas invented?

One of the cloaked Lumens stepped forward and pulled back his hood.

Martian ...

There was a loud clanking behind them. Cyrus turned and saw the Lumen guards inserting the spears back into the Atrium, twisting the door back the way it was. The entire lighthouse rotated and then made a huge *thud* as it locked into place.

Martin addressed Lady Marianne first.

"Your presence has been requested by High Duke Gabriel for a briefing on your new assignment. After you are briefed, meet us at The Lumen Caligo manor. I will escort the Lumen Caligo and his Virtus Latores to their quarters. You will report to me daily, understood?" said Martin as formal as ever.

Lady Marianne nodded and without a word, took an umbrella. from the other Lumen, turned left and walked into the night.

"Captain Ori, you have been around the Lumen Caligo the longest so I will be assigning you as an extra guard to aid Lady Marianne in her assignment. Before you are to fulfill this assignment, I will need an oath of silence from every person you came into contact with since you met the Lumen Caligo. I will also need yours. If we are not careful, the surprise will get out before the great feast ... News spreads like wildfire amongst the guards. We cannot allow it to spread any further at the request of Arch Duke Winston."

Ori made the Omniscius Salutatio and bowed deeply. Cyrus cheered internally.

"I am honored. I will dispatch at once."

With two quick flaps, Ori rose into the sky and disappeared.

"Lumen Caligo and Virtus Latores, you are most welcome to our great city of Aeolia. If you would follow me, I will lead you to your chambers. Lumen Caligo, if you'd be willing, could you please cover yourself with this cloak? We must keep your identity a secret." Martin handed him a black cloak.

Like you did from me? Thought Cyrus.

Cyrus put on the cloak without a word. He could feel the other guards peering at him curiously.

If only they knew.

Martin began walking to the right, up a different cobblestone road. With the umbrella overhead, he stopped, turned around and beckoned Cyrus forward. As they approached, Martin held out his hand. Cyrus let go of the twins and reached out to Martin but tripped on one of the cobblestones below his feet. Martin was quick and caught Cyrus before he hit the ground. The twins had instinctively reacted and grabbed the new black cloak Martin had given Cyrus.

Martin whispered softly, "I got him."

Cyrus was justifiably mad at him but his anger seeped away as Martin put his arm around him for support.

Cyrus couldn't wait. "Martian ... where is ..."

"Softer, Cyrus. We have eyes and ears behind us."

Cyrus lowered his tone to match Martin's. "Where is my mother?"

"You already met her father. Lady Marcella is the daughter of High Duke Gabriel so I imagine she is in the Bradford manor but I am not positive. You should accept the invitation extended by each of the dukes and visit their manors but you need to do it from highest ranking to lowest. It would be considered poor taste if you visited the dukes out of order."

"How long have you been here?!" hissed Cyrus. "Why didn't you contact us?!"

"I've been here two days. I did try to contact you but you must have been in the middle of the ocean. The Terram Chiefs deemed me a traitor and were about to sentence Akela and myself to death." Cyrus felt a twinge of guilt. He had been so wrapped up in his own feelings he had forgotten how anxious Kimo and Auli'i must have been.

"Did they ...

"No ... Manaia helped me Akela and I escape and then fought them off. By Manaia's request, I flew to Oahu by wing and dropped Akela off with Kamalani's brother." Martin dropped his head, closed his eyes, and turned slightly towards Cyrus.

"Manaia ... He stayed behind"

"Why didn't you fly Akela back to Kamalani?"

"Flying just yourself across the ocean is no small feat. Add another person ... nearly impossible. Just flying Akela to Oahu from Ni'ihau was difficult. Once Akela was safe, I called Ms. Palermo and she informed me that you, Auli'i and Kimo had left that morning for Acolia. I changed my flight to Florida, made it there by nightfall and then flew by wing to Aeolia."

"I thought they confiscated all of your documents?"

"Manaia got my passport back when he gave me Akela's. The Terrams may be flightless, but they do own and utilize swallows and godwits. I suspected they would send a message or two expressing their disgust to Aeolia. I was right in my assumption. Manaia informed me they had sent one the moment they sentenced me to death. I only beat the first swallow by a day. The next two came shortly after." Cyrus put his head into his palms. One question answered, three

more took its place.

"I have... no idea what I'm doing Martian," whispered Cyrus louder than he should have. "Why didn't you tell me? What else are you hiding? Why did you drug me all this time?! I want answers!" Martin looked over his shoulder and then back to Cyrus. Sympathy seeped from his eyes and then quickly returned to focus.

"Everything will be explained soon enough. Trust me. You won't have alone time with me since I am my father's personal guard. I will say two more things. First, you may ask me what you want to know the *most* and I will send a letter tomorrow along with the invitation my father will no doubt extend to you and the twins."

"Where is my mother and how do I meet her?"

Martin nodded. "Second, you must keep up the charade of unfamiliarity. You didn't meet me until tonight, understand?"

Cyrus nodded. More questions came to mind.

"Make sure the twins also keep up the charade. I am walking a very tight rope. Look for a falcon tomorrow morning ... Lumen Caligo! I welcome you to your temporary residence!" said Martin, speaking over the rain.

Cyrus hadn't even been watching where they were going. Two guards stood in front of an intricate two-story building. Kimo came to Martin's left side, Auli'i came to the right of Cyrus. They were both enchanted with the architecture. The guards began opening the gate.

The front entrance was decorated with sculptures of Lumens with wings outstretched and hands beckoning them in. The statues were at least 10 feet tall and as detailed as real Lumens. It was absolutely awe inspiring. Despite the beauty, sleep was starting to blur Cyrus' vision.

The guards by Kimo and Auli'i quickly folded up the umbrellas as soon as they were out of the rain and opened the doors to the great building. Torches adorned the entrance and as they entered, a chandelier with hundreds of candles lit the room. Great tapestries and smaller sculptures decorated the initial room. A great table had a vase full of flowers in its center surrounded by bottles of milk and plates of cheeses and fruit. Cyrus' mouth watered. Behind the table was a wide staircase leading to the second story.

The guards shook the water from their wings and then motioned to Martin the Omniscius Salutatio and quickly flew off. Martin motioned to the twins to take over for him. After the twins had Cyrus, Martin motioned for them to follow him up the stairs behind the table. Kimo grabbed a platter of the cheeses and a bottle of milk.

"This building is the Lumen Caligo manor but has been used as a guest house during the Lumen Caligo's absence. You will no doubt receive three invitations tomorrow morning from each duke. Promptly reply. Cyrus, you are to remain cloaked at all times if you wish to follow through with the Arch Duke's request."

"And, if I don't?"

"Then you must take that up with Arch Duke Winston personally," said a voice behind them.

Sleep left Cyrus very quickly.

Cyrus, Auli'i and Kimo whipped around. Lady Marianne stood three steps away from them. Martin had barely reacted.

"Nice of you to join us, Lady Marianne," said Martin cheerfully.

"She is right, though. You will have to take that up with my father as soon as possible. I, for one, do believe it to be the best course of action. This will prepare the Lumens to receive you all at once and in grand fashion. First impressions are very important."

Cyrus had heard that before, many times.

They reached the top of the stairs to a long hallway with three rooms. Martin led them to the first one.

"Lady Auli'i, this will be your accommodation during your time with us. Lady Marianne was gracious enough to find a suitable change of clothes. Should you need anything, Lady Marianne will be in the room across the hall."

Auli'i looked at Cyrus. "You gonna be OK?"

"I'll manage."

Auli'i nodded and slowly made her way into the room, waving as she closed the door.

They walked to the next door.

"Sir Kimo, your accommodations. I guessed as best as I could for your size ... Forgive me if I was a little off."

Kimo slowly let go of Cyrus and then tip-toed past Martin with the platter of cheeses and the jug of milk. With his mouth already full he made some unintelligible sounds and closed the door with his foot.

Martin led Cyrus to the last door and gestured.

"There is a bell next to your bed. Simply ring it to summon Lady Marianne, should you need anything."

Cyrus walked past Martin and looked back at him and Lady Marianne.

"Sleep well," said Martin with a smile.

Cyrus closed the door. A huge bed lay in front of him with a frame that was as extravagant as the architecture outside. On the bed lay a pair of clothes. Cyrus brushed them aside and collapsed in the bed, sleep filling his eyes. Cyrus wrapped his wings around himself and immediately fell asleep.

13

AEOLIA

CYRUS TEETERED BACK AND FORTH between consciousness and unconsciousness. Every time he fell asleep, he had a different dream. Caves, pyramids, wings, waves, Martian ...

CLACK CLACK CLACK!

Cyrus snapped his eyes open.

"Lumen Caligo... A falcon, a hawk and an owl have arrived for you," said Lady Marianne.

Where on earth am I?

Birds were singing in the background, the wind whistled and the faint sound of water rushing could be heard in the distance. Cyrus closed his eyes again. The bed was so comfortable. Cyrus recalled the shifting dreams he had the previous night.

CLACK CLACK CLACK!

"Lumen Caligo, may I enter your dormitory?" asked Lady Marianne with annoyance in her voice.

Cyrus rubbed his eyes and cleared his throat.

So much for sleeping.

"Yes, yes... enter," he said as he sat up.

The door swung open and Lady Marianne glided across the floor to the side of the bed. Cyrus blinked in rapid succession as light flooded through the door.

Lady Marianne held three letters in her hand. One had a giant eye sealed in purple wax. The other was sealed with a Phoenix in red wax and the last was sealed with a peacock in an emerald-green wax. The parchment was heavier than Cyrus thought it would be. Cyrus opened up the one with the eye first. He was pretty sure that was the one from Arch Duke Winston, or more accurately, Martin ...

Cyrus noticed Lady Marianne hovering. She hadn't moved since handing Cyrus the letters. Her green eyes remained fixed on Cyrus as if she were expecting something from him.

A tip? A high five? A thank you?

Cyrus decided to try the latter.

"Thank you, Lady Marianne. That is all for now."

She bowed her head slightly and made the Omniscius Salutatio.

"When you are ready, please join us downstairs. Breakfast will arrive shortly. You have your own private washroom just over there. Pull the lever and warm water will fill the basin."

Cyrus hadn't even noticed. The entire room was still relatively dark. The only light came from the door Lady Marianne opened and a little light shone from what seemed to be curtains. Lady Marianne followed Cyrus' eyes to the curtains. She promptly opened all the curtains in the room and left without a word. Light flooded the room and Cyrus shut his eyes. It was a stark contrast to last night.

The room seemed to be Greek-themed and the only difference that caught Cyrus' eye was the mural painted across the ceiling. It depicted ... him ...

A Lumen Caligo with pale skin pointed towards a series of islands with a numerous host of Lumens behind him. In the center was a larger island above the rest. Cyrus recognized it because of the light-house looking structure that sat on top of the Atrium. The island was floating. Birds flew with Lumens and the islands surrounding Aeolia had cattle and ships.

The letters ...

Cyrus grabbed the letter with the eye in purple wax and quickly opened it. Immaculate writing filled the thick parchment. A small letter with much thinner paper fell out. It was filled with Martin's cursive but was much smaller to utilize the space.

Cyrus glanced over the elaborate letter quickly. The visit was set for dusk at the Weatherford manor. It was eloquently worded in calligraphy. Cyrus didn't care. He quickly threw the letter aside and grabbed the smaller one.

Cyrus,

Your mother is Lady Marcella Bradford. My return will be announced with yours so only the dukes and militia know of my return. I was able to speak with a couple of the Bradford guards last night regarding Lady Marcella and was told she mostly keeps to herself in the Bradford manor. I was also told she was rescued 11 years ago and since her return to Aeolia, has remained a solitary creature. 12 years ago, it was my assignment to rescue her since we thought she had been abducted by a Caligo who had wandered into our midst named Cyrus...

Your father. By the time I caught up to them, they were somewhere in the Midwest of the US and your mother was pregnant with you. Rather than subject your mother and father to the punishments that awaited them for breaking the Isolation Order I fled west. Shortly after you were born, the second party following me must have caught up to them. Only your mother returned. The guards describe her as "someone in mourning". Again, this is all according to the Bradford guards. You'll have to ask her when you see her. I have planned your visits with the other dukes. You will see one of them each day before the feast, starting today with Arch Duke Winston and my family.

I'll do my best to navigate you and provide more information as things unfold. Give me until the end of the day to get a plan together to see your mother. I will have something more concrete then. Be *polite and on your best behavior. All will be explained soon. Promise.*

Sincerely,

Martian

Martian ... Cyrus couldn't help but smile.

He quickly reread the letter three more times.

My dad's name was also Cyrus. Was he going be called Jr? So many questions ...

He decided to mull it over in a bath. That sounded nice.

The other letters were quickly opened and read—all the same, just different dates.

Dinner at the dukes. Sounds like the name of a movie.

Cyrus slowly stood up, grabbed the clothes he had kicked to the floor last night and made his way to the washroom. Sure enough, there was a giant basin right in the middle of the room. It looked like a normal bath but it was shaped like a diamond and made out of the same whitish-grey stone that prevailed in Aeolia.

Pulling the lever, Cyrus heard water began to flow above him. A wooden tube had descended to start filling the basin. The water steamed as it filled the basin and smelled of citrus and something else ...

Lavender?

Cyrus slipped into the bath and found immediate relief. He unfurled his wings and let them float to the sides. He could understand why the bath was shaped like a diamond now. The wider diamond shape allowed his wings to spread out naturally with minimal effort. It was truly relaxing.

Cyrus allowed himself a luxurious 10 minutes in the bath. As the water began to lose its warmth, he dried off and grabbed the change of clothes Martin had left for him. Beige capris, an open white shirt with two slits in the back for his wings and a black hoody-like piece of clothing that looked three sizes too big. Cyrus shrugged and began putting on the strange outfit. Martin had also included sandals with two straps. He always had a pair for the beach he affectionately called jandals-Jesus sandals.

The shirt was an absolute game changer. He slipped his wings through the slits like you would put your arm through a sleeve-absolute freedom. It was a whole new world. Cyrus checked his phone. Zero bars and no service. Not surprising. Cyrus snapped a couple pictures of the mural on the ceiling and his surroundings. He then quickly turned it off and stuffed it back into his bag.

Cyrus had no idea what to do with the extra large jacket so he tied it around his waist.

Standing at the top of the stairs, Cyrus saw Auli'i and Kimo sitting around the table, Lady Marianne peering at them crossly. They were obviously frustrated. Kimo wore the same outfit as Cyrus except his shirt seemed too big. Auli'i wore a flowing white dress with sleeves that ended just below the shoulder. The white contrasted against her bronze skin. Cyrus found her new look refreshing. Cyrus wondered if she was frustrated with Lady Marianne, the fact that she was in a dress or both.

Cyrus began making his way down the steps. His foot thudded on the first step and echoed throughout the building. Lady Marianne's eyes flickered to him and then back to the twins. The twins turned quickly and faced Cyrus. Their expressions immediately lit up.

"Cyrus!" they said in unison.

There was a rustling of chairs as they both approached Cyrus, wanting to help.

Kimo was first to his side. Auli'i was annoyed Kimo had beaten her-always competing. Cyrus held up his hand as Kimo reached out to support him.

"Let me try ... Just catch me if I fall."

Kimo and Auli'i raised their eyebrows in surprise but nodded and gave Cyrus some space.

Cyrus felt refreshed from the bath but sore from the day before. Slowly, he made his way down each step.

One at a time.

Cyrus reached the bottom step triumphantly. Kimo and Auli'i provided some sarcastic applause with authentic smiles. Lady Marianne shook her head in disapproval.

Cyrus sat down between the twins and looked up at Lady Marianne who raised an unimpressed eyebrow.

"Kindly cover your wings with your taper, Lumen Caligo. I will usher in the servants after," said Lady Marianne.

Cyrus looked at her confused.

"The thing around your waist."

Cyrus untied it and looked at it. It had two sleeves and a v-cut. The clothing had an almost round shape to it. He pulled it over his head and wings.

Like a glove.

Cyrus' wings were completely covered. The material was breathable and made movement very easy. Another game changer.

Lady Marianne pursed her lips together and whistled loudly. The doors immediately opened and two Lumen guards robed in white entered followed by three Lumens in aprons, each carrying a giant platter. One had every type of danish you could imagine, another, a platter of cheeses of every kind. Kimo swooned. The last one had multiple jugs filled with different colored juices and milk.

Auli'i pouted her bottom lip up and nodded her head in approval.

The servers promptly left the platters on the table and exited as quickly as they'd come.

Lady Marianne followed them, "Shout if you need something." The guards shut the door behind them.

"Good food, good meat, good gosh, let's eat!" said Kimo, hurling himself at the food.

"Amen," said Cyrus with a smile.

"There is no meat here," said Auli'i dryly.

"Juuu know vhaatt I mean," said Kimo, already stuffing his face with a couple danishes.

Cyrus grabbed his fork and poked a couple of the cheeses.

"Dooose yellow ones are weeeally good!" said Kimo, pointing at the cheese platter while spearing another danish across the table. The danish fell off Kimo's fork and landed on the ground. Kimo quickly grabbed it and stuffed it into his mouth.

"KIMO! GROSS!" said Auli'i.

Kimo grinned.

Cyrus took a bite of the yellow cheese. It was good. Salty and sweet ... creamy and rich. Cyrus eyed the danishes next.

Auli'i ate properly with the fork and knife. One danish and three different cheeses adorned her plate.

Kimo poured a little bit of the first juice into each chalice. It was pink like bubblegum.

Auli'i sniffed it. "Guava."

They all sipped it at the same time. Sure enough, it was guava.

The others were orange juice, pineapple and passion fruit. Auli'i guessed correctly every single time.

The milk was also very rich. Cyrus didn't like it because it was warm.

Auli'i leaned in close to Cyrus.

"What did Martian say?"

Kimo stopped his loud munching and leaned in.

Cyrus swallowed deliberately before he spoke. "Akela is safe. Martian got her off of Ni'ihau."

They both exhaled in relief.

"Where did he take her?" asked Kimo, leaning in closer.

"He dropped her off with your uncle on Oahu."

"What about my father?" asked Auli'i with worry. "Did he get caught? Did the chiefs imprison him?"

"He stayed behind. I don't know what the chiefs did to him," said Cyrus apologetically.

"Did he say anything else?"

Cyrus shook his head. Auli'i looked worried. She peered past Cyrus to Kimo.

"If dad got caught, hypothetically, how long would it take for the chiefs to make a decision about him?"

Kimo looked up and counted as he chewed what was in his mouth.

"They would have to call another chief to take his place. No big decision can be made with less than three. That could take a while. Then again, it might be quick. I don't know," said Kimo.

"What would be the decision?" Cyrus asked.

Kimo looked at Auli'i with a wide-eyed expression. Cyrus turned to Auli'i.

"Probably the same as Akela's..." replied Auli'i. She no longer whispered.

"We don't know for certain ... Don't jump to conclusions, Auli'i," said Kimo.

"I'm not, I'm just considering the possibilities."

"Let's hope for the best. We just don't know," said Kimo with reassurance.

"What DO we know?!"

"That our sister is safe!"

"Kimo, that makes me so happy. Truly ... but did we just switch one family member sentenced to death for another?"

Kimo fell silent.

"Martin found my mother..." interjected Cyrus.

They both looked to Cyrus with surprise. Cyrus pulled Martin's letter out off his pocket and went back to whispering.

"Read this ..."

The twins read the letter quickly and silently.

"Your father's name is Cyrus?!" asked Auli'i.

"The red bearded guy is your grandpa?!" asked Kimo.

Cyrus blinked in surprise. High Duke Bradford was his grandfather.

Is my beard going to be red, too?

"Yeah... I guess so," said Cyrus with a chuckle.

"We need a plan of attack. What are we doing today?" asked Auli'i.

"Dinner at Arch Duke Winston's residence. Martian will be there too. I think Lady Marianne was going to show us around Aeolia as well."

"I'm sure she'll be a *wonderful* guide," said Auli'i, putting another piece of cheese in her mouth.

"Probably got jokes for days, said Kimo, leaning back in his chair.

"I'll ask her, LADY MARIANNE!" shouted Cyrus.

Kimo almost fell out of his chair. The door opened immediately and Lady Marianne was at Cyrus' side at once.

"Yes, Lumen Caligo?" she said making the Omniscius Salutatio. Her face was focused.

"Will you be showing us around Aeolia today before our dinner appointment with Arch Duke Winston?"

Lady Marianne raised an eyebrow. "I have been assigned to protect you, Lumen Caligo. IF you wish to walk around the city, I will accompany you. That is all."

Cyrus pouted his lip. Lady Marianne's expression remained unchanged.

"Very well, could you please ask one of the guards if they would be willing to tour us around while you protect me?" asked Cyrus unpouting his lip.

Lady Marianne nodded and whistled again. Both guards entered, white hoods covering their faces.

"Captain Johnathon, you may wait outside."

The guard on the left bowed while making the Omniscius Salutatio and promptly returned to his post.

"Captain Ori, at ease and de-cloak."

The Lumen put down his hood and sure enough, it was Ori.

"Lumen Caligo," he said gesturing with both hands in the Omniscius Salutatio. A smile crossed his lips.

"Captain Ori, the Lumen Caligo would like to be shown around Aeolia today before his dinner appointment with Arch Duke Winston. A tour, if you will. Aside from your skill with a bow, you are known for your tales and songs. Would you be willing to regale the Lumen Caligo with stories of this place?"

Captain Ori bowed.

"It would be a great honor. When would you like to begin?" asked Ori looking at Cyrus and the twins.

They all looked at each other while Kimo stuffed another danish into his mouth.

"Could we go now?" asked Cyrus.

"Of course. Allow me to find someone to fill my post and we shall be off," he gestured the Omniscius Salutatio, opened the front door and flew off.

"Three rules," began Lady Marianne. "Number one, stay within sight at all times. Number two, wings covered at all times and hood up. Number three, no Lumen Caligo mention or talk whatsoever. Should someone ask who you are, let us do the talking. You will be presented under the guise of new servants familiarizing yourselves with Aeolia. You are meant to stay a secret."

There was a *whoosh* followed in quick succession by another *whoosh*.

"Ready when you are, Lumen Caligo," said Ori with a slight bow.

"Refer to him by his name from here on. Do not address him as the Lumen Caligo again, understood?" said Lady Marianne.

"Yes, my lady."

The guard replacing Ori peeked in real quick and then closed the door. Cyrus recognized him from last night when Ori had flown Cyrus to Aeolia.

What was his name again?

Cyrus, Auli'i and Kimo stood up and promptly prepared. Cyrus made sure his wings were tucked away and that his hood was up.

Auli'i smoothed out the wrinkles in her dress. Kimo made a small mountain of crumbs on the floor by wiping them from his lap. Lady Marianne adjusted her belt and reached behind her to check a quiver that Cyrus was noticing for the first time. She counted the arrows silently behind her back.

"Off we go!" said Ori as he opened the doors.

Aeolia was even more breathtaking in the day than it was at night. The sky was crystal blue, a couple fluffy clouds whisked through the air.

The sun, coupled with the rain from the night before, had encouraged the vines decorating the buildings to bud. A row of trees and flowers lead to the entrance of the guest house. There were tulips in every color of red, yellow and pink. The statue with the outstretched hands had curly hair and looked like some of the statues he had studied when they had covered Ancient Greece. He adorned a toga and looked to the sky.

How would I meme this? Come at me bro.

He chuckled and kept walking.

The front gates were opened and they made their way into the street. Directly in front of them was the Atrium that seemed to be the pinnacle of the city. The manors decorated each side of the road. Lumens walked all about, garbed in flowing white cloaks and dresses. Their wings matched the brilliance of their garb and folded behind their backs in that v-like shape that Lady Marianne did as well.

They all seemed to be moving towards the Atrium which was now surrounded by tables, tents and chairs. Cyrus wondered what was going on over there ...

The details of the buildings were on full display. Each mural depicted stories of heroism and were intricately designed. Each one must have taken hundreds of hours to make. Some of the nicer manors had statues.

"Lumen Cal— Cyrus ... Kimo ... Auli'i ... We welcome you to Aeolia once more. The sacred residence of the High Dukes and homestead to all Lumens." Ori gestured grandly in front of him. He then began walking directly towards the Atrium.

"The first building every Lumen knows is the Atrium. It serves as a holy place of worship, a guiding light in the dark and the gathering place both inside and outside its walls. It is the center of our city and everything is built around its circular structure"

They approached the Atrium and saw hundreds of Lumens walking around, talking and negotiating with each other. It looked like a little farmers market was going on. Fruits and vegetables and all manners of meats decorated the tables. Delicious smells permeated from small fires in iron pits. The tables and tents completely encircled the Atrium. Most people were focused on getting what they needed but there were a few who stared as Cyrus and the twins as they walked by.

"We have the market six days a week. The fruits and vegetables are harvested from the many small islands and atolls surrounding Aeolia. Each one serves its proper function with Aeolia acting as the brain controlling and instructing the other isles."

Cyrus really wanted to see the other isles. He couldn't see the ocean because of all the buildings and the Atrium blocking the way. Seagulls shrieked overhead. Cyrus looked up and saw a falcon dive-bomb one. The seagull quickly flew away. The falcon pursued for a moment until the seagull was long gone. There was almost as much going on in the air as there was on the ground.

Besides the falcon and seagulls, there were at least fifty Lumens approaching Aeolia from the air. Most carried knapsacks and a pair of Lumens chased each other laughing. Cyrus couldn't take it in fast enough.

Captain Ori went to a fruit stand and smiled. "Morning, Darla, could I get two coconuts with lots of water in them please?"

"Morning, Captain Ori. You want the biggest ones?" the lady said with a smile in return. The woman had more freckles and sunspots than Martin. She was a middle-aged woman whose smile was completely genuine.

"Sure. The most filled one you got would be perfect," Ori responded while jingling for something in his pocket.

"You got it." She grabbed a couple of the coconuts and shook a few in rapid succession. After the third, she looked satisfied. She stabbed the coconut onto what looked liked a large, wooden stake and peeled the coconut with practiced efficiency. She grabbed a rock and struck the coconut two times with pinpoint accuracy. The coconut split into two perfect halves and dumped a lot of liquid as it opened into a dish below. She emptied the coconut completely.

"You want the pulp, the milk or the meat?" she asked.

Ori looked at the three of them and then back to Darla.

"Let's go meat today. Could you slice them thin please?" asked Ori as he placed a silver coin and two wooden cups on the table.

"You got it," the woman said back.

She grabbed a seashell and began shaving out all of the coconut meat. Once both sides were completely devoid of meat, she grabbed a medium-sized knife and sliced it into small french-fry-sized pieces.

She repeated the process with another coconut just as fast as the first.

Darla then promptly put the coconut meat into the two coconut shells and handed them to Ori along with the coconut water in his two wooden cups.

"You have a great day, darling," the woman said warmly.

"You too, Darla darling," said Ori with a wink.

Is that flirting?

He handed half of the shell to Kimo and one of the wooden cups to Auli'i.

"Let me know how it compares to Akhet," whispered Ori with a smile.

Kimo offered a piece to Cyrus first. The coconut meat was soft and slightly sweet. It was very pleasant. The coconut water was so refreshing. They ate as they weaved in and out of the outdoor market, taking in all of the sights and sounds.

Lumens bartered one with another, one ruffled his feathers when the merchant didn't lower his price on a bunch of bananas. People would immediately fly into the sky when they finished their purchases. A pair of Lumens strummed away on guitars.

A mother and father had one end of a rope attached to their hips while the other end was attached to a pair of boys. The kids looked to be five years old and had long flowing blonde hair. Cyrus wondered why they were connected by rope until the boys began flapping their wings and erratically flying in every direction, giggling and screaming.

"Follow me this way. We'll make our way to the outskirts," said Ori.

He led them away from the crowd to the other side of the Atrium. The only side they hadn't seen of the Atrium. As they weaved through the multitude of Lumens, they noticed that this way seemed to curve downward. The horizon was visible with no buildings blocking the view. The further they walked that way, the more the ocean came into view. Slowly, little islands appeared to dot the surface of the ocean and Cyrus could see a good 20 or so miles out to sea. They seemed to be looking down at everything.

How high up are we?

Ori took a sudden left down an open street and walked a little bit faster. Kimo looked at Cyrus who, in turn, increased his pace. The buildings shadowed them on both sides but the sun was shining very brightly at the end of the street. The opening grew closer and closer and Cyrus could see more and more of the ocean sprawling out in front of them. There was a gazebo at the end enclosed by a fence. Ori wrestled with the gate a bit and then opened it. He stood in the center of the gazebo and beckoned them to approach. The three climbed up and looked out towards the expansive ocean and gasped in unison.

"The floating city of Aeolia with all her children," said Ori with a smile.

Ocean as far as the eye could see encompassed Aeolia. Islands speckled her blue face like freckles. The sound of moving water was prevalent. It was the same one they had been hearing the last 24 hours. Ori looked down. Cyrus, Auli'i and Kimo did the same.

Below them was a giant whirlpool bigger than Aeolia. Auli'i gasped "Whoaaa ..." said Cyrus and Kimo in unison.

The water gurgled and swirled violently. The islands closest to the enormous whirlpool were very lopsided.

It's probably from that current constantly hitting them.

Cyrus could see hundreds upon hundreds of boulders on one side of the island redirecting the current.

The gazebo protruded from the island like a giant birdcage. It was from that vantage point Cyrus was able to see that Aeolia was shaped almost like a giant top. The top half carried the bulk of the buildings and then trailed down ever so slightly.

"Aeolia is a modern marvel beheld by few. It was initiated three and a half millennia ago and completed at the meridian of time. The giant whirlpool below us is named 'Wadjet' but everyone calls it 'the eye'."

"How ... how does it float?" asked Cyrus, still unable to wrap his brain around how they were suspended in the air.

Ori exhaled loudly. "Well ... We're not entirely sure ... We just know that the eye is the energy source that keeps Aeolia afloat."

Cyrus peered down at the center of the eye. It seemed to sink hundreds and hundreds of feet deep. The water turned darker and darker until he could no longer see the water due to the chasm that seemed to engulf the entire ocean. Cyrus shivered at the thought of what would happen if he got caught in the current.

As his eyes reached what he believed was the center of the whirlpool he saw something white poking out of it. Auli'i was to his right and had a slightly better vantage point. She cocked her head curiously and then looked at Cyrus. She'd seen it, too.

"Ori, there is something sticking out of the center of the whirlpool. What is it?" asked Auli'i.

"A giant spire that protrudes from the heart of the whirlpool. The spire houses a temple in honor of the Lumen Caligo and his past lives. Its proper name is Mentibus Oculis. The entrance is sealed and only a Lumen Caligo can gain access to whatever lies below. In the deepest part where Wadjet and Mantibus Oculis meet lies the *Sanctum*. The last Lumen Caligo never visited Aeolia so no one has stepped foot inside it for almost 700 years. No one knows what lies inside the Sanctum."

"The previous Lumen Caligo didn't come here?" asked Cyrus.

"Not to our knowledge, and we Lumens document everything. According to legend, Aeolia used to float much much higher than it currently does. If you look up you can see that we are below the clouds by a great amount. Seven hundred years ago, when the previous Lumen Caligo visited Mentibus Oculis, Aeolia soared upwards to a height so great you could not hear Wadjet. Since that time though, Aeolia has slowly descended back to the ocean."

What Ori said fascinated Cyrus. They were still hundreds of feet above the ocean. How would the view be if they were among the clouds?

"You saw how my guards and I found you a couple miles out last night. Well, there are two reasons for that. The first is to encourage anyone who is not a Lumen to turn back. We run perimeter checks nonstop in order to turn people away from our shores. Anyone who sees Aeolia is not allowed to leave to ensure we remain a secret from the rest of the world. The second reason is to prevent any damage to the Sanctum."

Cyrus looked down again at the white point sticking out of the ravenous whirlpool.

What does the Sanctum look like?

"Allow me to tell you one tale I know about the great eye," began Ori. "Seventy-five years ago or so, there was a fleet of metal ships with no sails that churned and howled as they moved. My grandfather was the commanding officer and was responsible for deterring the entire fleet from continuing towards Aeolia. They refused. My grandfather, with a large number of Lumens, commandeered all the vessels and docked them on the island we landed on yesterday. All of them, save one … One of the ships got caught in the great eye past our defenses. Despite our best efforts to hull the ship to the closest island, Mother Nature cannot be argued with. The great eye swallowed up the ship but on its way down to oblivion, the ship ran into Mentibus Oculis and lodged itself at the entrance. There, a piece of it still remains."

Auli'i, Kimo and Cyrus held their gaze then looked down, trying to see it. No dice.

Cyrus looked behind him and saw Lady Marianne down the street inspecting every person that walked by and then made eye contact with her. Fierce, no emotion, like she was unimpressed. Cyrus returned his attention to Ori. Ori's eyes also returned from looking at Lady Marianne. He seemed worried. Lowering his voice he said,

"I'm not sure how much I am supposed to tell you. The dukes might tell you the same story. If they do, hear them out and act surprised. I don't want them to feel like I took something away from them by answering your questions."

"Of course!" said Cyrus.

Kimo was looking down on the other side of Aeolia and the sheer drop of the wall.

"Why is the outside of Aeolia blue?" he asked.

Cyrus did a double take, ready to call out Kimo for a lackluster joke, but as he inspected, he noticed that the outside of Acolia all the way down was a dark blue. Looking around, he noticed it was a vibrant blue in the sun.

"We call it Iris Stone. Its function is two-fold. It beautifies Aeolia but the mineral also reacts to Wadjet. It has an energy about it. We have a mine on one of our islands called Alumnus that's filled to the brim with it. We use it for good health, jewelry and maintenance of Aeolia's underside. We call the gradual point going downwards 'the spire.' It is the most difficult to maintain."

Between the blue sheen of Aeolia, the giant whirlpool and all the islands dotting the horizon ... It was an unbelievable sight. Cyrus pinched himself to make sure he wasn't dreaming.

Cyrus saw a small bird fly past him and straight to Lady Marianne.

She held out her forearm and let it land. The bird had a small piece of parchment attached to its leg. Lady Marianne quickly untied it and read the note.

"The Arch Duke has finished all appointments and has offered to move up the timetable. Due to his declining health, he would be unable to receive you properly tonight. Do you accept his proposal, Cyrus?" It almost sounded like a threat.

"Of course."

"Very well, let's go then." She quickly wrote a note, attached it to the leg of the bird and lifted it into the sky. Lady Marianne took off in a brisk walk after it.

Ori and the three shrugged and then took the view in real quick before following Lady Marianne. They reached the end of the street where they had turned left and made their way past the Atrium back towards where they had stayed last night. The Atrium was truly circular and the guards remained ready at each entrance. They passed by a pair who nodded and made the Omniscius Salutatio with one hand as they walked by. The five of them returned the signal.

Lady Marianne walked past the manor that they had stayed in the previous night and walked to the end of the street where a massive building stood. It looked like it had been constructed for Zeus himself.

Lady Marianne looked around cautiously, then spoke. "Announcing the Lumen Caligo with his Virtus Latores and escorts. We request entrance to the Weatherford estate."

"Granted!" came a voice. The gates then swung open.

Cyrus was going to meet the Weatherfords.

14
THE WEATHERFORDS

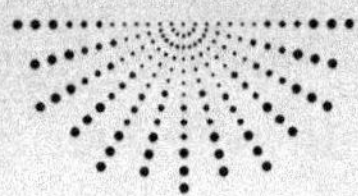

TWO GUARDS APPEARED as if from nowhere, bowed and then opened the gate toward the luxurious manor. Lightning bolts decorated the gates and statues stood on either side of the entrance. Flowers and trimmed bushes led the way to the manor which had giant pillars and a series of friezes engraved across the building.

The first frieze started at giant pyramids surrounded by a Lumen, Caligo, Terram and the Lumen Caligo. The frieze depicted many travels and places all around the top of the manor. It was filled with Lumens flying around Aeolia. It was so detailed. Cyrus felt like he could look at it for hours.

They made their way up a few steps, and as they reached the front, the doors opened as if by magic. Cyrus walked through the doors and saw two Lumens who had opened the doors for them.

Not magic.

Servants brought platter after platter to an enormous table. More servants dusted the manor while others cleaned the windows. None of them had wings.

The door shut and then a Caligo dressed in a white suit laced in purple trim stood in front of them. Cyrus was dumbstruck at the sight of this man. His wings were charcoal black and he looked Latino. His wings were folded back neatly, and with every shadow behind him, his wings seemed to disappear.

He glanced at them with a smile and loudly proclaimed, "Announcing The Lumen Caligo, Cyrus Ganymede with his Virtus Latores, Sir Kimo Fualautoalasi and Lady Auli'i Fualautoalasi."

The servants momentarily stopped what they were doing, made the Omniscius Salutatio with both hands and then went to their knees in a prostrated bow. Cyrus was caught off guard and didn't know what to do. The Caligo did the same.

The Caligo with the purple trim stood back up, made a loud but quick whistle noise and then all of the servants stood and resumed their duties.

"Should you need anything, Lumen Caligo, my name is Fernando, and I am the head butler of the manor." He then bowed and ascended the stairs out of sight.

The inside of the manor was as impressive as the outside. Hand painted ceilings, flowing stone work, and a chandelier that looked like unfurled Lumen wings made out of crystal. The enormous table was the darkest item in the room while everything else was light and colorful. The table was covered with a white table cloth and silver platters of meats and an assortment of dishes. At the top of the stairs, there was a large painting of a singular eye. It stood out above everything there.

"Good afternoon, Lumen Caligo, came a familiar voice at the top of the stairs.

Martin glided down the steps and made the Omniscius Salutatio to Cyrus and the twins and then to Lady Marianne and Captain Ori.

Cyrus rolled his eyes and returned the gesture. The twins followed suit. Lady Marianne and Captain Ori obliged.

All this Omniscius Salutatio business is getting really tedious.

"You are well received, Lumen Caligo," came another voice from the top of the stairs.

Arch Duke Winston was being escorted by the same Caligo that had announced them in the purple trim. Arch Duke Winston wore a purple robe accentuated with white clothing underneath. Behind him was a woman in a flowing purple dress with blonde hair, blue eyes and full, red lips escorted by a man in a white robe adorned with a purple sash. He looked very similar to Martin and carried himself with his chin held high. Arch Duke Winston moved slowly and deliberately.

The servants seemed to move even faster as Arch Duke Winston made his way down the steps. Plates were set in place, silverware adjusted and the last dishes full of food made their way onto the table. As Arch Duke Winston made it to the last step, there was silence.

Arch Duke Winston coughed loudly, his entire body shaking as he coughed. A single feather fell to the ground. After he composed himself, he made his way to the chair in the center of the table and gestured for everyone to also grab a chair. As soon as Arch Duke Winston sat down, everyone did the same.

"Welcome to my manor, Lumen Caligo, Cyrus Ganymede. You are most welcome here. Good conversation accompanies good food, so without further ado..." He clapped his hands twice.

The servants revealed the food promptly and what a feast it was.

An entire pig with an apple in its mouth lay at the center of a sprawling arrangement of food. There were pies, soups and cheeses of every kind. There was smoked fish, clams and lobster. So many different types of fruits surrounded the cheese spread that Cyrus could hardly wrap his mind around it. Mangos, apples, papayas, starfruit, pieces of coconut and bananas—to name a few. Kimo's eyes were glued to the cheeses. That boy loved him some cheese.

With another clap of his hands, the servants backed away until they disappeared behind those sitting at the table, giving all the attention to the elaborate display of food.

" ... Bon appétit. Please help yourselves or ask the servant behind you and they will accommodate you in any way."

Cyrus looked behind him and saw a teenage girl with jet black hair. She smiled at him and then looked down timidly. Cyrus smiled back and then looked around. There was a servant behind every single person at the table. The couple that walked behind the Arch Duke sat on his left with Martin on his right. Cyrus, the twins and Lady Marianne sat facing Arch Duke Winston and his family. Captain Ori stood off in the distance.

The Weatherfords (excluding Cyrus) turned to their servants and handed them their plates while pointing and telling them what they would like. Promptly, each servant moved around the table as if it were a choreographed dance. A red liquid was poured into each of the cups, and then the servants faded into the background. Cyrus decided to give it a go.

"Could I have a small slice of the pig, some of that pie and an apple please?" he asked with a smile.

"Would you like a fresh apple or the apple from the swines mouth?" the girl asked intently.

"Uhhh... a fresh apple would be fine."

"Would you like the apple peeled or cut into slices?"

"Slices would be fine. Thank you."

The girl went and retrieved each item. As she got the apple, she set the plate down, pulled out a knife and quickly cut the apple into thin slices with precision. In less than 10 seconds, Cyrus had exactly what he'd asked for. Cyrus could feel eyes on him from every angle. He looked up to see the couple staring at him. They quickly looked down at their food when he looked up.

"Wine?" she asked.

Cyrus eyes bulged. "No ... Water would be great." She grabbed another pitcher and filled his chalice.

"If you need anything, summon me with a finger or say Naomi." She then faded to the background.

Cyrus looked around and saw that Auli'i had a healthy serving of pork and fruit. Lady Marianne had a single slice of the meat pie. Kimo had one of everything and a separate plate filled with an unholy amount of cheese.

That poor servant ...

"Now, Lumen Caligo, allow me to introduce to you my family. You have already met my eldest, Sir Martin Weatherford, our most skilled hunter who has returned to us after 12 years looking for you. This here is my youngest son, Sir Guthrie Weatherford, accompanied by his fiancé, Winifred Medina. They were informed of your arrival only moments ago so forgive them if they appear to be staring."

"No problem at all. I am used to the staring. If you have any questions, I am an open book," said Cyrus to the couple. They smiled politely.

"Have you visited any of the other nations, Lumen Caligo, or just Ahket?" asked Sir Guthrie.

"I have yet to visit the islands of Ahket. It is the Lumen city of Aeolia that I chose as my first stop in the three nations."

Arch Duke Winston raised his chalice. The rest of his family did the same.

"And we are honored by that decision. You chose wisely!" he said as he downed some more wine. He coughed loudly and spilled some wine on his purple robe. Sir Guthrie spoke up while his father covered his mouth with a napkin.

"Then, how did you meet your Virtus Latores?"

Cyrus panicked internally. He had nothing. He felt his temperature rise as he racked his brain for an explanation.

"Have you ever had a dream you couldn't explain?" began Auli'i.

"Why yes, Lady Auli'i. Most dreams of mine are difficult to explain if I remember them."

"I had a reoccurring dream that started about a year ago. Over and over thoughts wove it into my mind. My home was being swallowed up by the sea. Despair filled my heart. Then, a hummingbird appeared and poked me with its beak until I followed it. The hummingbird was the brightest green I had ever seen with a red chest as red as the rising sun. I got in my family's way finder and began sailing across the sea. Each night I grew further and further away from home until one day I reached land. The hummingbird guided me to Poseidon's lair where he landed softly into the very hand of Poseidon. Poseidon spoke to me in a language I could not understand, but in my heart I knew I must leave. After that, I never had the dream again."

Everyone had their eyes fixed on Auli'i.

"A beautiful dream," said the fiancé.

"How did you interpret this dream, Lady Auli'i?" asked Sir Guthrie.

"You see me before you now? I found the Lumen Caligo and he made us his Virtus Latores. We acted rather than interpreted."

Ask Auli'i more about this dream later.

"A riveting story... Good thing you actually found the Lumen Caligo, otherwise we would have to throw you into Wadjet per the Isolation Order," said Arch Duke Winston with a small smile.

Auli'i gave a shiver.

"Now, I am most curious, where was Poseidon's lair? Or, put plainly, where did you meet?"

This time Auli'i looked a little panicked. With Akela and Kamalani hiding with Ms. P, it was probably best they didn't tell anyone where home was. Cyrus couldn't help but think of Ms. P.

What would she say?

She loved her theater. All those plays and musicals she made him watch ... wait... musicals ...

"Oklahoma..." began Cyrus.

Kimo stopped mid munch. Auli'i coughed loudly. Martin took a large sip of whatever was in his glass.

"A place called Oklahoma. The wind comes right behind the rain. The wheat waves, it's a wonderful place," finished Cyrus with as much conviction as he could muster.

"It sounds intriguing," said Martin, lowering his chalice. "My father is quite the cartographer. I'm sure once the Isolation Order is lifted you could show him a few maps of this Oklahoma that you speak of."

"Ah, yes," said Arch Duke Winston with a smile. "My oldest is right. I yearn to catch up on what we have missed these past 350 years in isolation. Lumen Caligo, when do you intend to lift the Isolation Order and allow us to begin studying the world's events and technologies?"

"Well... I don't see the need to impose it any longer. How would I go about doing it? Do I just say the word or do you need my signature?"

"You need an official declaration saying it has ended for us Lumens and ... You must seal it with one of your feathers."

"OK ... That doesn't sound ... so bad."

"Would you like me to summon the other dukes father?" asked Martin.

"No, no need my son. Let us handle that later." He began another coughing fit.

Martin gave Cyrus a quick look.

"Father, I believe it is time for you to rest. I'll have Fernando take you up to your room. How is everyone doing? Anyone need anything? More food? More wine? Use of the bathrooms?" Martin looked right at Cyrus with that final suggestion. Catching on, Cyrus raised his hand.

"Oh, don't be silly. We have an honored guest with us, Martin. One I would very much like to play a game of chess with. Do you know how to play chess, young master Cyrus?"

"Absolutely! I would love to! Could I use the bathroom first, if you don't mind."

"Of course! Of course! Martin, would you escort the Lumen Caligo to our facilities?"

Cyrus stood up, and everyone else did the same. Kimo was midbite in another piece of cheese and fumbled to get up quickly.

"Right this way, Lumen Caligo."

He followed Martin down the hall to a door that was still in plain sight of where they were dining.

"I'll be right outside if you need me," said Martin, opening the door. "Pull that lever for fresh water, and here is a fresh towel for when you are done."

Martin closed the door without another word. Cyrus was left in a Lumen bathroom with a purple towel and confused thoughts.

Did I misread that? Maybe I need to pull the lever.

He went to the basin and pulled the lever. Sure enough, water came out just as Martin had said. Cyrus watched the water flow and then let go of the lever. Frustrated, he threw his towel to the ground. He did his business and washed his hands. He begrudgingly picked up the towel and dried his hands. Opening the door, Martin was outside with his back turned. He casually turned around with a smile.

"The towel can stay in the restroom, Lumen Caligo. Please, allow me," said Martin, taking it from him. As Martin took the towel, a piece of paper fell out. Martin caught it and quickly put the piece of paper in Cyrus' robe pocket.

Cyrus internally smacked himself on the head. He reached for the piece of paper but saw Lady Marianne whip her head towards him.

Guess the note will have to wait.

Cyrus returned to his seat. The pig with the apple in its mouth had been moved to a smaller table and in its place was a chess board set up and ready to go. Arch Duke Winston had his hands in a power pose. He smiled with anticipation.

"Seeing how you are tonight's guest, you may begin," he said, gesturing towards the board

Cyrus looked at Auli'i who gave a nod of encouragement as she nibbled on the little food she had left on her plate.

Here goes.

Cyrus moved his pawn forward to f4. In quick succession, Arch Duke Winston moved his pawn to d5.

"Do you know how long chess has been around, young master Cyrus?" asked Arch Duke Winston.

"Off the top of my head, no, Arch Duke Winston." Cyrus matched his tone.

"Since the 600's. It was originally called Chatarung and originated from India. Persian traders brought it with them to Europe at the millennia where it was enhanced and perfected," he said as he took Cyrus' third pawn.

Cyrus took the High Duke's first pawn shortly after.

Finally.

"How long have you been playing?" asked Cyrus, looking up.

The Arch Duke continued to look at him. He wasn't paying attention to the board and yet he was outplaying Cyrus.

"Oh, I was a teenager when I first started playing, just a little older than you," he said with a smile.

Cyrus smiled back and then returned his attention to the board. Cyrus had opened aggressively but felt he was being cornered. He needed to readjust his strategy so he decided to play more defensively.

"We hold chess tournaments weekly here in Aeolia. Although it is open to all Aeolians, our warriors are required to participate in at least two per month," said Arch Duke Winston, taking a knight.

"Why is that?" asked Cyrus, taking the Arch Duke's rook.

"Because it is the mind that wins battles, not the muscles. A man who has mastered his mind is more deadly than the man who can swing the heaviest sword." The Arch Duke looked at the board, and surprise filled his eyes.

"You are very good, Arch Duke Winston," said Cyrus.

"You are not half bad yourself, master Cyrus. Tell me, who was your teacher?"

"Uhhh... experience."

The Arch Duke let out a laugh. "Well, experience is the greatest teacher, master Cyrus, no argument there."

"Our father's chess record is impeccable, master Cyrus. On occasion, he also participates in the chess tournaments and never loses," said Sir Guthrie.

"Ah, but you are mistaken, my son. I have lost only once in the Aeolia chess tournaments... My eldest, Sir Martin, played a flawless chess game the month before he passed the Iris Ascension. Some would view it as a tarnish to my record. I could not have been more proud," he said, putting his hand on Martin's shoulder.

"You flatter me, father. I'm pretty sure you let me win that one out of pity."

"Nonsense! You adapted and changed on the fly. Truth be told, I thought I was winning until the very end when you flipped it." The Arch Duke took Cyrus' queen.

Ouch. This game is over. He adapted to my defensive strategy and has me backed into a corner.

"Anything done only once is a fluke, father," said Martin, folding his arms with a fake pout.

"Oh, come now ... It can also be said that the taste of one win leads to many others. I can promise you I never took it easy on you. To borrow what the Lumen Caligo and I were talking about earlier, experience is the greatest teacher, is it not, master Cyrus?"

"You're not wrong ... Check mate in three for you, Arch Duke Winston. You are exceptional at this game." Cyrus bowed his head and offered the Omniscius Salutatio.

The Arch Duke completed the three moves on the board and then knocked over Cyrus king. Only then did he return the gesture.

"Well played, master Cyrus. I enjoyed that very much." The servants began clapping as did everyone else at the table.

Kimo clapped awkwardly with food still in his hand.

Kimo is still eating?!

"Perhaps we can play again sometime?" asked Cyrus inquisitively. He was starting to regret not paying attention as much when he played with Martin.

"Yes, of course! Now, please do excuse me for the time being, Lumen Caligo. I must rest. It was a pleasure dining with you and playing with you. Tonight, I will be meeting with the other dukes about the document we have created for nullifying the Isolation Order. I could have that sent to you by tonight if you are interested in seeing it. Would that be something you'd be interested in?"

"Of course! Send it over. I'll gladly read over it."

"Thank you, Lumen Caligo. Your return has been greatly anticipated. I am grateful to you for visiting my home and blessing our family with your presence." He made the Omniscius Salutatio with one hand while coughing into a napkin with the other. He then gestured to everyone and said, "May your light illuminate the darkness."

Everyone stood up and returned the gesture. "May the darkness never overshadow your light."

Fernando appeared next to the Arch Duke and helped him up the stairs. Cyrus slowly reached into his pocket and removed the paper from Martin. He opened it as quietly as he could, keeping the paper just under the table in case someone looked up. The anticipation was killing him.

Midnight. Be ready.

15

MARCELLA

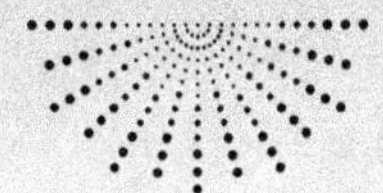

CYRUS DIDN'T REMEMBER MUCH after he'd read the note. Not anything detailed at least. There were some deserts, they saw more of Aeolia and Captain Ori told some stories but one thing kept repeating in Cyrus' head.

Midnight. Be ready.

Everything else faded into the background. By the time they reached the Atrium again, Auli'i and Kimo knew something was up.

"Hey ... What's on your mind? You've been here in body only since we left the Weatherford's," said Auli'i.

Cyrus peeked over his shoulder to see how far Lady Marianne was behind them. Ori was going on about how they caught the rain water and the intricacies of the aqueducts.

"Martian is coming to get me at midnight. I'm pretty sure I'm going to meet my mom," whispered Cyrus.

Kimo tripped over his feet and fell to the ground. Ori stopped his story and Lady Marianne was right next to them in an instant.

Kimo got up clumsily.

"Not too late to swap Virtus Latores," said Lady Marianne.

Cyrus chuckled.

So she's not made of stone.

"Sorry! Sorry ... I got distracted looking at ... um ... that ..." he said, pointing at the Atrium.

Skepticism was plastered across Lady Marianne's face.

"Let's hurry and get you guys back to the manor. The sun is going down," she said.

"On an ending note, allow me to tell you about how the city is organized," Ori began. "There are five precincts on Aeolia. The 1st precinct is where the dukes, the Lumen Caligo and important guests reside. The 2nd precinct is occupied by those whose profession has the most value ... military commanders, blacksmiths, and healers. The 3rd and 4th precincts tend to have Lumens who deal with day to day items. Farmers, ranchers, wood workers, and seamstresses to name a few. The 5th precinct is where all of the servants reside."

Cyrus furrowed his brow.

Servants ... Is that their way of saying slaves?

He would ask Martin later.

Cyrus and the twins walked by the Atrium and looked up at the towering pillar leading up to the lighthouse. A Lumen had just lit the fire and shadows began to dance up and down the Atrium.

"Can we see the sunset?" asked Cyrus.

Captain Ori looked directly at Lady Marianne. Cyrus, Kimo and Auli'i followed suit.

"Sure... to the bird cage."

Lumens were closing down their little shops around the Atrium and flying off.

Wonder where they nest for the night?

Cyrus chuckled as he thought of a Lumen nesting like a hen instead of lying down and sleeping. There were a lot of Lumens in the air. Many of them flew together, carrying heavier items. The circular space in front of the Atrium was almost empty.

It was Kimo's turn to support Cyrus while he walked so the moment they saw the opening overlooking the ocean, Auli'i ran ahead.

"Hey! Wait up!" said Kimo apprehensively.

Cyrus supported himself more and leaned less on Kimo. He

wouldn't put it past Kimo to drop him and chase after his sister. Kimo stayed steady though. Auli'i laughed as she caught up to Lady Marianne who was opening the cage.

Auli'i looked out at the horizon and then turned back towards the boys and beckoned for them to come quicker. Kimo picked up the pace by essentially carrying Cyrus. Only Cyrus' tippy toes touched the floor.

"Two minutes, then we head to the LC manor," said Lady Marianne, keeping her eyes on the street behind them.

The sun was going down and the water glimmered and danced faster because of the whirling vortex underneath them. Comfort and familiarity filled Cyrus from head to toe. With all this new information, new location and new reality he was living, it was nice to see something he was familiar with ... sunsets on the ocean. He didn't have to think. He allowed himself to feel.

Lumens dotted the sky as they went every which direction to the various islands.

"How many islands surround Aeolia, Ori?" asked Auli'i.

"One hundred thirty-seven. Five are atolls, though. There used to be more but the eye's current is ravenous. It has eroded about 20 islands over the years despite our efforts to prevent it. Do you see those boulders surrounding the south side of that island?" he said pointing.

Sure enough... there were large boulders sticking out of the water directing the current around the island.

"The boulders take the brunt of the current instead of the island itself. The island still gets washed away from the eye's current but at a much slower pace because of our efforts. One of the islands has servants directly responsible for the sculpting of such boulders. Another island is responsible for transporting and placing them."

"I bet that's difficult," said Kimo, shaking his head.

"Extremely ... We lose vessels and servants almost every time," he said with a tint of sadness.

"What's worse? That or working on the spire?" asked Cyrus.

"Depends on the man. For me, it's a tie. I wouldn't want either of them."

"I wonder what Aeolia looks like from one of those islands. I thought Aeolia was just an island with a huge mountain when we got here last night," said Auli'i.

"It is a sight to behold. Living here, I am used to it. But to any outsider who sees it for the first time ... It is a wonder. One of our past Lumen Latores was named Hippotes. He brought with him a young storyteller by the name of H-"

"Time's up. Let's go you three," said Lady Marianne behind them.

They took one last look out at the horizon, soaking up every bit of it.

The west was sunny and optimistic. They began walking back towards the Atrium and what a change. Mist and darkness began to roll in from the east. The circle was almost empty except for a few straggling Lumens and the guards that stood at the three entrances to the Atrium.

They made it back to the manor with the last sliver of light at their backs. The night had come.

The doors were opened for them by the two Lumens standing guard. They bowed and made the Omniscius Salutatio as Cyrus entered the Lumen Caligo manor.

Herald. Herald was his name!

"Thank you Johnathon. Thank you Herald," said Cyrus.

They both nodded and smiled. Especially Herald.

"If you are still hungry, let me know now and I will have a couple servants bring a couple trays. Cheese?" said Lady Marianne, pointing at Kimo.

Kimo nodded emphatically. Auli'i rolled her eyes.

"I'm glad you have your own room," said Auli'i. "I can only imagine what that's doing to your stomach."

Lady Marianne nodded, whirled around and began giving orders to Captain Ori who nodded at every pause. Once she finished, Lady Marianne went through the front door and promptly flew away.

"How does she command someone like you, Captain Ori? What makes her so special?" asked Kimo curiously.

"Her abilities ... She is one of six people alive to have completed the Iris Ascension. Not only that, she did it when she was fourteen. She would have tried it sooner to beat Sir Martin's record.

Unfortunately, she injured herself while training with the Jocovics just a couple days before, which forced her to wait an extra three months before she tried again."

"What is the Iris Ascension?" asked Auli'i.

"In the center of the great whirlpool below us, there is the structure I pointed out to you, the Mentibus Oculis, to refresh your memory. The structure has an arch that is no bigger than both of my arms held out wide. The Iris Ascension is where you begin at the top of the Atrium, the highest point in Aeolia, do a nose dive until you reach Mentibus Oculis, maneuver through the arch and then fly back up to where you began."

Captain Ori gave a shiver.

"And that's ... hard?" asked Cyrus.

"Hard? You have to be slightly crazy to even think about attempting it. To actually do it, you're either mental or have no fear. If you avoid going into the swirling current of the eye you have to turn up at the *perfect* time, otherwise, you will splat all over the entrance of the Mentibus Oculis. If you happen to pull up at the right time and line yourself up to go through the arch, you have to have enough speed AND fold your wings *perfectly* in order to make it through a hole this big," said Ori gesturing.

"If you make it through the arch without getting stuck or scraping yourself up, you then have to unfold your wings *perfectly* and turn up without running into the swirling current of Wadjet. A current that, may I remind you, pushes anyone and anything to a watery grave. *If* you can do that... you *then* have to battle the unpredictable air currents inside Wadjet, gravity AND the weight of the water sticking to your wings until you reach the top of Aeolia where you jumped off!" Cyrus and the twins looked at each other with raised eyebrows and mouths slightly open.

"Flying straight up is like me telling a Terram they have to swim 200 yards... underwater ... against the current... as fast as you can."

Auli'i and Kimo exhaled loudly. Kimo did a smile that portrayed a mixture of yikes and admiration.

"That sounds tiring," said Cyrus.

"It is ABSOLUTELY exhausting. Now, if you can make it to the top of the Atrium, you must land on your feet and stand without any support for one minute. Otherwise, you fail. Doesn't matter if you did everything perfectly until that moment. You don't stand on your own for one minute? You fail."

"Do a lot of people fail at that part?" asked Aul?'i.

"Almost all do. That specific part of the trial is the most difficult mentally. You put your body through the most excruciating test and then after all that, all you have to do is stand? It messes with people's heads."

"How many people try to do it every year?" asked Cyrus.

"Every year we have anywhere from 3 to 10 Lumens attempt the feat. Lady Marianne was the first to pass in seven years. That makes her the sixth person alive to complete it. Most who attempt the Iris Ascension live, despite failing. We have our strongest fliers at the entrance of Mentibus Oculis and their family members on the spire. It isn't uncommon for the men and women to faint from exhaustion mid-flight."

"That's scary ..." said Auli'i, grabbing Cyrus' arm.

"It's terrifying. Most people don't attempt more than once. If they fail the first time, that's it. Most of the Lumen men attempting the feat go limp from exhaustion. When that happens, the other Lumens fly into action, attempting to snatch them out of the air before they fall to their deaths. A couple years ago, a couple drowned together because when the man fainted halfway up, the wife caught him too close to Wadjet's spiraling walls. Sadly, Wadjet pushed them to the bottom of the ocean."

"Who was it?" asked Cyrus.

"It was actually Karlovic's older brother and a blacksmith's daughter. Aeolia mourned that day ..."

"Are boy Lumens stronger than girl Lumens?" asked Kimo.

Auli'i furrowed her brow. Cyrus looked down. Captain Ori chuckled.

"Yes, male Lumens are physically stronger than their female counterparts. Similar to the Terrams, I'm sure. You must remember, Sir Kimo, the test is not a test of strength alone. It is a test of endurance, precision and force of will. I guess you could say how someone uses their strength determines how successful they are. More men have passed the Iris Ascension than women by a large margin. However, men have failed the task by an equally large margin."

"Why do it?" asked Auli'i, softening her expression.

"Prestige. If you complete the Iris Ascension, you have done the toughest feat in flight and demonstrated mastery over all its concepts. Exceptional flying abilities are important to Lumens. Nose diving, wing tucking, directional manipulation and maneuverability. Not only do you earn the respect of every single Lumen, the highest positions, outside of duke, are opened up to you. Security detail, ranking officer, anything really. Aeolia opens her arms fully and abundantly, if you succeed. That is incentive enough to keep us Lumens trying."

"Who are the six?" asked Kimo.

"Lady Marianne Evynwood. Karlovic Jocovic. Sir Martin Weatherford. Lady Marcella Brad ford. High Duke Gabriel Bradford and Arch Duke Winston Weatherford."

Cyrus bulged his eyes.

Did he just say ...

There was a sudden flap of wings. Three Lumens trailed Lady Marianne carrying trays-one covered in nothing but cheese. Kimo licked his lips in anticipation.

"My room, one hour," Cyrus whispered to the twins.

They nodded.

"I will have one piece of cheese and then have a bath," said Cyrus, grabbing a piece from the tray. "Thank you." Lady Marianne bowed slightly and made the Omniscius Salutatio.

"Sleep well, Lumen Caligo," she said with the same flat expression. Her voice sounded warmer, though.

Cyrus gestured the Omniscius Salutatio and then climbed the stairs slowly with Auli'i. Kimo had his hands full with the cheese.

The servants had lit the torches again leading to his room. The flickering light reminded Cyrus of the time Martin took him camping when he was nine.

I would kill for some s'mores right now.

Cyrus drew himself a bath and thought about the day. His mind anticipated meeting his mother for the first time.

What will she be like? Will I look like her? Will she want me? Why did she abandon me?

Cyrus floated underneath the water on that last thought. His heart hurt. Maybe he didn't want to meet her ... oh, but of course he did. He always wanted to have a mother. Ms. P was the closest thing to a mother he had growing up ... and she was crazy.

Cyrus dried off and changed into a white shirt and some black pants that were left on the bed for him. The clothes were soft and smelled like citrus. Cyrus got his phone out and turned it back on. Still no signal. Not that he expected there to be. Cyrus began taking photos of the paintings by the lit torch. He had missed some earlier. He made a mental note that he would take pictures of Aeolia when there was daylight. A knock at the door interrupted Cyrus' thoughts.

"Come in."

Auli'i and Kimo tip toed into Cyrus' room.

"Wow.. Your bed is nicer than mine," said Auli'i. "And you have your own bathroom?! Someone is the favorite."

"Get used to it."

"Never."

Cyrus smiled. All three sat on his bed.

"OK, enough flirting you two. Cyrus, what don't we know?" asked Kimo.

Cyrus pulled out the note and showed it to the twins.

"So... nothing new."

"That's all I got."

"Can we stay with you until he gets here?" asked Auli'i.

"Sure ... I don't mind..."

"If that's the case.." Kimo got up, ran out of the room and quickly returned with the platter of cheeses.

"Do you ever stop eating?" asked Auli'i in disbelief.

"It's so I stay stronger than girls."

Auli'i punched him in the arm.

"See? Maybe you should eat more cheese."

Auli'i swiped a handful of cheese and stuffed them into her mouth with a frown. Cyrus suppressed his laughter. Soon, all three of them were laughing as they munched on some Lumen cheese.

"Lumen Caligo," said a voice with a knock at the door.

All three stopped laughing and looked behind them. Kimo got up and opened the door. Lady Marianne stood at the entrance with the same unimpressed expression.

"A letter from Arch Duke Winston just arrived. There is a falcon perched just down the hall whenever you are ready to respond," she said, walking past Kimo and handing the letter to Cyrus.

"Thank you, Lady Marianne."

Lady Marianne bowed and then promptly left. Kimo shut the door slowly behind her.

"You're welcome," he said sarcastically after her.

Cyrus ripped the letter open and began reading aloud.

Master Cyrus,

It was a joy receiving you into my home earlier this afternoon! My meeting

with the other Dukes was successful (and fortunately short). Attached is the Isolation

Order Nullification. All that is needed from you is your signature and one of your

feathers. Should you have any questions please speak with any of the Dukes, myself included.

May your light illuminate the darkness,

P.S. Should you find yourself with a little bit of free time tomorrow around noon, please stop by for another game of chess, You've put me in a gaming mood.

Have a wonderful evening!

Arch Duke Winston Weatherford

Cyrus smiled at the Arch Duke's letter.

A game of chess tomorrow sounds nice.

Cyrus turned the page and read the nullification of the Isolation Order. It was written much neater.

By decree of the Lumen Caligo. all stipulations outlined in the Isolation Order of 1690 A.D. are now declared null and void. The Lumen Nation will now be permitted full access to the world and her technologies under the guidance of it's appointed Dukes

May the Lumen Nation be a beacon to the world as in times of Old.

———— Approved by ————

Arch Duke Winston Weatherford

High Duke Gabriel Bradford

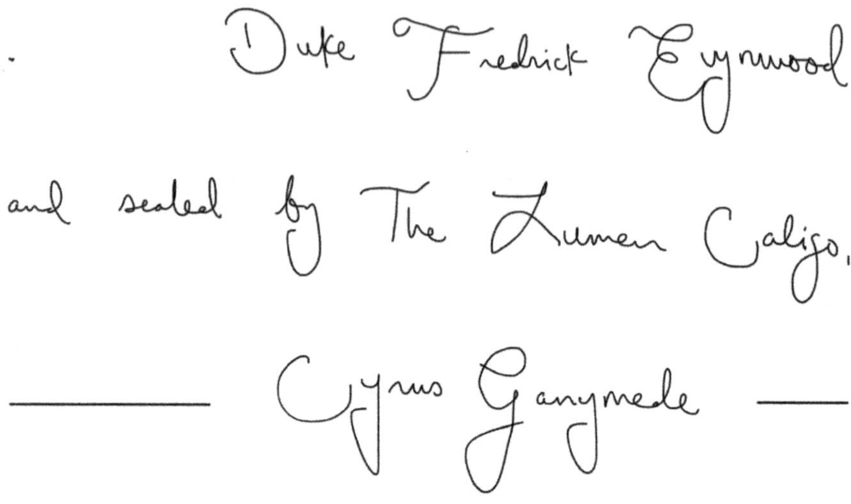

There was space below the document for the letter to be signed. The presentation of the letter was impressive.

Cyrus re-read the letter to himself and then looked at the twins.

"Sooo ... Should I sign it?"

Kimo looked at Auli'i. Auli'i raised her eyebrows and pouted her lips.

"Honestly... I think you should wait for Martian," she said.

"You're probably right."

"Probably?! I am right, young master Cyrus," said Auli'i with a grin.

"The progress of an entire nation hinging on the signature of an 11 year old ..." said Cyrus trailing off.

"Don't forget the feather," said Kimo with a yawn.

"That too ..."

"Want me to pluck it now?" asked Auli'i with a grin.

"Ut tuh duh duh," said Cyrus, putting his finger up. "You said to wait for Martian."

Auli'i smiled and then made herself comfortable on Cyrus bed.

"I was only trying to help," she said, closing her eyes.

"No she wasn't," said Kimo also making himself comfortable.

Auli'i gave him a half-hearted punch. Kimo smacked her back in similar fashion.

The night deepened and so did the sleep in the twin's eyes. Not

Cyrus though. He was attentive and awake. Every second that clicked by seemed an eternity. Eventually, the twins fell asleep on Cyrus' bed.

Martian, where are you?

Cyrus was so desperate to know the exact time he kept his phone on.

After what felt like an eternity, midnight ticked into existence. Cyrus felt his heart accelerate. Cyrus looked at the front door and saw two eyes floating in the shadows. Cyrus jumped from fright. It was Martin. He motioned to his lips in a shush and then motioned towards him.

He slowly got up and made his way to Martin with the papers in his hands. Cyrus turned the flashlight of his phone on and handed Martin the letter he had received from his father. Martin quickly read them and then whispered to Cyrus.

"Do NOT sign these. We can go over them tomorrow. Are you ready to go?"

Cyrus nodded with a look of surprise. Martin walked past him and placed the letter on Cyrus' bedside table.

Kimo snored loudly. Cyrus went to Auli'i who had wrapped herself into a little ball on his bed. He shook her gently awake.

"I'll be back. I'll tell you all about it in the morning," he whispered.

Auli'i snapped up and looked right at Martin. She then rushed over and gave him a hug.

"Take care of him, Martian," she whispered tiredly.

Martin smiled and nodded. He then gestured to Cyrus.

"We have to go now. Night guard is making his rounds," he whispered.

Cyrus grabbed his black cloak and followed Martin.

Martin closed the door behind them silently and moved like a cat to the window sill. Martin unfurled his wings, and to Cyrus' great surprise, they were covered in a black material just like his outfit. It was almost like a bed sheet, it was so thin. Martin looked left and then right. He grabbed Cyrus and then opened his wings and whooshed into the night sky.

Martin flew low and jumped from building to building, keeping his head on a swivel. Cyrus could see the lighthouse burning brightly. Everything was quiet except for the sound of Wadjet below them. Cyrus shivered. The whirlpool spooked him even more during the nighttime.

Martin landed on a roof and then jumped to an alleyway to the side of the house. He put Cyrus down and then peered around the corner. Satisfied with what he saw, he beckoned Cyrus to follow him. Silently, they made their way through a garden as lavish as Arch Duke Winston's and up to the front entrance of a manor.

"Where are we?"

Martin put his finger to his lips. He then grabbed Cyrus again, this time putting him on his back and lept into the air toward the overhanging ceiling above them. Martin grabbed the top and placed his feet against the building. There was a large stained glass window in front of them. In the center was a giant lotus that formed a perfect circle as big as Cyrus. Martin put his hands up against the lotus and pushed.

Creak ...

Martin pushed again.

Creeeeak ...

Martin inhaled and pushed forward one more time.

Creeeeeak ... Click.

The stained glass window must have been held together by a metal lever. The stained glass folded outwards in either direction, giving them access to the inside of the house.

"Crawl under the lotus. I'll go through the top half," he whispered.

Cyrus gulped but did as Martin asked. Martin placed him right at the entrance and Cyrus slowly clawed his way through. There was a *whoosh* above him and he found Martin suspended in the air with his arms outstretched, waiting for him. Cyrus reached out. He felt himself lose his balance on the thin metal outlining and began to plummet. Right before he could gain momentum, Martin's strong hands plucked him out of the air. Cyrus breathed heavily, terrified.

"Will you look at that..." chuckled Martin softly.

Cyrus, confused, saw Martin looking behind him. Cyrus looked and saw his wings were outstretched behind him.

Did I do that? I must have.

There was no way they were open when he was crawling underneath the stained glass lotus.

They landed on the floor of a sprawling dining hall. The room connected to the main entrance which had a flickering torch ... that was moving.

Martin grabbed Cyrus and threw him under the large table that was in the center of the room. Together they hid as a Lumen guard walked into the room. Cyrus trembled and felt his heart beat faster.

The guard walked nonchalantly around the table, humming some flimsy tune. He did a circle around the table and then left.

Martin quickly got up and peered into the entrance hall.

"Let's go," he whispered.

They quickly made their way to a staircase, to which Martin grabbed Cyrus and with one giant flap of his wings, made it all the way to the top. A fountain with a winged woman holding a pot pouring water greeted them at the top. She was decorated in gold leafing. Cyrus' stomach was churning from all this up and down. He shouldn't have eaten that cheese Kimo had given him.

"Your mother is down that corridor, the last door on the right.

Knock three times and she'll think you're the house butler. We are in the Bradford manor. I don't know much about your mother aside from what the guards told me. All they said is that she has been in mourning ever since she came back. She sleeps during the day and stays up all night. The Marcella I knew will rejoice when she learns you are here. I can only imagine how much she must miss you and has dreamt of having you back in her arms. Now go ... I'll knock one time to let you know it's me," said Martin, pointing Cyrus down the hall.

Cyrus turned around and started walking. He turned back one last time and met Martin's eyes. He smiled and gave the thumbs up. Martin then jumped towards the ceiling and disappeared.

Cyrus was a bit nervous. He had a mother ... an actual mother who was living, breathing and, from what Martin had told him, missed him more than anything in the world.

"Dreamt of having you back in her arms." Cyrus' thoughts echoed.

He walked through the long corridor decorated with gold leafing as he approached a large red door. Reaching the door, he took a deep breath and knocked three times.

"I do not wish to eat, Constance, as I told you earlier. Please give the food I would have been given to those in the 5th precinct. They would be most grateful to receive it in a time like this," said the voice.

Normally Cyrus would have been entertained by the assumption he was someone else ... but not today.

"It's not Constance ... It's ... er ... um ... It's Cyrus ..."

Silence.

Then a rustling and rushing with hurried steps and clanking of locks. The door opened and light flooded into the corridor where Cyrus stood. An involuntary gasp escaped Cyrus' lips as he beheld his beautiful mother.

The color red for the door now made more sense to Cyrus. Long, flowing red hair sprouted from his mother's head, curls tugging up and down her fiery strands. It was thick, like his. Or better yet, his hair was thick like hers. A soft white dress draped over her sun kissed body and freckles adorned her arms. Behind her, wings matching the exact tone of her dress majestically sprawled out into an embracing shape.

A soft white glow seemed to be pulsating with emotion that warmed Cyrus from head to toe. Vibrant blue eyes brimmed with tears and an expression of sheer joy spread across her face. Her shade of blue was only slightly darker than his left eye but the eye shape and the eyebrows matched his perfectly. Her expression was now mixed with utter disbelief. Up and down she inspected Cyrus. She then rubbed her eyes a couple of times and turned away. She composed herself and then slowly turned back around, staring Cyrus directly in the eyes.

The two maintained their timeless stare. Cyrus let a smile tug at his lips. Tears began to stream down his mother's face as she looked at him like no other person had looked at him before. A look of love so deep ... so pure ... it had to be maternal. This look of unfathomable love unlocked a dormant feeling inside of Cyrus. Something he had been without for so long but something, he now realized, he did not want to live without. Satisfied it was actually him, Marcella smiled the most heartwarming smile and then opened her arms.

"It can't be ... Cyrus ... Is it really you?"

Cyrus, gently but hastily embraced his mother. She wrapped her arms around him first and then her soft arid wings. Cyrus had never felt so safe. Warmth spread across his chest like a warm drink on a cold day. Tears flowed freely between the two without shame. Cyrus had felt like an outsider his whole life. Embracing his mother, he felt accepted. He had a mother ... *She* was his home.

16
SURVIVAL

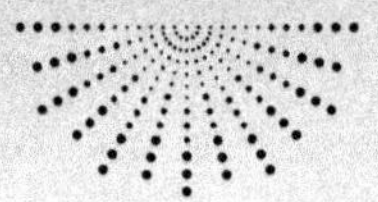

YOU'RE ALIVE?!" SOBBED MARCELLA, stroking Cyrus' head. "Oh, my baby is alive! I hoped you were ... I can scarcely believe it!" Marcella squeezed him tightly. Cyrus could feel her entire body quivering. She grasped at him like he was about to disappear.

"Oh, Cyrus ... Oh, Cyrus ... I ... am so happy. My ba- My baby is alive."

Cyrus squeezed her back in what felt like an eternal hug. The raw emotion made him choke up again.

Marcella composed herself and looked back at Cyrus. She stroked his face and then smothered him in kisses.

Cyrus scrunched his nose.

"Oh my!" Marcella started laughing. "You did the same thing as an infant! It was just as cute then!"

Her smile warmed Cyrus from head to toe.

"It was probably cuter then," said Cyrus with a smirk.

Marcella giggled and stroked his face. "If this is a dream, I pray I never wake up."

"I'm very much real. I'm having a hard time believing you are too ... mom."

Fresh tears came to her eyes and her smile returned.

"How? How did you find me, Cyrus?"

"It's kind of a long story, but after I found out you existed, I made my way to Aeolia."

"I ... I can't believe it. I thought you were dead all this time," she said, covering her face.

"Dead? I thought you were the one who left me with Martian?" Marcella looked at him with an incredulous look on her face.

"No ... The last time I saw you, you were with your father as I tried to lead our pursuers away, only ..." she paused and put her head down.

"They weren't after just me."

"Who was pursuing you?"

"Stragglers from the search party Martin led. When I ran away from Aeolia with your father, the story was I had been 'abducted?' Martin found us first and was about to fight your father until I explained it was my choice to leave. My choice to be with Cyrus. My choice to have you," she said, stroking his face.

"Wait, wait, wait ... Start at the beginning. Why did they think you were abducted?"

"Have you seen the Caligo at the Weatherford manor?"

Cyrus nodded

"His name is Fernando Constantinople. Fifteen years ago, your father arrived to Aeolia with six other Caligos seeking an audience with the dukes ... unannounced. There was panic and whispers of a surprise attack so instead of a peaceful solution, the Arch Duke reacted with violence. All of the Caligos were shot down and killed ... save your father and Fernando. I happened to be training with Martin for the Iris Ascension that day and flew to their aid right before the Lumen Air Force was able to finish him off."

"Martin said we shouldn't interfere, but your father was wounded, protecting Fernando and desperately trying to keep another Caligo afloat-even though that Caligo was long gone... His care for others despite his own perilous situation moved me deeply. So, I stood in their way and pleaded for them to spare him. Eventually, I got my way, but that was only half the battle. They would stand before the dukes and surely be sentenced to death. Even my own father would vote in favor of the Caligo's execution for violation of the Isolation Order but ... I was persistent and found a loophole," she said with a cheeky smile.

Cyrus soaked in every word coming out of his mother's mouth.

"I asked my father that if I completed the Iris Ascension at that very moment, would he change his vote and petition the dukes to instead commit the Caligos to indentured servitude instead of execution. That's what happens to the Civilized, why not the Caligos? The Caligos did break the Isolation Order so they needed to be punished.

"Now, my father-your grandfather—is a great man ... and all great men are suckers for two things. More glory for the family name ... and their daughters. So, naturally, he said yes. In that moment, I flew to the top of the Atrium and completed the Iris Ascension flawlessly. Fernando was assigned to serve the Weatherford household and Cyrus was assigned to serve our household."

"How old were you when you completed the Iris Ascension?"

"Sixteen. Martin had been training me for a year prior to my attempt and told me I was ready. I just didn't have the courage to do it. In that moment, when my father agreed to my plea, I found my courage. That was something your father always brought out of me. Courage to question. Courage to act. Courage to follow through ... The next three years, he was nothing short of perfect to me and my family. He gained my family's trust and through small acts of service, he claimed my heart. We knew our desire to be together would never be allowed so in the dead of night one summer, we flew away to the United States and settled in a small town in the Midwest. There, we were married and I became pregnant with you." She stroked his face again.

Cyrus closed his eyes as the flood gates opened. He felt slightly embarrassed but trusted his mother. He felt a comfort with her he couldn't explain.

"Oh, Cyrus, your wings are pulsing," she said with admiration.

The white sides seemed to be pulsating light while the black sides seemed to make the other half of the room darker with each pulse.

"I'm so happy to see you," said Cyrus.

Marcella smiled warmly as another tear fell from her angelic face.

"I'm so happy to see you too. Words cannot express how full my heart is." She embraced him with her arms and wings again. It was warm inside her embrace like a cocoon.

"Martian never talked about you... He ... He would always avoid the subject when I asked."

"Why do you call him Martian?" asked Marcella curiously.

"Oh. I couldn't pronounce my T's very well when I was younger so that's how I used to say it and, well... it just kinda stuck ... he does act like a Martian sometimes."

Marcella giggled and pinched Cyrus nose softly. "You're not wrong. Was Martin the one who raised you then?"

"Yes ... So you didn't leave me with Martian?" Marcella shook her head.

"Do you know who did?"

Marcella shook her head again.

Cyrus scratched his head.

"What happened when Martian found you and dad?"

Her smile slowly faded. He almost regretted the words as they'd left his mouth. He wanted to see that smile again.

"I was eight months pregnant with you when Martin showed up. I heard a commotion in the kitchen and was surprised to find Martin and Cyrus crossing blades. I immediately told them to stop. After they didn't listen, I stood between their blades. I turned to show Martin that I was pregnant and told him I had left Aeolia on my own free will and that it had actually been my idea to leave. Martin ... he said nothing and then left. That was the last time I saw him."

The memory seemed to cause physical pain and discomfort for her. She sat up straight and continued.

"Almost four months later, they arrived. A company of Lumens and two Caligos hot on our trail. I didn't recognize any of them save Karlovic's older brother. We tried to outrun them but they were persistent and caught up to us. You were three months old at the time. I thought they only wanted me so in a last ditch effort, I left you in your father's care while I tried to lure them away. I thought my plan was working until I saw smoke in the distance where I had left you with your father." Her voice faltered.

"I ... flew faster than I ever have ... but when I reached the farm house, it was a raging inferno. I tried to go in but they had finally cornered me. Despite my best effort to go in after you and your father ... they wouldn't let me. They tied me up like a hog and transported me back to Aeolia. Delirious and depressed, I have simply existed since that day. Nothing has brought me joy. Nothing has taken me out of my sorrow ... until tonight."

Dang it.

Cyrus began tearing up. He wrapped his arms around her.

After releasing him, she inspected every inch of him.

"I love your eyes, darling. Always have. They reflect both myself and your father. He had eyes as dark as night. Yours have a bit of amber in them but still remind me of him. Your skin is almost the perfect shade between myself and him. Some of those freckles might give him a run for his money," she said with a smile.

Cyrus touched his nose, trying to imagine what his father looked like.

"Is it possible he survived?" asked Cyrus.

Marcella looked up hopefully.

"I don't know, Cyrus... There were two Caligos and six Lumens chasing us that day. By the time I got back to the burning farm house, there was only one Caligo and three Lumens left. While they were transporting me back to Aeolia, they mourned the loss of their companions, citing your father as the cause of their demise. He took three Lumens and one Caligo with him before he died ... or at least that's what they said ... I don't know, sweetheart.."

A sliver of hope surged through Cyrus.

What if he is still out there?

"Let me look at you," she said, running her fingers through his hair.

Cyrus felt a little self-conscious.

"Can you open your wings for me?" she asked sweetly.

Cyrus opened his wings as wide as he could. Marcella circled him, touching his wings and wiggling them from end to end. She circled back to the front with a worried look in her eye.

"You're so thin ... Can you fly?"

Cyrus shook his head and exhaled. His wings drooped from the exertion.

"Martian had me confined to a wheelchair and drugged up. I just started walking this month. I learned I had wings about the same time."

Horror filled her face. Then pity. "Wh….. Why would he do that?" Cyrus shrugged. "I'd like to know, too.

"You just started walking?!"

"Yes."

Marcella turned away and shook her head.

"Martian and I haven't exactly had a lot of time together since he left for Hawaii. We've maintained this charade pretending we met here in Aeolia. I don't know what he is up to, but he told me to trust him."

"Do you?"

Cyrus thought about it for a while.

"Yes ... He just needs to fill me in."

"Well, allow me to teach you something all Lumen mothers teach their children. They are called the 'A B C's'"

"I can read, mom."

Marcella smiled. "You better. These are actually for your wings, silly."

"Ahhhh, yes. Proceed." Cyrus' cheeks turned red.

"These cover almost all movements for flying. First, with your wings, you will make the letter 'A'." She started making an 'A' with her wings. Cyrus made an 'A'... slowly.

"When doing them in the same direction becomes easy, try reversing the 'A. The 'B' is easy. It's like rolling your shoulders. In fact, I would recommend you do this with your arms and your wings," she said, looping her wings and arms in constant circles.

Cyrus once again did the letter ... slowly.

"Then there is 'C'" She stopped her wings mid-loop and started looping them into a 'C' shape over and over. Her arms followed suit.

Cyrus felt a couple sweat droplets form on his forehead as he imitated his mother.

I have a long way to go.

"I wish Martian had prepared me better. I feel so behind," said Cyrus panting.

"You'll catch up. Martin is one of the best men I know and I have always trusted him. His reasons will be made known soon enough."

Cyrus nodded.

"Is he close?"

"Somewhere in the house."

Marcella walked to the door, opened it and jumped from fright. Standing in front of the door was a woman with flowing blonde hair with strands of red.

"Good evening, Marcella. You're ... looking healthier. All that day sleeping must be doing you some good," she said with a smile.

"Malinda! Goodness gracious you startled me ..."

"I'm so sorry. I heard voices in your room and was worried you were talking to yourself again so I came to check on you. Who is your friend?"

"Cyrus, this is my sister, Lady Malinda. Malinda this is Cyrus... The Lumen Caligo," she said with a smile.

Malinda couldn't hide her surprise. She approached Cyrus slowly with eyes bulging and mouth agape. She circled him slowly, hardly believing her eyes.

"Oh my! ... It really is you! He ... he looks ... oh my ... ohhhh my ..." stuttered Malinda in disbelief.

"Forgive the intrusion, Lady Malinda," said Cyrus politely. "Me and my Virtus Latores are not due until tomorrow. Your father, High Duke Gabriel received me last night in the Atrium alongside the other dukes."

"So that is what all the commotion was about!"

"I heard father come in last night ... When I asked what happened, all he said was I had to attend dinner in two days time to find out. I wasn't feeling very playful so I didn't pursue it further," said Marcella.

"You haven't felt playful for the past eleven years, Marcella. Let's be honest. This is the most energized I've ever seen you. I can see why ..." she said, looking directly at Cyrus.

Cyrus felt uncomfortable. Every observation Malinda made sounded like an accusation.

"Oh, quit acting coy. The Lumen Caligo is amongst us. That is plenty of reason to be energized," said Marcella with a tone of annoyance.

"A Lumen Caligo named Cyrus ... What a coincidence ..." she said wryly. "I see you have much to catch up on. Cyrus it has been a pleasure meeting you. I'll be sure to act surprised tomorrow at supper when father presents you to us for what he thinks is the first time. How is this for my look of surprise?" Malinda put her hands to her cheeks with her mouth open.

"Needs work. Now, go practice in your room," said Marcella.

"Night night ..." said Malinda, waving her fingers as she shut the door.

"Should I be worried?" asked Cyrus.

"I don't know yet ... Malinda... acts on whims."

There was a single knock at the door.

"That's Martian."

Marcella opened the door and sure enough there was Martin. Marcella inhaled sharply.

"Martin..." she said.

"Lady Marcella," he said with a slight bow. "Cyrus, we have to go. Malinda isn't the only one up. High Duke Gabriel is roaming the halls now."

"Why did you drug Cyrus all those years?" blurted out Marcella.

The question caught Martin off guard. "Can this wait?"

"No," Marcella and Cyrus said at the same time.

Martin looked back and forth and then nodded. He then reached into his pocket and pulled out a small bottle with a soft yellow liquid inside. The liquid looked familiar to Cyrus.

"What is it?" asked Marcella.

"A powerful sedative. This is what was given to me twelve years ago when I was sent to rescue you. My instructions were to inject you with it but here is where I became suspicious ... I was also told to save enough for the Lumen Caligo, should I encounter him or her."

"So ..." said Marcella.

"So, doesn't that seem suspicious to you that I should be instructed to use this for a Lumen Caligo that was about to be born?" said Martin, raising an eyebrow.

Marcella nodded

"It gets worse. A couple of your house guards just received a bottle of this four hours ago. They were admiring it while I spied on them. They said they were instructed to use it on enemy forces arriving in Acolia. We need to get back to the LC manor quickly and come up with a plan."

"Who sent this instruction?" asked Marcella.

Martin paused and looked at Cyrus.

"Legion."

Marcella gasped and horror filled her eyes. "I thought he was gone. After the execution ..."

"Well, apparently not, Marcella. We need to move Cyrus now!" Marcella nodded and then grabbed a black outfit similar to Martin's.

"You should really stay here, Marcella. Malinda has already seen you and who knows who she'll tell."

"I'm going with you. I'm not leaving my son's fate up to chance. Did you come through the lotus?"

Martin nodded.

"Go close it up and get back here quickly. I have a safer way out." She disappeared into her wash room.

Martin nodded and then silently disappeared.

His mother reemerged dressed head to toe in black.

"The stained glass window with the lotus is what Martin and I used to use to sneak in and out of my family's manor..." she said as she began to tie her hair. "If you ever want to sneak into the Weatherford manor, there is a secret entrance underneath the statue on the left by the front entrance." Martin reemerged. "Done."

"Do we need anything else?" asked Marcella.

"Yellow Death."

Cyrus looked at his mother who was giving a 'you can't be serious' face to Martin.

"Crocea Mors?" she asked.

"Now or never. I don't think there will be another opportunity."

"We don't know what will happen to him! Plus, the dukes will take that as an insult for not deciding that with them. Aeolia will be in an uproar!"

"We need it. With everything in motion, I doubt Cyrus will be safe at day break."

Realization came into Marcella's eyes. She nodded in agreement. Cyrus remained as confused as ever.

"If you distract your father, I can sneak into his chamber," said Martin.

"I just changed..." huffed Marcella, grabbing her white gown and going back to the wash room. She reemerged in the white outfit and brought a bag filled with the black clothes.

"The pipes in my wash room have made the mortar connecting the stone soft. I rearranged them so there is a hole just wide enough for us to squeeze through. Behind the wall is a bigger fountain that always has flowing water. We will hide behind the wall of water until it is clear and then leave. We may get a little wet on the way out but it is away from the guards and exits."

"Sounds good. Can we go get Yellow Death now, please."

"Tsk-tsk... patience, Martin. How are we going to play this?"

"Keep him in the entrance hall. I don't want him to feel any draft I may create," said Martin.

"How long?"

"Sixty seconds."

"Cyrus, honey, follow me."

She led him to the washroom. Cyrus felt a slight breeze coming through the cracks in the stone.

"Could you move these stones to this corner, darling? Martin and I will be back in a jiffy."

Cyrus blinked in surprise at the word. Must have picked it up when she was living in the states.

"What is Yellow Death?" asked Cyrus as he lifted the first stone.

It took considerable effort from him.

"Crocea Mors, or'Yellow Death,' is a sword and a Bradford family heirloom. It is also a key that grants access to Mentibus Oculis ... Or so we think. Now, go ahead and start stacking. Love you!" She kissed his nose and ran off.

Cyrus was left with a mixture of feelings. His mother had said love you for the first time he could remember. Cyrus began stacking the stones in a straight line, one after another. He decided to count in his head.

30 seconds.

Cyrus could hear muffled voices outside-one was his mother's. It surprised him how fast he could recognize it.

45 seconds.

Cyrus had four stones left. He could feel himself sweating. The voices trailed off.

55 seconds. All done.

The voices had ceased. Cyrus grabbed the wall and used it to help himself up.

65 seconds. Maybe they started the countdown when they left the room.

Cyrus grabbed the bag his mother had asked him to hold.

75 seconds. Should I be worried?

Cyrus looked at the hole he had made in the wall.

"INTRUDERS IN THE MANOR!" someone yelled.

Cyrus jumped at the sound. Martin and Marcella appeared in front of him.

"Cyrus, give mommy the bag. I need to change."

"We leave for the Atrium at once. They'll comb this place first and then the LC manor," said Martin.

Cyrus looked at Martin, fear in his eyes. "The twins!"

"Who are we talking about?" asked Marcella.

"His Virtus Latores are in the LC manor," said Martin.

Marcella stopped tying her hair, thought for a second and then promptly finished.

"Here is our plan. Martin, go get the twins and meet me at the entrance of the Sanctum. Cyrus and 1 are going to the Atrium to try Crocea Mors."

"Be careful. Keep him safe," said Martin with a nod. He handed something gold to Marcella and then disappeared into the night.

Cyrus heard a splash as Martin went through the fountain and into the night sky.

"What is going on? Why are we going to the Atrium?"

"I need you to move through the hole in the wall, sweetheart. I'll explain on the way. Come on ... Let's go," she said sweetly but urgently. She strapped the gold item to her back as she walked forward with Cyrus.

Cyrus squeezed through the gap in the wall with his mother right behind him. She replaced the stones quickly. The wall of water was about as tall as Cyrus. Marcella grabbed his hand, and together, they jumped through the water. The night was warm and the water felt refreshing.

"Into mommy's arms, we have to fly and fast." Cyrus wrapped his arms around her neck.

"Oh my goodness, you've gotten so big. I don't think you remember our first flights but I do. Those were a little bit easier."

She leaped into the air and flew directly to the Atrium, keeping to the shadows of the buildings. There was a crescent moon out and a sky full of stars.

Cyrus looked back and saw torches and Lumens in white robes flying towards the LC Manor. Cyrus felt guilt for leaving the twins.

Marcella flew quickly though the air. Her grip on Cyrus kept slipping but she always readjusted. Before they knew it, they were at the entrance to the Atrium. The sky was beginning to lighten.

What time is it?

"Command the guards to open the Atrium. Make sure you show

your wings. Be quick about it. We have maybe 10 minutes," whispered Marcella as she set him down.

The two of them walked towards one of the entrances to the Atrium.

"Halt! Return to your homes at once!" boomed the guard on the right.

Cyrus looked back at his mom and then towards the guards with the long metal spears.

"I, Cyrus Ganymede, the Lumen Caligo, command you to open the Atrium," said Cyrus, extending his wings.

His wings were still pulsating and the light side facing the guards seemed to mesmerize them. Bowing while making the Omniscius Salutatio, the two guards made the whistling noise to the other guards and in unison they put their spears into the slot and began turning. The entire island shook as the Atrium rotated. The entire process was as amazing as when he saw it the first time.

The guards retrieved their spears and gestured inwards. Marcella and Cyrus began their entrance when the guards clanged their spears together blocking Marcella.

"I, Cyrus Ganymede, grant Atrium access to Marcella Bradford."

The guards lowered their spears and made the Omniscius Salutatio.

Marcella picked up Cyrus and ran into the Atrium. Cyrus' questions finally caught up to him.

"OK, why are we running? What happened when you went to get Yellow Death?" asked Cyrus as his mother set him down gently and reached for something attached to her hip.

Marcella pulled a sheathed sword out from behind her.

So that was what Martian gave her.

"This is Yellow Death. As for why we're running, Martin is certain the sedative isn't for capturing these supposed invaders. It's meant for sedating YOU. What's worse ... My father was wearing a black cloak outlined in white ... Just like those who hunted me all those years ago."

"Why?"

"I don't know, sweetheart, but I didn't stay long enough to find out.

There was an extra guard with my father. Malinda 'sneezed' right as Martin was making his way back to my room. Unfortunately, the guard saw Martin and sounded the alarm. Martin lost him fast enough but the damage is done. We have to move fast."

As soon as they made it inside the Atrium, Marcella grabbed Cyrus and flew into the air. They made their way to the pillar of crystal in the center of the Atrium. The mirrors bounced the light up and down the Atrium illuminating its intricate displays.

"What are we doing in the Atrium?"

"Something only you can do. Unlocking the Sanctum below." Cyrus looked around for a key hole. Nothing. He looked at his mother who pointed to the top pillar.

"There is a small slit on the top pillar. You need to stick the blade of Crocea Mors into that slot. Nothing ever happens when a Lumen, a Caligo or a Terram does this ... but from the documented history of my people, it is different when a Lumen Caligo does it."

Cyrus nodded and gulped loudly. He was apprehensive with all the uncertainty.

"Do I have to? Why don't we just fly away?"

"Can you fly?"

The question cut him deeper than it should have. He could barely walk.

"Last time I ran from these guys, they still caught me. I was 11 years younger and only carrying myself. I won't make the same mistake twice and try to outrun them. We're going to hide from them. If this doesn't work, then we'll try something else but I'll be damned if I let them take you from me again."

"Mom?"

"Yes, Cyrus?"

"I'm scared."

Marcella stopped flying, landed in front of the largest pillar and turned to Cyrus. She grabbed him and kissed his cheek.

"I love you more than life itself, Cyrus. It is time to be brave," she said smiling, tears in her eyes again. She flapped her wings forcefully, and in the blink of an eye, they were on top of the spire.

"GET DOWN FROM THERE IMMEDIATELY," came a voice from another entrance.

Cyrus and Marcella whipped their heads around and saw five Lumens in black cloaks lined in white coming at them.

"South entrance," said Marcella.

Cyrus turned around and sure enough there were more.

So much for me granting entry.

"Northwest entrance now, too. Cyrus hurry and insert Crocea Mors in the slit of the crystal. If nothing happens we'll make a dash for the northeast entrance."

Cyrus unsheathed Crocea Mors ... it was very underwhelming. The blade was rusted, chipped and dull. It looked like it would fall to pieces at any moment.

The Lumens cleared the hallway leading to the Atrium and ascended into the air. Most had bows and arrows, while some had long spears like the guards at the entrance of the Atrium.

"PUT DOWN THE SWORD AND SURRENDER TO US NOW!" came the voice from afar. His voice was rough and bled cruelty. He walked slowly towards the crystal spires.

Cyrus lined up the sword with the slit in the crystal and looked at his mother. She nodded with approval.

"IF YOU INSERT THAT SWORD INTO THE CRYSTAL, LUMEN CALIGO, YOU WILL JEOPARDIZE ANY AMNESTY YOU HAVE HERE IN AEOLIA," said the voice continuing his slow approach.

Cyrus began pushing the sword downwards.

"STOP NOW AND I WILL SPARE YOUR MOTHER." It sounded like a smile had followed the sentence.

Cyrus stopped dead in his tracks. "Who are you?!"

The man stopped in front of the crystals with his hands behind his back. He lowered his voice to almost a whisper.

"I ... am Legion. You escaped me once, Lumen Caligo ..."

The last entrance was now blocked. They were completely surrounded.

"... you will not escape me again."

Cyrus started to panic. He felt like he was caught in Wadjet's current. No matter what he did, he felt like he would lose.

"Cyrus," came his mothers voice. "Let's try ..."

Marcella put her hands on his and together they pushed Crocea Mors into the slot.

"NOOOO!! SEIZE HIM THIS INS-" began Legion jumping into the air.

BOOOOOOOOOOOOOOOM!

The ground shook loudly and everyone standing fell to the floor.

The Atrium began to spin counterclockwise around the crystal pillars.

Faster and faster the Atrium spun. Ten airborne Lumens remained unaffected and began closing in on the mother and son.

Marcella let go of the sword and lept into action. She drew a dagger and small sword from her back. Cyrus heard the clang of metal as Marcella crossed blades with the first Lumen.

Cyrus felt a strange energy flow through him from the sword. The energy felt like it was going from the tips of his fingers to the tips of his wings, building through each strand of every feather on his body.

The Lumens were right on top of him. Their bows were drawn, and their ropes were out.

"NO!" screamed Marcella as she catapulted herself toward the three Lumens about to grab him.

She kicked one square in the face who crumpled and fell to the floor. She began crossing blades with the second. The third got through and grabbed Cyrus' right wing and pulled forcefully. Cyrus winced at the pain but quickly forgot it as more energy pulsed through his body, traveled through his wings and into the hand of the Lumen. Like a stick of dynamite, there was a loud bang and the Lumen flew through the air and hit the wall of the Atrium with a loud crash.

Cyrus felt the energy continue to grow until it reached a peak in his body and exceeded what he could hold. Like an overflowing cup of water, it had to be let out.

VOOOOOOO!

The dark side of his wings pulsed and every light went out in the Atrium. It was so dark you couldn't see your own nose. Shrieks and despair filled the air.

Cyrus felt depleted as the energy left. He breathed heavily as sweat fell from his face. The sword then began to seep energy back into him. More and more energy rushed through his body until ...

VOOOOOOO!!

The light side of his wings pulsed a blinding light that lit up the Atrium brighter than the noon-day sun. Cyrus choked on his own surprise. The energy began to slow from the sword.

Cyrus inspected his wings. The inside of his wings were glowing like he was the sun but the outside of his wings were like a black hole absorbing all light.

"Cyrus! I can't see, guide me with your voice," said Marcella.

"This way, mom... Warmer. Warmer. Take my hand."

His mother was covering her eyes with her right arm and reaching out with her left. Cyrus carefully grabbed her arm, avoiding the dagger in her hand.

All of the previously airborne Lumens were now on the floor sliding toward the edge except two. One of them heard Cyrus and quickly flew towards him letting out a yell. His sword was drawn and coming right at them. Marcella turned to face the noise, still blinded.

"Duck!" said Cyrus, yanking his mother down.

The Lumen swung his sword right where Marcella had been. He clipped the crystal next to Cyrus and spiraled to the floor with a loud 'Ooof'. The spinning Atrium carried his momentum until he hit the side of the wall.

With the Atrium spinning as fast as it was, all the Lumens were stuck to the walls like flies caught in honey. In the air remained one Lumen with his back to the pillars.

What is he doing? Is he blinded, too?

Cyrus turned his attention to the crystals. The top pillar was now swirling with shades of light and darkness. The second pillar glowed brightly like a white flame. The third was pitch black like obsidian. The last pillar looked like swirling mist.

HISSS ...

The four crystals circled outwards like a pupil dilating, revealing a straight drop into a heart of darkness. The sound of Wadjet entered the room faintly. Cyrus could feel the wind rush into the Atrium and he grabbed onto his mother for support. Marcella blinked rapidly.

Cyrus felt filled to the brim with energy. He felt ... good. For the first time, he felt... strong. His wings lightened and darkened the room at the same time. Marcella placed her hands on his and together they pulled the sword from the crystal. His mother quickly put it back into the sheath on her back.

Cyrus panted loudly.

"You are incredible, child," said Marcella with a smile:

"YOU HAVE NO IDEA..." said the voice with his back turned.

Cyrus shivered. It was Legion.

Marcella stopped smiling and looked first in Legion's direction, then to the gaping hole that had been exposed. Cyrus looked where the entrance to the Atrium had been. The Lumens kept yelling as they spun around, and he heard one of them vomit loudly. They were not leaving the way they'd come.

"We have to jump," Marcella began. "It will be a tight squeeze so wrap yourself around me, and don't open your wings. Once we're out in the open, then open your wings and catch as much wind as possible. Can you do that for me, Cyrus?"

Cyrus nodded.

"On the count of three. One." Legion began to turn around.

"Two."

"GET BACK HERE! YOU MUST SUSTAIN ME!"

"Three."

Cyrus grabbed his mother and lept into the abyss.

17

SANCTUM

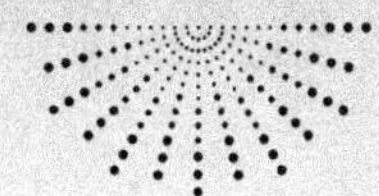

SILENCE … UTTER SILENCE. The wind gradually grew louder and louder as they fell faster and faster.

Focus … complete focus. His mother kept herself and Cyrus tucked in as they spiraled through the gaping hole.

Blue … deep blue. That was the color that bounced back to Cyrus off the walls from the light of his wings as they nose dived.

Shine … sunshine. Cyrus longed to see the sun. The night had felt too long.

"NOW, CYRUS!" yelled Marcella.

The moment of silence and mesmerizing blue was gone. It was now met with the thunderous sound of moving water. They shot out of the bottom of the spire under Aeolia like a bullet out of a gun.

Cyrus opened his wings and felt his mother do the same. She quickly veered them off to the right just in time. Had she not, they would have been skewered by the flag pole attached to Mentibus Oculis. Cyrus gasped at the site. Wadjet was a terrifyingly powerful whirlpool. He felt the air currents and gravity sucking him downward. The whirlpool diameter was easily a mile long, if not more, and swirled around angrily. Hundreds of thousands of gallons of ocean water churned mightily as it began its descent to what seemed to be the very center of the earth.

Cyrus looked down and saw an intricate building descending within the whirlpool. Cyrus couldn't see how far down the whirlpool went or how steep its descent was ... Frankly, he didn't want to. The building was made with the same greyish white stone as all of Aeolia. As they circled around, Cyrus audibly gasped.

Just like Ori's story, part of a metal ship stuck out of the platform. Jagged metal attached itself to the building like a decapitated vampire. It was a sight to behold.

Cyrus saw four figures standing on the platform, two of them were waving their arms back and forth and hopping up and down.

As they drew closer, Cyrus could see it was Kimo, Auli'i, Martin and Captain Ori.

"There is the arch," said Marcella as they descended below the flag pole. It was a half-moon shape and was big enough for Cyrus to crawl through, but hurl yourself through it at a blinding speed with wings folded perfectly? No, thank you.

"Imagine yourself catching as much wind in your wings as you can when we land, OK, Cyrus? Kind of like this." She opened her wings wide and curved them so she could catch as much air as possible. They slowed as she did so.

Cyrus nodded nervously.

They swooped towards the massive entrance of Mentibus Oculis, Cyrus opened his wings feeling the wind push against them like a sail and then they landed on their feet.

Kimo and Auli'i rushed to Cyrus and threw themselves on him in a backbreaking hug.

"O ... K ...You're ... breaking ... me ..." Cyrus said between each squeeze.

They were both playing with his wings in awe.

"Cyrus... why are you glowing and ... why are you ... um... darkening?" asked Auli'i.

"And what happened up there?" asked Kimo, pointing to Aeolia.

"There was this crazy burst of light right as we got here and it shot down into this temple and shook the ground and the water started spinning wider ..." Kimo sounded excited but frantic.

"Probably me. How did you guys get away from the manor?"

"I woke up after hearing all this commotion on the rooftop. It took a few tries but after I woke the bear, we hid behind your bed. They kept yelling, 'He's in the Atrium' and 'To the Atrium' over and over until it went quiet. Then Martian and Captain Ori appeared and flew us here. They had to make two trips because of Kimo."

"I can't help that I have an incredible physique. It's my curse," Kimo said with a shrug.

Cyrus shook his head.

"You were a curse to carry, young Kimo. If you didn't struggle so much, it would've gone smoother," said Martin behind them with a smile.

Auli'i leaned in and whispered to Cyrus, "He was practically crying when they landed."

Marcella stepped forward. "Is the Sanctum entrance opened?"

Martin shook his head.

"Are you Lady Marcella?" asked Aulii with a vibrant smile.

"Cyrus' mom?" added Kimo.

"I am, and who might you be?" asked Marcella, returning the smiles with one of her own.

"I'm Auli'i Fualautoalasi and this is my brother Kimo. We're Cyrus' Virtus Latores! Of course, we're also his friends."

"That makes me happier than your title, even though it is important," said Marcella, making the Omniscius Salutatio to the twins with a slight bow.

The twins made the gesture back.

"You kinda look like her," said Kimo, looking back and forth from Cyrus to Marcella.

"I would hope so ..." said Cyrus dryly.

"Sir Martin!" interrupted Captain Ori, pointing up to Aeolia.

Like a swarm of bees leaving a hive, hundreds of Lumens were now in the sky.

"We better move before they spot us," said Captain Ori, flying ahead.

Kimo looked up at Aeolia and put his hands on his hips while he sighed loudly. "I'm going to miss that cheese."

Martin began moving toward the Sanctum. Captain Ori was already at the entrance looking dumbstruck. As they arrived at the archway, Martin pulled something off of his back and handed it to Cyrus. It was his backpack with his passport, tablet, charger and wallet.

"Thank you, Martian!"

They stood under the great arch. The right side of the arch had three giant crystal pillars sticking out of the walls like thorns on a rose. They resembled the crystal pillars in the Atrium. The arch was an intricate design of carved flowers and trees. In the center below them was a single crystal surrounded by a perfect circle about 10 feet in diameter. Cyrus scanned the crystals for a slot similar to one they had seen in the Atrium. Cyrus spotted one in the middle crystal protruding from the wall 30 feet above him.

"That one!" he said, looking at his mother.

Marcella swooped over, grabbed Cyrus and accelerated upwards. Martin flew up as well and supported Cyrus in mid-air with his mother. Grateful for Martin's support, Marcella unsheathed Yellow Death with her free hand and gave it to Cyrus. He inserted the sword and twisted. A resounding click echoed from within the giant arch.

The inside of Cyrus wings lit up like a Christmas tree while the backside grew darker and darker. The floor beneath them began to shake and then the towering temple began to rotate clockwise. Cyrus gasped as he felt the same energy flow through his body. Instead of it charging his body, he could feel the energy being taken from him. His eyes bulged and he gritted his teeth.

"OUCH! I ... CAN'T ... HOLD ... ON ..!" yelled Marcella as she was sent hurtling into the other side of the arch.

"ORI! CATCH ... HER ...!" yelled Martin as he was flung to the other side.

Both Martin and his mother began falling off the wall of the arch.

Cyrus flapped helplessly in the air. He wanted to let go but it was as if the energy was holding him there. All of his weight was now being supported by his fragile back and bicep muscles. Ori leaped into the air after Marcella. Kimo and Auli'i moved towards Martin.

There was a loud *hiss* from below and an unholy amount of mist surrounded them completely. Visibility became almost nonexistent. There was a shriek from Auli'i down below. The muscles Cyrus was using gave out. The energy from the sword wouldn't let him go. It kept taking what he had stored in his body from the Atrium. Cyrus was now being supported by his forearm strength alone.

The giant arch of Mentibus Oculis began a 360 degree turn. Cyrus felt his arms tremble.

"Master Cyrus!" said Ori from the ground.

The arch settled back into place with an earth shattering *THUD!* The water inside Wadjet vibrated and rippled through the current. It was silent for a split second and then returned to its violent form, circling Mentibus Oculis. Cyrus felt some of the energy begin to return to his body but not nearly as much as before. He gasped loudly as the energy flowed back to him. Simultaneously, the crystals began to light up in the exact same fashion as they had before. The one with the sword in it was pulsating rhythmically with darkness while light swirled throughout it simultaneously. The one above was as dark as the backside of his wings and the one below swirled like a misty grey cloud.

The energy stopped. Cyrus was free from its grasp. He let go of the sword and began to free fall.

One second. Two sec... Ori caught Cyrus halfway and slowed his descent to the middle of the carved design on the floor. The crystal on the floor was lit up like a beacon... and moving.

"The platform is descending!" yelled Captain Ori.

Sure enough, the carved platform rotated slowly downwards. Through the haze, Cyrus could just make out Auli'i and Kimo on either side of Marcella, helping her walk towards the carved platform. Martin walked behind, inspecting Marcella.

"Captain Ori, retrieve the sword," said Martin.

"Right away, sir," said Ori, leaving Cyrus on the platform and then propelling himself upward.

Marcella lifted her head and saw Cyrus. Her face immediately lit up.

"Are you all right, sweetheart?"

They hopped down onto the platform that was starting to descend faster.

"Yeah," said Cyrus shakily. "I'll be fine. What about you? Are you OK, mom?"

"Never better," she said with a smile. "Just bumped my head is all."

"She might have a concussion," said Martin, ripping off a piece of his shirt. He began wrapping Marcella's head.

Ori landed with the sword in hand. Marcella waved her hand to the twins who stopped helping her. She stood up straight, took the sword from Ori and sheathed it. She then looked at Martin with a fierce look in her eye.

"I'll be fine. I am still of use."

"Never said you weren't. Simply that you are probably concussed."

"Are you OK?" asked Marcella, now inspecting Martin.

"Never better," said Martin, imitating Marcella's tone.

Cyrus chuckled as he rubbed his forearms. They were tender to the touch. His fingers throbbed from over exertion too.

"How ... How do you feel handling that much energy?" asked Marcella with a look of admiration.

"Like a battery going from 10% to 100% in the matter of seconds. Then, that 100% keeps getting doubled over and over again until it fills every cell in my body. It ... it wasn't painful. Just hanging up there on my own was ..."

"What's a battery?" asked Captain Ori.

"Later, Captain. Was it the same both times?" asked Martin.

"Kind of... In the Atrium, I felt like a battery absorbing electricity. Just now, I felt like I was giving it instead."

"Are you alright?" asked Auli'i.

"Fine." Cyrus stood up straight.

"The twins caught me," said Martin.

"You were already floating down to us, Martian, we didn't do much," said Auli'i.

"I can assure you, you caught me. I was seeing stars, even if I was conscious. Thank you, Fualautoalasis. I am in your debt."

"Let's just call it even since you saved our sister," said Kimo.

"Fair enough. Cyrus could you hand me the robe in your backpack?"

Marcella made her way to Captain Ori and gave him a kiss on the cheek.

"Thank you for saving my life, Captain," she said making the Omniscius Salutatio.

Captain Ori blushed and returned the gesture.

The robe was a black robe outlined in white. The same one the Lumens who had been chasing him wore ... The same one Legion had on.

"Martin, why do you have this?" asked Cyrus, handing it to him.

"If Legion is still around, I need to find out who he is. Best way to do that is to appear as an ally, not an enemy." Cyrus felt someone playing with his wings.

"You're missing a couple feathers ... and your wings aren't as bright as they were a moment ago," said Auli'i, running her fingers through his feathers.

"But they are still glowing brighter than normal," said Kimo.

"They are also darkening everything. Look at the crystal when you have your back turned."

"It's ... incredible..." said Captain Ori in awe.

Sure enough, when Cyrus had his back to the crystal, the light would wane and visibly appear dimmer. The moment he turned and faced it with his light side, the light would grow brighter to the point where everyone had to squint.

"Captain Ori, did you see how close the others were before the mist rose out of Wadjet?" asked Martin looking up at the entrance as it got smaller and smaller.

Captain Ori shook his head.

"How far does this go down?" asked Auli'i.

Captain Ori, Marcella and Martin all looked at each other and then shrugged.

"We've only read about it," said Marcella.

"Do you remember the story I told you about my grandfather and the ship crashing into Mentibus Oculis?" asked Captain Ori. "The ship got the worst of it. However, the build of this tower is second to none ... There is a reason it has withstood Wadjet's current for over a millennia."

"The inner Sanctum ... no one has seen it in over 700 years. Scattered songs and very few written records are all we have," said Martin. "My father has always been fascinated by them."

The platform kept whirling as it took them deeper and deeper into Wadjet's eye. They began to slow down and entered a giant dome. It was incredibly dark beneath them so much so that none of them could make out where the platform was going or what was around them.

Cyrus rummaged through his backpack and grabbed his phone. He turned on the flashlight and Captain Ori flapped his wings in surprise.

"HOW ARE YOU DOING THAT?" he said with fright.

"Oh, wow... is that on a phone, Cyrus?" asked Marcella intrigued.

"Yes! Did you used to have a phone, mom?"

"Yes, we did. Your father and I would take odd end jobs to get by and we wound up purchasing one. It wasn't as fancy as that one."

"When the light is better, we should take a selfie," said Cyrus peering over the edge.

"Ah, yes... that word was circulating while we were stateside," said Marcella.

"What is a selfie?" asked Captain Ori.

"You take a photo of yourself with your phone," said Cyrus. All Cyrus could see was a bunch of support pillars above and below him.

It was an absurd amount.

"What's a photo?" Captain Ori asked.

Cyrus looked at Ori with surprise.

Man, there is a lot for them to catch up on.

"It's kind of like an instant painting with modern technology. You point it at something and it instantly captures that moment to look at later," replied Martin.

Cyrus could see they were coming to another entrance. He backed up and turned his phone light off.

A wall immediately appeared next to them again. The light from the crystal bounced off the walls illuminating intricate paintings decorating the walls. A Lumen Caligo held up a sword that resembled Yellow Death triumphantly. Cyrus turned his phone to selfie mode and stood in the center of the platform next to Captain Ori and his mother. Auli'i quickly hopped next to Marcella. Kimo crouched next to Cyrus and Martin leaned in.

Click.

Cyrus showed the photo to Captain Ori who stared at the phone incredulously.

"Wow."

Cyrus pocketed his phone and turned his attention back to the art on the wall.

It showed Aeolia with a pillar of light leaving the Atrium going towards Mentibus Oculis. The four crystals were exactly how Cyrus had left them moments ago. One was a mixture of black and white, one white, one black and one grey. The painting kept revealing itself as they descended.

Cyrus felt his ears start to pop.

It then showed the descent they were currently doing and a great room at the bottom. It then showed a Lumen, Caligo and Terram gathered with a Lumen Caligo who was standing in front of what looked like either a mirror or a door. Cyrus couldn't tell what it was.

He tilted his head in confusion as he inspected it closer. There were *two* Lumen Caligos. If it was a mirror, the one that was looking back had trees and blue skies behind him.

Twip! TINK ...

Cyrus saw a sudden movement in the corner of his eye. A crushed arrow ricocheted to Cyrus' feet. Martin picked it up and quickly examined it.

"The Apollo Archers," he said, looking at Marcella.

"Everybody, stand away from the center!" she whispered forcefully.

Everybody moved in unison as more arrows began to hit the floor. Cyrus hugged the wall and felt his skin slide against the paint.

"We are sitting ducks right now," said Martin putting up his hood

"It can't be that much further! The moment it opens, we jump!" said Marcella.

Martin pulled out a bow, loaded an arrow and returned fire. Captain Ori did the same.

"Should we go up and run interference?" asked Captain Ori.

"Absolutely not! They have the high ground!" said Martin.

Despite the fear he felt, Cyrus smirked at that comment.

Arrows began to shower down, each making a tinking sound as metal met rock. The subsequent sound of crunching wood from the shaft breaking followed shortly after.

"SEIZE THE LUMEN CALIGO!" shrieked a voice from above.

Cyrus felt his blood run cold.

There was a push of air from the ground moving upwards. Cyrus felt it rush through his feathers.

"It's starting to open!" said Marcella.

The arrows ceased and two Lumens landed on the platform.

Martin and Ori lept into action. Swords clanked in a flurry of rapid movements.

Martin avoided the swing of the Lumen's sword, turned around quickly and bashed him in the back of the head with his sword hilt. The Lumen crumpled to the floor. Kimo went to the fallen Lumen and grabbed his sword and the shield. Auli'i grabbed the bow and quiver of arrows.

Captain Ori made quick work of his Lumen as well but there were already four more Lumens to take their place.

"Cyrus! To me!" said Marcella.

The gap between the descending platform and the dome wall was just big enough to crawl under. Kimo had stepped up and was now crossing blades with a Lumen. The metal clanked off of the shield as Kimo parried an oncoming strike.

Auli'i fired an arrow with little success as it bounced off of the side of the wall and landed close by Cyrus' feet.

There was a loud clang as the Lumen knocked the sword out of Kimo's hand. The Lumen began to laugh triumphantly but Kimo remained unfazed and hid behind the shield. Strike after strike reigned down on Kimo, each one bouncing off of the shield. The Lumen's laugh faded away as he began cursing under his breath. He raised his sword high, leaving himself open. That was all Kimo needed. Kimo punched forward with all his weight and knocked the Lumen to the ground right by Martin. Martin repeated the motion with his hilt, bashing the Lumen in the head with one precise swoop. The soldier went still. Martin had already taken down two Lumens and was now working on his third.

"Auli'i! Kimo! Let's go! NOW!" said Cyrus.

The twins gathered around Marcella and the four of them jumped into the dark abyss. Cyrus opened his wings and tried to catch us much air as he could. Kimo yelped loudly and Auli'i clenched on to Cyrus for dear life. There was rapid flapping of Marcella's wings trying to keep them from plummeting completely. She did a good job, for the most part... but the weight was too much. With the light of Cyrus' wings, he could see the ground approach faster and faster.

They fell for what seemed like a minute until they hit the cold floor. Grunts and groans filled the air as they quickly tried to gather their surroundings. Cyrus heard a crunch from his bag.

The light from the crystal on the platform began to fill the room and what a room it was. It was a huge dome that was shaped like a giant igloo. The paintings on the roof showed the entire world. Oceans and a rather accurate depiction of the land masses decorated the walls. Above the igloo-like opening at the end of the room was the depiction of Aeolia and thousands of Lumens and Caligos flying around it and Terrams sailing its waters. Something was depicted under all of it but Cyrus couldn't make it out. They had made it to the Sanctum ...

The smell was musty and the sound of thousands upon thousands of gallons of water enveloped them. Even through the walls, it felt like it would break through at any moment.

Light continued to flood into the room as the platform descended further and further down. Kimo was first to stand and quickly lifted Cyrus to his feet. Auli'i was trying to help Marcella.

"Lady Marcella! Are you OK?!" asked Auli'i.

Fear spiked through Cyrus' body. He went over to his mother as quickly as he could. She was grimacing in pain.

"Where are you hurt, mom?!"

She pointed to her foot. Her right foot was turned at an odd angle.

"I think I took the weight of all of you and broke it," she said through clenched teeth.

Cyrus felt tears come to his face.

"I'm so sorry, mom ... I ... I tried to open my wings ... I just ..." said Cyrus, looking down.

Marcella immediately lost her look of pain.

"Honey... It's not your fault! I would have broken more had you not helped me," she said caressing his face.

There were more clangs and a couple whooshes of wings from above. The sounds reverberated throughout the Sanctum and were quickly drowned out by the thundering noise of water.

"Kimo! Auli'i! Help my mother and follow me!"

Cyrus did his best to help his mother put her arms around the twins but he quickly realized he was just getting in the way. He took a step back and let them take care of her while he quickly scanned the room. There were precious jewels that began to glimmer in the light of the crystal and piles of treasure in another corner of the room. The place was starting to look more and more like the cave of wonders.

Cyrus' eyes were drawn to the the arch under the igloo-shaped entrance. Underneath the depictions of Lumens, Caligos and Terrams was a large yellow stone. It was translucent, so much so that Cyrus could see the water rushing from Wadjet. The yellow-tinted window was 20 feet tall and looked equally as thick. In front of this enormous window was a pedestal with four crystals in a half circle. The half circle was significantly shorter, only coming up to Cyrus' knee, and faced the yellow stone.

Cyrus walked over to the pedestal and looked on either side of the wall. There were two Lumens painted on the walls with their arms outstretched. One of them had curly hair, a full beard and wore a toga while the other had slitted eyes like an Egyptian and wore a crown. From each of their hands was a crystal pillar protruding its way outwards, pointing right at the pedestal.

"WATCH OUT!" screamed Captain Ori.

He tackled Cyrus as another Lumen dove from above. Cyrus found himself caught in a tussle between the two men. Cyrus felt a rope around his neck and choked as they ascended into the air.

Blades clanged. With one quick slash, Cyrus was in a free fall. Cyrus braced for impact and opened his wings.

Swoosh.

"I got you," came the reassuring voice of Martin.

He set Cyrus in front of the pedestal and then turned around and shot three arrows in quick succession. Three Lumens began to spiral to the ground.

Thud, thud, thud.

Kimo and Auli'i moved quickly towards Cyrus and Martin.

"Auli'i! Give Marcella the bow you grabbed. Marcella, I need you to help me hold them off while we buy Cyrus some time," said Martin.

Marcella didn't wait for Auli'i to give her the bow. She grabbed it from her and pulled the quiver over her shoulder. She handed Cyrus the sword.

"I'm immobile on the ground, Martin, broken foot. I'm going airborne. What do you need?"

"The entrance to the Sanctum is a natural funnel. Shoot down as many as possible but aim for the wings."

Marcella nodded and opened her wings to fly off.

"WAIT!" shouted Cyrus.

"Cyrus ... I'm no use to you here. Listen to what Martin says. I promise I will be right back. I love you." She kissed his cheek and few off. She headed straight for the gaping hole they had just come out of.

"Captain Ori!" yelled Martin.

Captain Ori finished another Lumen with a resounding *thud*. He was next to Martin in an instant.

"Assist Marcella. She's going to funnel the-"

Thwp.

An arrow pierced Ori in the chest.

Thwp.

Another arrow pierced Ori's right thigh.

Martin leaped into the sky, bow drawn and hood up.

A Lumen emerged and hovered in the air. Cyrus turned his gaze towards this Lumen and the light of his wings illuminated the face.

With green eyes and a serious expression, it was Lady Marianne.

There was a shriek near the entrance and another Lumen appeared, dragging Marcella by her hair.

Cyrus heard himself scream but it was drowned out by the water.

"You have been commanded to return topside at once. Do not make us harm your mother in order for you to comply," said Lady Marianne.

"What happened to protecting the Lumen Caligo?!" yelled Cyrus furiously. "Was that all just for show?!"

"No. It was not. You were protected for a purpose. This ..." she said, gesturing to the Sanctum. "Is not it."

A rough voice spoke from behind Lady Marianne.

"Legion wishes to speak to you. You can still walk out of here in once piece."

"There is no way I am going with you," spat Cyrus.

The cloaked individual put his sword up to Marcella's throat. Cyrus' wings illuminated the face of the other Lumen. It was Karlovic.

"Don't test me," said Karlovic.

"Wait, wait ..." said Cyrus pleading.

Martin landed behind Cyrus.

"Cyrus ... Put the sword in the slot ... Now."

"Cyrus! Don't you dare surrender. I will—"

Karlovic struck Marcella with the hilt of his sword and she went unconscious.

Cyrus grabbed the sword, turned around and through tears and screams, thrust the sword into the pedestal in front of the yellow stone.

18

THE PORTAL

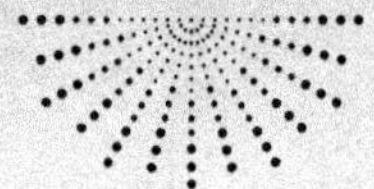

"CLOSE YOUR EYES" YELLED Lady Marianne, turning away. Martin leaped into the air.

The two light flashes Cyrus had made before looked like small candles compared to what erupted from him now. His wings extended fully on their own and both sides of his wings blazed a light so bright there was nothing to see except white in the entire room. The light traveled all the way up the deep tunnel. It lit up everything and blinded everyone.

It knocked everyone close to it out of the air and off their feet.

The light reached a climax and then shot out of Cyrus' wings towards the yellow window. The window started to glow bright. The two crystals next to the pedestal began to glow. The one on the left, a bright light, and the one on the right, a misty grey.

Cyrus felt as if his very soul was being sucked out of him. The energy that had flowed through him so freely seemed to be leaving his body and taking every spare inch of strength he had with it. It was like ice water being pulled out of his veins.

The light on his wings began to dim as they grew darker and darker until all the light in the room was gone except for the yellow window, pulsating light rhythmically.

Cyrus felt his wings stretch out further and further. Both sides grew darker and darker until, like a bullet, the darkness shot out of him and joined the light in the yellow window. The dark crystal and the crystal with light and darkness lit up.

Cyrus felt faint and struggled to stay conscious. The yellow stone began pulsating in sync with the four crystal pillars.

Then, the pulsating stopped.

VEEEEEEEW!

The four crystals shot their unique quality at Cyrus. Light, darkness and everything in between surged through Cyrus.

Cyrus felt like a battery going from 1% to 100% in a second. He felt strong and alert... but it was short lived. Brimming with energy, Cyrus' body shook erratically as the light and darkness shot out of his wings toward the yellow stone. He felt his body start to collapse and an unbearable pain began in his left wing. A thousand needles stabbed at him as he watched his feathers begin to turn around individually so the black side of his left wing faced inward and the white side outward. The light in the room changed with his wings. Half of the room lit up brilliantly while the other half stayed as dark as night. Light and darkness pulsated from him faster and faster while every feather on his left wing turned the other way.

Cyrus was certain he was going to die. His body, his mind, his soul ... Everything was leaving him as the light and darkness shot into the yellow stone. He didn't know how he was still holding on to the sword. There was no strength left in any part of his body. He felt like he weighed 1000 pounds. Then, all at once ... It stopped

The light faded and darkness crept into the Sanctum once more.

There was a brief pause as the light and darkness swirled in the yellow stone like Wadjet. It spun faster and faster, transforming into a swirling vortex. Then, light filled the room once more as the vortex began to change shape and open.

Cyrus fell to the ground, utterly spent. His kept his right eye open as he hit the floor and saw trees and grass. There was a nice breeze that smelled like lavender. The sun was shining and he could hear birds singing.

Is this death?

Everything was peaceful.

" ... KIMO!"

That's Ori's voice.

" ... GRAB CYRUS AND GET THROUGH THERE, NOW!"

Why is he yelling? He's ruining the peace and quiet ...

Cyrus felt someone pick him up and put him over their shoulder like a rag doll.

Kimo ...

Kimo turned around and Cyrus saw a flurry of activity. Martin was rushing towards Karlovic who was still covering his eyes from the flash of light. His mother was on the floor starting to come around. Auli'i was tapping Cyrus on the cheek, trying to say something he couldn't understand. Captain Ori snapped the shaft of the arrows and picked up his sword.

What is going on? I just want the sunshine ...

Martin grabbed his mother from Karlovic who began swinging his sword wildly, trying to retrieve his prize.

"GET GOING, YOU TWO!" screamed Marcella.

Lady Marianne turned toward them, drew her sword and wildly started running, flapping her wings for added speed.

"GO NOW!"

Martin had Marcella and began retreating toward them, trying to stop Lady Marianne.

Kimo grabbed the sword, adjusted Cyrus and began running toward the warm sunshine. For some reason, the sunshine, grass and birds started to get smaller and smaller. The scene had been as tall as the window but was shrinking fast. Cyrus tried to lift his head to get a better look at it but couldn't find the strength.

"HURRY! THE PORTAL IS CLOSING! YOU HAVE TO HURRY!" said Marcella while Martin hopped into full-flight. He carried Marcella in his arms and they desperately tried to catch up with Lady Marianne to no avail.

"AHHHH!"

Ori clipped Lady Marianne in the air, only getting her arm. She spun around wildly as her sword clanged to the ground. She quickly recovered and continued pursuit. Ori remained on the floor.

She was hot on their tail again and closing. The portal grew smaller and smaller.

Kimo and Auli'i were in full sprints toward the portal. Auli'i reached it first and thrust herself forward, tripping on the pedestal. Kimo came barreling behind and full-on jumped and tucked with Cyrus in his arms.

Cyrus felt the sun on his face and grass on his skin.

Bliss.

Kimo left Cyrus on the ground and raised his shield. Lady Marianne hurled through the portal and met Kimo head on. She may have been faster but Kimo was a brick wall. Kimo stepped forward and bumped his chest as Lady Marianne met him. It was no contest. There was a *thump* followed by a *thud*. Lady Marianne fell to the ground, discombobulated.

"Tie her now!" said Kimo, getting on top of Lady Marianne and holding her down.

"With what?!" screamed Auli'i.

"I don't know, but do something! The portal is about to close!" Cyrus lay on the ground, looking back on the portal that was no bigger than a Frisbee now. He could see two faces looking at him ...

Mom? Martian?

"You come back to me, Cyrus," she said with tears in her eyes. "I love you ..."

The portal was only inches tall.

"I'll take care of her. I be-"

The portal closed.

Cyrus went unconscious.

V oices ... muttering voices ... Wheels ... wheels turning. *Am ... Am I alive?*

Cyrus felt his thoughts start to swirl in his head. Pain everywhere reminded him that he was very much alive.

Cyrus heard wheels turning and feet marching. He tried to open his eyes, but they were still too heavy. He tried to move his arms. Not possible. He tried to move his wings. They burned painfully.

He felt like he had just had his insides squeezed out and then set on fire. Everything hurt. His energy was completely gone. He went unconscious again.

He dreamt vivid dreams. Two hummingbirds circled each other endlessly. Round and round they went until one turned to ash.

"Cyrus .. Cyrus ... Wake up," said a voice.

Who is that?

"Cyrus ... Please, wake up ..." the voice said again. It was a female voice.

Mom?

"Cyrus ... You have to see this," said a male voice.

He felt someone sit him up and lift his eye lid with their finger. His eyes rolled up into his head.

"Kimo!"

There was a slapping sound and everything went dark again.

"Be careful with him! You saw what just happened! We have no idea what that did to him!"

"Sorry ... Sorry ... Cyrus, if you can hear me, make a sound." Cyrus inhaled and exhaled a soft wheeze.

"Cyrus, " said Auli'i, grabbing his hand. "If you can hear us, squeeze my hand."

Cyrus mustered what little strength he had and gave a slight twitch.

"OK, good. Cyrus, we're in a city. Some soldiers found us shortly after we went through the portal. We couldn't understand what they were saying," she said softly.

There came some muffled grunts from a female voice close by.

"Knock it off!" said Kimo.

"Lady Marianne tried to fight the guards. She's tied up real good," said Auli'i.

Cyrus slowly opened his eyes. It felt like his eyelids were rusted shut. Directly above him were Auli'i and Kimo.

"Good morning, sleepy head," said Auli'i with a smile.

Cyrus breathed in deeply and attempted a smile. Looking directly to the sky, Cyrus noticed he was moving. Cyrus used his fingers to feel the texture of whatever he was laying on.

Hard, but definitely made of wood.

They were bumping around on a wooden cart. Cyrus heard a horse whiney and the hum of hundreds of people all around. Buildings shadowed over him, none bigger than two stories high. Cyrus heard Kimo and Auli'i gasp in unison. Kimo sat Cyrus up and pointed.

"Look! Look at that!" said Kimo excitedly.

To their right was a giant edifice towering over everything. Cyrus could hear the roar of a huge crowd growing louder as they passed.

The cart continued straight and entered into a mysterious city. Hens clucked, dogs barked and people bartered in a strange tongue. Hushed murmurs and whispers passed through the crowd. Cyrus strained to understand. He heard two words he recognized... Lumen Caligo.

Where are we?

The phrase 'Lumen Caligo' was heard over and over again as they continued through the city. Cyrus felt his strength sapping again and closed his eyes to preserve energy. The moment he did, he fell asleep.

Shadow ... light ... Cyrus' mind swirled with more dreams. All of the colors.

The sudden stop of the cart woke Cyrus from his slumber.

Someone picked him up. He was carried like a rag doll through a giant entrance. Cyrus felt shade cover him and the temperature drop.

The sound of boots marching echoed through halls. Men arguing in a great number grew closer and closer. Cyrus heard the creak of giant doors opening and the sound of the men arguing exploded into a deafening roar for a moment. Then, everything fell still.

"Cyrus ... Wake up ... You need to see this," whispered Auli'i. Her voice seemed frightened.

Cyrus mustered all the strength he could find and lifted his head and opened his eyes. He couldn't believe what he saw.

Cyrus was in the center of a great hall. On both sides were rows and rows of Lumens, Caligos and Terrams staring adamantly at Cyrus. The guards maintained their perimeter around Cyrus and continued marching forward.

The rows of people made a semi-circle angling towards an elevated seat where a Lumen with sprawling wings and an adorned toga sat.

He wore a thin laurel crown, had a Caligo on his right hand side and a Terram on his left. He stared at Cyrus intently.

One Lumen made a comment in a strange tongue on the right side of the hall and then another made a comment on the left. Pretty soon the noise resumed its deafening sound as it echoed through the great hall. Cyrus looked around, utterly confused. They pointed and yelled, screamed and argued.

The Lumen on the elevated throne stood up and held up his hand.

The room fell silent. The Caligo and the Terram stood up as well, their eyes fixed on Cyrus.

The Lumen with the laurel crown began to speak slowly, addressing the Lumens, Caligos and Terrams on both sides. Cyrus understood nothing. He felt his strength fading away by the second. He didn't have much time left.

Cyrus looked forward and locked eyes with the crowned Lumen who cocked his head to the side and beckoned them closer. The guards surrounding the twins clanked their spears on the ground and stepped out of the way. Kimo walked forward slowly with Auli'i next to him and Cyrus in his arms. The crowned Lumen lifted his hand. Kimo halted immediately. The Lumen took a deep breath and then addressed the three of them loudly.

"ROMANUM IMPERIUM SUSCIPIT!" he said grandiosely gesturing to the entire room.

There were hushed whispers and muffled voices throughout the rows. Cyrus was on the brink of collapse again. His mind was already going dark.

The Lumen then looked directly at Cyrus, and in perfect English said, "I am Emperor Gaius Julius Caesar, father of the Roman Empire and protector of her interests"

Auli'i and Kimo gasped. Cyrus felt the darkness about to take him completely.

"The Roman Empire welcomes you, Lumen Caligo."

Cyrus blacked out.

Lawrence C. Cobb

From the Author

The story and images depicted in the Lumen Caligo have lived within me for as long as I can remember. The world I've written about is a remnant of the scattered dreams I have pieced together which always seems to whisper, *'write'*. The story was born in darkness and nurtured by light. The first words of "Fallen" were written during a sunset very similar to the one in *Isolations Visitor*. Covid-19 gave me the ultimatum to let the story live rent free in my head or put pen to paper and share this story with the world. You are reading this book now because of my choice to do the latter. "Fallen" is the first book of the seven book "Lumen Caligo" series. I hope you find something that speaks to you while reading about Cyrus' adventures. May it serve you well, and as always . . . May your light illuminate the darkness before you.

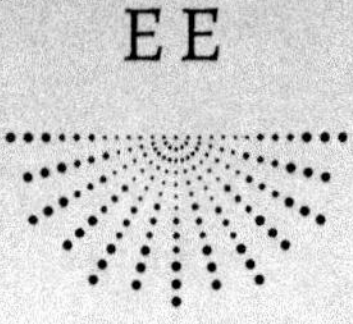

2/10

Misspelled Message.